THE LOOK

Y

THE LOOK

Sophia Bennett

SCHOLASTIC INC. / NEW YORK

All rights reserved. Published by Chicken House, an imprint of Scholastic Inc., *Publishers since 1920.* CHICKEN HOUSE, SCHOLASTIC, and associated logos are trademarks and/or registered trademarks of Scholastic Inc.

www.scholastic.com

First published in the United Kingdom in 2012 by Chicken House, 2 Palmer Street, Frome, Somerset BA11 1DS.

www.doublecluck.com

Library of Congress Cataloging-in-Publication Data

Bennett, Sophia.
The Look / Sophia Bennett. — 1st American ed.
p. cm.
Summary: When she is spotted by a modeling agency and her beautiful sister falls seriously ill, gangly fifteen-year-old Edwina "Ted" Trout must choose between fame and family.
ISBN 978-0-545-46438-3
[1. Models (Persons) — Fiction. 2. Sisters — Fiction. 3. Family life — Fiction. 4. Cancer — Fiction. 5. London (England) — Fiction. 6. England — Fiction.] I. Title.
PZ7.B44705Lo 2013
[Fic] — dc23
2012002704

10 9 8 7 6 5 4 3 2 1   13 14 15 16 17

Printed in the U.S.A.   23
First American edition, March 2013

The text type was set in Book Antiqua.
The display type was set in Zurich and Zapfino.
Interior book design by Kristina Iulo

To my brother Christopher, and Sarah.

And to my friend Rebecca K. You are *amazing*.

ONE

busk:
to perform music in the streets and other
public places for money

That's the official dictionary definition. I checked it on Dad's computer before we came out, while I was waiting for Ava to remember where she'd put her flute case. But there was another version underneath:

busk it [informal]:
to do something as well as you can, without
much preparation

That's the one we need, my sister and me. We aren't so much busking as busking *it*. And I have a feeling it shows.

"Are you sure this is working?" I mutter, as Ava puffs her way through the final chorus of "Yellow Submarine."

She finishes with a flourish and a smile.

"We're fabulous. Trust me."

Trouble is, I don't. The last time I trusted my older sister was in grade school, when she assured me that it was perfectly normal to wear a Buzz Lightyear costume (complete with wings) to gymnastics class if you accidentally left your leotard at your granny's. The teacher made me do the whole class in that costume, including the hula hoop sequence. Ava giggles whenever she thinks of it. Some memories haunt you to infinity and beyond.

However, she promised me a third of the proceeds today, which sounded tempting at the time. I was hoping to earn enough for some new shading pencils.

"Jesse's cousin got fifty pounds last week," she says, reading my mind. Her eyes have the dreamy look she always gets when she mentions her boyfriend in Cornwall — or even, it seems, his relatives.

"What, Jesse's cousin, the classical violinist?"

"Uh-huh."

"Who's in an orchestra?"

"Well, yes," Ava admits. "But she was busking in Truro, which is miles from anywhere. And look at us."

I look at us. Location-wise, we're perfect: Carnaby Street, in the heart of London's West End, surrounded by Saturday shoppers taking advantage of some early summer sun. If we were Ava's boyfriend's cousin, we'd probably make a fortune. But I bet she wasn't playing *Easy Beatles Tunes for Beginners*. And I bet she didn't give up her instrument at fourteen, like Ava did three years ago. And I bet she wasn't accompanied by a girl who only took up the tambourine that morning, like I did.

It. We are so busking *it*.

"I figure we can make at least double what she did," Ava says confidently. "All those people have been stopping to look at us."

"That might have something to do with that top you're wearing."

"Why?" she says, looking down. "What's the matter with it? It's a lot more interesting than your T-shirt."

"Nothing's the matter with it," I sigh.

Ava spent forty-five minutes this morning choosing the skimpy lilac top and cutoff jeans she's wearing now, and another twenty-five perfecting her makeup. She looks fantastic as always: glossy-haired and violet-eyed, curvy and sparkling — well, not quite as sparkling as usual due to her virus, but still superhot. We must make an odd couple: the stylish student looking like an undercover film star, and her gangly younger sister, looking like a lamppost in shorts.

I wish I could copy her, but I've tried and it doesn't work. I just don't have the required va-va-voom. When she bent down to pick up her flute she actually got a round of applause from a group of passing construction workers. As soon as she started on her version of "Yellow Submarine" they moved on pretty quickly, though. It seems even construction workers have sensitive hearing.

"Anyway, how much have we made so far?" she asks hopefully.

I check the open flute case at our feet.

"Two Starburst wrappers, a piece of chewing gum, and a parking ticket."

"Oh."

"But there's a guy down the street who keeps staring at us.

Over there, see? He might give us a pound or something if we're lucky."

She sighs and looks tired for a moment. "It's hardly enough for a ticket to Cornwall. I'm never going to see Jesse at this rate. Let's give them 'Hey Jude.' My last performance 'had to be heard to be believed,' remember?"

I grin. I do indeed remember that quote from the school newsletter. I'm not sure they meant it the way she took it, though. I'm starting to understand why she couldn't con any of her friends into coming along today, before she asked me.

Ava does a couple of test breaths, then launches into the opening bars. I rattle my tambourine as best I can, trying not to catch the eye of anyone nearby. I think I'm supposed to "take a sad song and make it better," but that's beyond my musical ability. I'll just have to settle for making it louder.

Meanwhile, the guy down the street is slowly heading in our direction. It suddenly occurs to me that he might be a plain-clothes policeman, if plainclothes policemen wear leather jackets and carry orange backpacks. Maybe we're not allowed to play here and he's about to arrest us. Or worse, he could be a kidnapper, staking out victims.

Thank goodness I took judo in my last year of grade school. And for once, my height could be useful. While Ava got her movie-star looks from Mum, I got all the genes from our tall, lanky dad, who's six foot five, even without the mad hair — which I also inherited, along with his bushy unibrow. I'm not Dad's height yet, but I'm definitely taller than Leather Jacket Guy. I'm pretty sure I could take him on in hand-to-hand combat, if I had to. As long as he hadn't taken judo, too, of course.

When I look around, Ava's not there. Then I realize she's sitting down on the cobbled pavement, with her head between her knees.

"Are you OK?" I ask. She should definitely eat more breakfast.

"Yeah. Just needed a rest. 'Hey Jude' is a lot tougher than I remember. I finished ages ago, by the way. You've been rattling that tambourine by yourself for five minutes."

"Oh, have I?" I bet she's exaggerating. I hope she's exaggerating. I stop rattling. "I've been watching that guy over there. D'you think he's a policeman? What's that he's holding? Is it a walkie-talkie?"

Ava follows my gaze. "No. I think it's a camera. Ooh! He might be a scout." She gets up to have a better look.

"I don't think so," I say. "He's too old and he isn't wearing a woggle or anything."

Ava rolls her eyes. "I mean model scout, not Boy Scout, you idiot. Lily Cole got scouted round here."

"Lily who?"

"Famous supermodel. Do you know *anything* about fashion, Ted?"

"Mum says, 'blue and green should never be seen,' although I've always thought —"

She interrupts me by digging me in the ribs. "Hey! He's coming over. Act natural."

Oh, no. He *is* a policeman. I can just feel it. We're about to get a criminal record. At least Ava is. I think I'm too young for one. Plus, her rendition of "Hey Jude" was definitely more criminal than my tambourine playing.

"Hi, girls," the man says, with a disarming grin. "How are you today?"

"Fine," Ava answers coyly. She looks up at him through her long lashes, while I try to remember my defensive stance and blocking maneuvers.

"My name's Simon and I'm from a model agency. D'you mind if I take a picture?"

"Oh, I don't think so." Ava blushes. "I'm not really —"

"I meant you, actually," Simon says, gazing past her.

Ava's watching me now. Come to think of it, Simon's definitely looking in my direction. But that can't be right. I stare back at him, confused. He looks straight into my eyes and his grin widens to a dazzle.

"I've been watching you and you're amazing. Have you thought about modeling?"

What? Amazing? Me? *Modeling?* No.

Suddenly I feel dizzy. This must be some sort of prank. I assume we're being filmed. Is Ava in on it? She looks as bewildered as I feel. Why is Simon talking to the flat-chested freak with a unibrow, when the gorgeous one with the film-star face is standing right beside him?

He hasn't stopped staring at me. I guess I'm supposed to say something, but my mouth has dried up. I shake my head.

"You should consider it," he goes on. He delves into the pocket of his trendy black jeans and hands me a card. It has a logo on it of a jagged black *M* inside a pale blue circle. He says the name of the agency, but I don't catch it because my ears are buzzing. "Look us up. How old are you, if you don't mind me asking?"

My mouth is still dry.

"Fifteen," Ava tells him, less bewildered now and more suspicious. "She's too young. Look, we've heard about people like you."

He looks confused for a moment. "Actually, she's not," he says. "Fifteen's great. Too young for catwalk, but we've got fourteen-year-olds on the books. Come and talk to us. Bring your parents. We're one big family. Picture?"

He holds up the camera again. It's larger than average: a Polaroid, designed to spit out instant snapshots. I wonder what they're like.

"No, you can't," Ava says firmly.

"Well, at least tell me your name," he says, dazzling me with that smile again.

"Ted." My voice is a croak. "Ted Trout."

"Trout? Seriously?"

I nod, but is anything serious around here? I'm still waiting for the camera crew to leap out from wherever they're hiding and fall into the street laughing.

"Nice meeting you," he says. "And think about it. Call us. You've got something."

You've got to be kidding, he means. As he looks away, the spell is broken. There will be a comedy video of me on YouTube any day now: the human beanpole who thought she was Kate Moss. But by the time I've stopped feeling dizzy and the buzzing in my ears has faded, it's all over. Simon has disappeared into the crowd and if Ava wasn't standing there, staring at me like I'd just sprouted a second head, I would swear I'd just dreamt the whole thing.

TWO

As the shock fades, Ava dumps her flute and gives me a hug. "Are you OK? Look, let's just give up and go home."

I nod. I'm shaking. That whole experience was just too weird for me to handle.

"Do you think he said it as a joke? What did he expect me to do?"

"I think he was a scammer," Ava says, staring angrily after him. "There's a lot of them about. They'll go up to anyone and say you could be a model, then next thing you know they're charging you five hundred pounds for photographs. Then they disappear. It's fairly evil."

"How do you *know* this stuff?"

"Happened to a girl named Holly last year. She had to miss the volleyball trip to France because she'd spent all her travel money on the photos. Turns out they were useless for proper modeling, but it was too late."

"That's terrible!"

"Yup. But don't worry, you're safe now. Come on — let's go."

I look at her gratefully. "But what about the money? Do you want to do another song?"

"No, it's fine. I'm tired anyway. Didn't sleep too well."

"Were you hot again last night?"

She nods and rubs her neck. It looks a bit swollen.

"And sweaty. My pj's were soaked again this morning. Exam stress, Mum says."

"You don't look stressed."

"I'm not."

And it's true — she doesn't look it. Ava doesn't really do stress. Whereas I've just been doing it enough for both of us.

We collect our bags and head for the subway. Now that we're not standing around in front of a bunch of strangers, I can start to enjoy myself. It's not often I get to wander around town with my big sister. Carnaby Street is full of trendy boutiques with pastel-painted shop fronts, and cafés with tables spilling onto the sidewalks. On the corner, a group of shopgirls from Liberty's are standing around in their chic black outfits and scarlet lipstick. They must be on a coffee break. I wonder if they know how cool and sophisticated they look.

Ava follows my gaze again.

"Lucky things. Mind you, that could be me in a few weeks."

"Really? You've applied for a summer job at Liberty's?"

"Not exactly," she says. "Constantine & Reed."

She pauses, waiting for me to be impressed. I'm sure I would be, but I've never heard of Constantine & Reed.

"Who?"

"Oh, come on, T. It's the biggest new fashion company in America. They're opening their first UK store in July. Everybody's talking about it."

"Not to me."

"Big surprise," she says, sighing at my T-shirt-and-shorts combo.

Ava is the fashionista of the family, and I'm the . . . well, I'm the normal one. I'm interested in all sorts of things. Trees. Drawing. Music (as played by actual musicians). People. But not shopping. It's too complicated. Finding jeans long enough to fit me is a nightmare.

"Anyway, this is by Constantine & Reed," Ava says, pointing at her bag, which has green and white stripes, with a logo of a snake in the middle. "Jesse bought it on the internet for my birthday. They're opening this shop in Knightsbridge, and Louise and I applied. It pays OK and they give you a discount. If we get the job, I can afford to go surfing with Jesse for at least two weeks in August, and Louise can pay for driving lessons. It'll be brilliant."

"So, you mean we didn't have to go busking after all?"

She looks uncomfortable. "Well, I don't know if I've got it yet, do I? And besides, it was fun."

She can see from my expression that "fun" is not how I'd describe the last half hour of my life.

"Tell you what, you can have all the takings, to make up for the creepy guy accosting you like that."

"Takings? But there aren't any."

"Aha! Well, that's where you're wrong. One of the wrappers still had a Starburst in it. Strawberry. Your favorite. It's yours."

She hands it to me as we reach the Underground station. It's hot and sticky and half unpeeled. I stick it in the pocket of my shorts, along with the card from Simon the scammer.

On the bright side, at least we didn't get arrested.

★

All the way home — standing in the crowded Tube train while Ava smiles at the man who gave up his seat for her — I try to work out why I was the girl Simon chose.

On the wall outside our bedroom there's an old clip frame stuffed with snapshots of my sister and me. Mum's favorites, mostly. Occasionally Ava sticks something in there, too. I know each one by heart.

In the top left-hand corner, I'm a baby in Ava's arms. She's two and she's sitting in a big green armchair, proudly holding me up like a school project. She is dark-haired and gorgeous, with long bangs over her big violet eyes. A toddler-sized Suri Cruise, without the designer shoes. I am round. And hairless. And crying. Why Mum chose that particular one, I don't know. I have a feeling it's the only one she's got of the chair.

In the middle: school photos. Ava looks like a fresh-faced beauty queen. I look like a frightened blob. Then something changes. I'm about ten. This would be the start of my judo phase. Now I look like a blob with purpose.

Party shots: me and my friends at various birthdays, all with our arms around one another's shoulders. Then I hit twelve and start shooting up. Now my friends have their arms around my waist.

Bottom right-hand corner, recently added: Ava's seventeenth birthday. I'm stooping down so my eyes are level with my sister's. From the side, I look like a question mark — Mum always threatens to make me take ballet if she catches me like this. Ava, meanwhile, looks like a young Elizabeth Taylor. I know this because she's been told it so often that we looked up Elizabeth

Taylor on the internet, and she was hot. She had the same violet eyes, the dark, wavy hair with its own special luster, and the perfect curves. Afterward, I googled a load of other movie stars from the same kind of time: Ava Gardner, Vivien Leigh, Jane Russell. My sister looks a bit like all of them, but with a better handle on eyeliner.

I know what true beauty is. I've grown up with it all my life and . . . well, that Simon guy must have been on drugs or something. Or else I look like the most gullible idiot in history.

THREE

When we get home to our flat in South London, Ava goes straight to our room to put her flute away and makes some noises about studying for exams. I'm about to follow — I have exams, too — but the man who is genetically responsible for my freakiness calls to me from his bedroom, where he's at work on his computer. He leaps up as soon as I come in, with a worried expression under his bushy unibrow.

On Dad, the height and the hair and the gangly limbs just about work. He looks like a mad professor — which is what he would have become if his university hadn't suddenly sacked half the history department last summer in a fit of cost-cutting. To be more accurate, he looks like a mad professor crossed with an eager collie. He has so much pent-up energy. He used to get rid of some of it by bounding around the lecture hall, inspiring his students with the delights of the English Civil War. Now he spends most of his time at home, writing a novel about Cavaliers and Roundheads, or working on job applications. I'm pretty sure the energy will turn into actual electricity if he doesn't do something soon. Maybe we'll be able to use him to power the apartment.

His worried look makes me nervous. My father is not a man to be left alone in a place with electrical equipment, or indeed any equipment. It's why I like to "help" him with stuff. Otherwise, somebody usually gets hurt.

"How are you, love?" he asks innocently.

"Fine." I hold my breath. "What happened?"

He scuffs a toe on the carpet. I sniff for smoke. The air smells clean enough. Nothing's blown up this time, then. That's good.

"So . . . is there a problem?"

"Ah. Well, I thought I'd help your mother with the laundry while she was working today. Your sister's sheets were soaking this morning. That's the second time this week. She's not hiding a Jacuzzi in there, is she?"

"She said she was sweaty. Oh, and her neck's a bit swollen."

"Anyway," Dad sighs, looking guilty again, "I got a bit distracted and twiddled a few knobs I probably shouldn't have."

This sounds bad. Really bad.

"Is something broken?"

"Not exactly."

He's still scuffing the floor with his toe.

"Do you want to show me?"

He nods. Like a guilty toddler, he leads me through the flat to the scene of the crime, which turns out to be the bathroom, where the washing machine lives. Placed over the bathtub is a clothes rack where various bits of laundry are hanging out to dry. So far, so good. Except I don't recognize some of the things. They look vaguely familiar, but small, like dolls' clothes.

"Sorry, love."

I look closer. Oh.

Two of the little things are my school skirts. At least they were.

"The prewash got a bit hot. Shrinkage problem. Didn't quite realize in time."

I look at Dad. He grins bravely. "They'll be OK, won't they? I mean, you're stick thin. You're a string bean, you are. Anyway, Ava'll probably let you borrow one of hers."

Yeah, Dad. And then Rihanna will call and ask to sing a duet. My father may be an expert on the English Civil War, but he's pretty rubbish at the history of his own family. Does he not remember that four years ago I went through a phase of being inspired by Ava's outfits and she forbade me from dressing like her, or borrowing any of her stuff, EVER AGAIN? She's recently made an exception for iTunes, but school uniform? I don't think so.

We stand in front of the clothes rack for a moment, not saying anything. We're both thinking that before Dad lost his job this wouldn't have been much of a problem. We'd have gone to Marks & Spencer and got some new skirts. But we can't do that anymore. Dad's overqualified for most of the jobs he goes for. We don't know how long his severance package will have to last, so every penny counts. It's why Ava and I don't have allowances anymore. He feels so bad about it that I can't really say anything, so I don't.

All the same, he senses my hesitation about approaching Ava.

"Tell you what, I'll ask her for you, if you like."

"Thanks, Dad."

But he can't — at least, not straightaway. When we finally track her down in the living room, she's asleep with her head on a pile of untouched practice tests.

She's still asleep when Mum comes in from work hours later, looking as glamorous as anyone can in a green nylon polo shirt and matching trousers — which, given my mum, is surprisingly glamorous. Imagine a middle-aged Elizabeth Taylor in a green nylon pantsuit.

Mum's the one keeping us going at the moment. It was her idea to move out of Rose Cottage, our pretty, old home in Richmond, so we could rent it out, and find somewhere smaller. She got a job at a local superstore, as well as doing occasional translating work, which is what she's qualified for. And she still cooks all our meals, like she used to. I think this might be because she doesn't want Dad to break the oven.

"Suppertime soon," she says, holding up a bag of fresh vegetables she picked up on the way home. "Can you set the table, Ted? Get Ava to help you. Goodness."

She gently wakes Ava, who looks surprised to have drifted off.

"Oh, hi, Mum. I'll do this later," Ava says, yawning and looking at her blank tests. "I'm just going to Louise's. She wants to hear all about Carnaby Street."

"No, you're not," Mum says firmly. "Suppertime is sacred, as you well know."

"But I can grab something at Louise's."

"A packet of crisps and raw cookie dough doesn't count as 'something,'" Mum insists.

Ava looks sulky. They have this argument several times a week. Ava claims that Mum's stunting her social skills; Mum says if she misses a decent meal it will stunt her growth. I leave them to it. Mum learned French by working in a restaurant in

Lyon when she was young. I wouldn't miss one of her meals if you paid me.

I only wish there was more of a table to set. After we rented our cottage out, we moved into this flat above a travel shop, on a main road in Putney, two bus rides away from school. No garden. Only two bedrooms, so Ava and I have to share. (She cried.) Green walls. Brown furniture. Tiny kitchen, which is why I'm setting out the knives and forks on a small folding table that we've squeezed into the back of the living room.

At least it's beside a window. There's a tree — an ash — in the messy, built-up yard between us and the house behind. Every day I look for signs of leaf growth and changing color. I miss the open spaces of Richmond Park so much it hurts. It's May, so the ash tree's feathery leaves are fully formed and starting to flutter in the gentle evening breeze. Tonight, I don't draw the curtains, so I can keep watching it as the daylight fades.

They join me, one by one: Mum with a dish of ratatouille, Dad bearing a massive salad bowl, and my sister, bearing a grudge.

"I'm fine, Mum, honest. Why shouldn't I go out later?"

"You had your head on the table when I got in. I think you need an early night."

"It was a refreshing nap. I'm OK now."

"Well, I worry about you."

"Well, don't."

"Anyway," Dad breaks in hurriedly, "tell us about busking this morning. How did it go?"

"Not as well as we hoped," Ava sighs. "Ted got approached by a scammer with a camera, did she tell you? You can stop staring at yourself by the way, T."

I look around guiltily. OK, so I was checking my reflection in the window. I happened to be thinking about what Simon the scammer said, and I wanted to see if anything had changed, but no. There's still a blonde caterpillar where my eyebrows should be, and my hair still looks as though a half-finished bird's nest has accidentally landed on my head. My face is as moonlike as ever, with wide-apart eyes and almost-invisible blonde lashes. Back when I was eleven, Dean Daniels said I reminded him of E.T. That was before my growth spurt. Then he started calling me Friday, short for Freaky Friday, which is short for plain Freak. Class comedian, that's Dean. And I'm his favorite source of material.

"No," Dad says. "We were talking about . . . other things. What's a scammer?"

Ava rolls her eyes and tells him the story about Holly and the five hundred pounds. He looks horrified.

"They're really convincing, these people." Ava shrugs. "They advertise in local papers, too, and on the internet. They say you look totally stunning and you just need to pay for some photos or training or whatever. They charge you a fortune for it, then — bam!"

"What?"

"Nothing happens."

"That's 'bam'?" I ask. *Nothing happens* doesn't sound very "bam" to me.

"They run off with your money and don't get you any work. Google 'modeling scams.' There's millions of them."

"You didn't pay anything, did you?" Mum asks, hand on her mouth.

"No, of course not."

"And they picked on *Ted*?" Dad says, astonished.

Thanks, Dad.

"Don't worry, darling," Mum says to me with a reassuring pat on the arm. "We'd never have let you go through with it. No way is any daughter of ours getting into the clutches of the modeling industry, is she, Stephen?"

"What?" Dad asks with a start. He was miles away, staring from me to Ava and back — from freak to fabulous — and frowning in confusion.

"I said," Mum repeats, "we'd never have let her go through with it. It's all drugs and anorexia, isn't it?"

"Hmm, you're right," Dad says, still not listening. "Mandy, love, have you noticed Ava's neck? I've been comparing it to Ted's just now. That's a real lump there."

"My glands are up," Ava grumbles, touching her neck gingerly. "It's been like this for ages. Oh, it's bigger now, though."

"Goodness, you're right," Mum says, peering closely. Then she puts her fork down, looking grim. "No school tomorrow morning, Ava Trout. I'm taking you back to the doctor's."

"But, Mu-um, I've got volleyball tomorrow morning!"

"Tough. You'll have to miss it. It's only one practice — I'm sure they won't mind."

"If you don't need it, can I *please* borrow your skirt?" I ask quickly.

Ava raises one eyebrow, to remind me of our many conversations on the subject. That would be a "no," then.

I wait for Dad to back me up, but he's forgotten already. His brain's still elsewhere.

Mum catches me glaring at him. She doesn't know about the laundry, so she assumes I'm cross with him for being so surprised that it was me who got scammed, not Ava.

"Never forget, darling," she says, "you have your own inner beauty. You'll always be lovely to me."

"Thanks, Mum. Great."

I was just about OK before, but when your own mother starts talking about your "inner beauty" you know you're officially doomed.

FOUR

Two weeks later, I'm modeling handbags in Paris.

SO not. Obviously. On Monday, I'm in choir practice in the assembly hall. My singing is about as impressive as my tambourine playing, but my best friend, Daisy, kindly drowns me out most of the time with her P!nk-esque go-for-it vocals. Besides, we've got a new Head of Music called Mr. Anderson, who bounces around in front of us like a ball in a lottery machine and makes us do hip-hop versions of Haydn and Mozart — or, as today, One Direction as arranged by Debussy. It's usually great.

As always, Daisy and I stand at the back so we can chat in between the singing bits.

"So, did you bring it?"

"What?" I ask.

"The card, of course."

I told her about it on the phone yesterday. I still can't quite understand what happened.

"No. It wasn't in my pocket when I checked. I think I've lost it."

I think back to the pale blue logo with the jagged line. I've searched everywhere for it but it's gone.

"But he could be back in Carnaby Street this minute, taking advantage of some poor girl. You've no idea what some people would do to be a model."

"No. What?"

"Well, stuff. Letting people talk them into bad situations."

She furrows her angry brow. Daisy does a lot of angry brow furrowing. When she was born, I'm guessing her parents were picturing a little bundle of natural goodness, with curly blonde locks and a sunshine smile to go with her name. What they got was a mop of black hair, an obsession with classic indie rock, and an easily aroused sense of grievance. Venus Flytrap would suit her better. I always think of daisies as black and spiky now.

"My mum said last night that a friend of hers had a daughter who got scammed. There was supposed to be this big audition for a tropical juice commercial. You had to go to this hotel room in your bikini. She went along and there were lots of girls in the room, milling about, and this guy was taking photos of them. Turned out, though, nobody knew who he was. There was no commercial. He was just some guy who liked looking at girls in bikinis."

"Ew! That's disgusting."

"I know."

"Well, this guy only asked my age," I say. "I don't think that's illegal."

"It should be," she grumbles. "Going up to strangers in the street and taking photos."

"He had this really nice Polaroid camera. Sort of retro. I'd love to have seen how it spat out the —"

The room has gone strangely quiet. Mr. Anderson is staring angrily in our direction.

"Oi! You there! The boy at the back. Stop talking and pay attention."

Everyone looks around. There isn't a boy at the back, just Daisy and me.

"Yes, you," he goes on. "The tall one next to the girl with the spiky hair."

A snicker goes around the group as people start to catch on, and the temperature of my face goes up by about five degrees.

"D'you mean Ted?" someone calls out.

Mr. Anderson nods. "Thank you. Yes, you, Ted. The boy at the back. You haven't been paying attention for the last five minutes. Will you come down, please?"

This isn't fair on so many levels. Daisy was doing most of the talking, for a start. I try to do as he says, but I can't move. My body's numb. My face must be so bright by now that you could use it as a homing beacon. I always thought Mr. Anderson liked me. I thought he was pleasantly surprised by my reggae interpretation of "Ave Maria." I had no idea he didn't even know I was female.

Daisy nudges me. Her eyes are completely round. "Sorry," she mouths. Then she glances down at my legs and looks sympathetic. Oh, no . . . I'd forgotten about *that*.

Somehow, Dad managed to shrink my skirt vertically, but not horizontally. On my waist it's still fine, but the length is different. Very, very different. *Length* is not a good way of describing it.

Short-th might be better. Because this skirt is super-mini. So short that if I tuck my shirt in, it pokes out at the bottom.

"You'll be fine," Daisy says, unconvincingly.

I glare at her. Then back at my legs.

"I'm waiting," sighs Mr. Anderson, tapping his foot.

Gradually some sensation returns to my limbs. Feeling like a human glowstick, I make my way down through the tiers of snickering singers. Then I walk across the assembly hall stage until I'm close to Mr. Anderson, beside the grand piano. I stand there, swaying slightly. The only thing keeping me going is the fact that suddenly he's more embarrassed than me.

"It's understandable," says a voice from the front row. It's Dean Daniels, naturally. The class comedian and wannabe *X Factor* star. "She's got no boobs. Boy's name. Easy mistake to make, sir. But she's definitely a girl — you can tell from the color of her knickers."

What? I look down in a panic. What color panties did I put on? How can he see them? Is the skirt that short? I yank it down as far as it will go, and half the choir erupts into laughter.

Oh, fabulous. Thanks, Dean. This is turning into *such* a perfect day.

"Er, I see," Mr. Anderson mumbles gruffly. "That's enough from you, Dean. Sorry about that, er, Ted, is it?"

"Short for Edwina," I whisper.

"Right. Edwina. Well, don't do it again . . . the talking, that is . . . Back to your place now. Um, where were we, everybody?"

"Admiring Friday's knickers," says a voice from the second row as I go past, not quite loud enough for Mr. Anderson to hear, but easily loud enough to make Dean grin.

Cally Harvest, sitting smugly in her cloud of poufy hair and signature perfume — Radiance by Britney Spears. I can smell it from here. I'm pretty sure it will always remind me of this moment. And make me want to be sick.

Cally smirks at Dean. I avoid everyone's eyes as I dodge my way back up to my place at the back, wondering who, in an ideal world, I would take my revenge on first: Cally, Dad, Dean, or Daisy.

Daisy looks suitably apologetic when I sit back down beside her, eyes stinging. She even hands me her sweater so I can put it over my legs. I can't bear to see them right now. They look pretty silly at the best of times — bits of spaghetti hanging down where my thighs should be — but at this moment their endless, bony paleness is more than I can take.

Mr. Anderson holds up his hands.

"'What Makes You Beautiful,' everybody. From the top."

The others stand to sing, while I sit where I am and regret ever coming to school today.

How come in my head I'm Ted Trout — decent ex-gymnast, friendly, artistic, a loyal supporter of the Woodland Trust — whereas in public I'm "the boy at the back"? Or Freaky Friday? Or, as of now, "the girl with the knickers"?

They hit the chorus. One voice sings out above the others, doing his famous Harry Styles impression.

Dean. If I could take my revenge on anyone first, it would be him. The guy everybody loves, because he's always cracking jokes and having a laugh. He's not bad-looking, if you happen to like walking bowl-banged early Bieber impersonations. I happen to know that Cally has had a crush on him since

Christmas, and it certainly looks as though she's got his attention now. He keeps turning to grin at her.

If Dean's on your side, everything's perfect. It's just that there has to be another side, to even things out, and that's the side I'm on. Me and all the other freaks and losers. But mostly me.

FIVE

"**A**nd what color knickers *are* you wearing?" Ava asks. We're on the bus home.

"That's not the point! Lilac, sort of, since you ask."

Somehow, I've managed to get a seat next to her for once. I wanted her to share my pain, but she's not taking this nearly seriously enough.

"I bet they're gray by now," she says. "All our clothes seem to go gray when Dad gets involved in the laundry."

"This is all *your* fault, you know, for not lending me your skirt last night."

She looks guilty. "All right, you can have the one with the dodgy waistband."

"Oh, great. Now that it's too late."

"Or I can always keep it —"

"No! I'll borrow it," I say quickly.

There's sulking and there's self-preservation. I'm not stupid.

She grins and looks out of the top deck front window. My favorite place on the bus. It's always full when I try and sit here, but somehow, when Ava wants to, it's free. It must be magic or voodoo or something. She's always been like this.

She scratches her arm and I spot the Band-Aid near her elbow.

"Oh, did the doctor give you another blood test?"

"Uh-huh," she says, "and he wants me to have a biopsy on my neck."

"What's that?"

"They stick a needle in and suck out what's inside so they can test it."

She knows how much I hate needles, so she says it with flailing hands and bulging eyes, looming over me like a mad scientist.

"Ew, get off me! Sounds yuck. You seem in a good mood for someone who's given blood."

"That wasn't the good bit," she says. "I got a text from Constantine & Reed this morning. I got the job! Louise did, too. Four weeks as a salesgirl. Longer if we want it. So that's the summer sorted." She does her singsong, happy voice. "I get to see Jes-se. And I get to go surf-ing. And I get a dis-count."

"So we *didn't* have to go busking!"

"It was a useful experience, T," she says, digging me in the ribs. "Just think — now you can put *professional musician* on your résumé."

"I don't have a résumé."

"Well, you will one day."

"Does a Starburst count as professional payment?"

She looks sleepy again and rests her head on my shoulder. "Just hope they don't ask you too many questions in your interviews. It'll be fine. Trust me." She closes her eyes.

Various students come to check out the front of the bus, see

Ava resting beside me, and give me a friendly wave. I take a deep breath and try to hold on to this moment. For five minutes, I'm not "the girl with the knickers" — I'm "Ava Trout's sister." Maybe this makes me temporarily cool by association. I sit back in my seat while the burning finally fades from my cheeks. Meanwhile, the Elizabeth Taylor look-alike beside me starts gently snoring into my collar.

Looking back ten days later, the sleeping was a clue. There were other clues, too, but we missed them. We all thought it was a combination of being a teenager, moving house, exam stress, and a virus. Instead, we worried about math and sociology tests, gray underwear, finishing a book chapter, and underdone potatoes dauphinoise.

Then the doctor called one morning to say the biopsy results were in. Mum and Ava arranged to get them that afternoon, while I was at school. I thought nothing of it.

By coincidence, as I get off the bus, I spot them walking back to the flat from the doctor's. I call to them and they turn to look at me.

It's the first of June. A beautiful summer's day. All the sycamore trees along the road are a vivid green, their leaves standing out against the crystal blue of the sky. But Mum's face is as gray as our knicker collection. So is Ava's. They won't talk to me. Not a single word. It is . . . not good. I have the same buzzing in my ears as when I was scammed on Carnaby Street. I want to say something but I can't think of the right question to ask, because I'm not sure I want to know the answer. Instead, I wait beside

Ava while Mum struggles to get her key into the lock of the front door. Her hands are shaking.

The sky doesn't make sense.

That's what I'm thinking. The blue sky doesn't make sense. Today it is the wrong sky.

Dad's waiting at the top of the stairs. I don't know if Mum phoned him from the doctor's office or if he just knew, but his face is gray, too. He looks as if something heavy is about to fall on him and he's worried he'll be knocked over.

We somehow get into the living room and, without thinking, we sit at the table in our usual places. Four gray faces, framed against a blue sky, with the ash tree waving cheerily through the open window, caught by a summer breeze.

Dad just looks at Mum. Something in his expression makes me reach out to hold his hand.

"It's lymphoma," Mum tells him. "The biopsy was pretty certain. They'll need to do more tests, but they think she's had it for months. *Months*, Stephen. And those other blood tests said she was fine . . ."

She stares at the tabletop. Her hands are still shaking. She's talking about Ava as if she's not there, and something about Ava isn't there at the moment. There's a far, faraway look in her eyes.

"What's lymphoma?" I ask.

Mum tries to answer, but can't.

"It's cancer, love," Dad says, surprising himself with the sound of his voice. "I think. Isn't it?"

Mum nods so microscopically you can hardly see it.

But cancer is for old people. Dad's mum died of it two years ago. Cancer kills you. Ava can't possibly have it. Maybe it's just a really bad flu. Or asthma?

"They're referring us to a pediatric oncologist," Mum says. "He has a space on Saturday morning. Apparently he sees patients on the weekend, which is good. It's not always so quick, but there was a cancellation and they didn't want to waste time . . ."

She stops as suddenly as she started, and gazes out the window at the tree, as if she's just noticed it. I stare at Ava's neck, just as Dad did when he first pointed out the swelling. It's very obvious when you look. Could it be an actual tumor, like they talk about on *Grey's Anatomy*? I can feel my whole body going cold. I don't want to worry anybody, but I think I'm going to faint.

Dad squeezes my hand to steady me. "Don't fret, love. It'll be fine. She'll be fine. Won't you, Ava, my sweets? Won't she, Mandy, love? What else did the doctor say?"

There's a coded signal in Dad's voice that clearly says to Mum that we need some good news, and quick.

Mum snaps out of her reverie and nods.

"He said it's quite common in teenagers and they know exactly what to do. He said this man at the hospital — Doctor . . . I've forgotten his name. *Damn.* Doctor . . ." She wipes a hand over her forehead and gives up trying to remember. "Something. Anyway, he's highly respected and he'll explain everything on Saturday."

"And it will be fine, right?" Dad checks.

Mum smiles a tight smile and says nothing. Clearly the doctor didn't say it would be fine.

"I'm going to bed," Ava says, getting up without glancing at any of us. "Wake me later."

Three gray faces nod. After she goes, nobody speaks. The breeze keeps blowing somehow. It's the only sound in the room.

Ava's favorite pictures are stuck to the inside of the closet door.

She's standing on a beach in Cornwall, wearing a wetsuit and clutching a surfboard. Next to her is a bleach-haired boy with a muscled torso and deep gold tan. This is Jesse, teaching Ava to surf last summer when we went camping near Polzeath. Oh, and falling in love with her, but that's quite normal. Ava has to deal with boys who fall in love with her all the time. The difference was, this time it was totally mutual. Jesse's surprisingly sweet for someone so gorgeous. Mum and Dad were convinced their romance wouldn't survive several months of not seeing each other — apart from one weekend at Christmas when he came up to visit — but it has so far. The photo's pretty tattered by now, because she regularly takes it down to kiss and stroke it, despite the fact that she has an identical version on her phone, which she also strokes and kisses.

I *know*.

Ava with her best friend, Louise Randolph, who's captain of the volleyball team. They're in matching skinny jeans, lacy camisoles, and smoky eyes, and look as if they're about to get signed up to a record label. Actually, I think they were going bowling.

A group shot of several girls in short skirts and sweatshirts, clutching field hockey sticks and grinning. Ava's in the middle, holding the silver cup they won last year at the South London

Schools Tournament. The team is going on tour to Belgium next term, if they can raise the money.

This is Ava's life: Jesse, surfing, and volleyball in the summer; her friends, looking good, field hockey in the winter — never mind A-level exams, which she takes next year. I don't think she's got time for cancer.

SIX

On Saturday morning, we show up at a building in central London that Dad assures us is not far from the British Museum. Mum gives Dad a stiff look at this point. We don't care if it's on top of the British Museum or, frankly, in London Zoo. It's a hospital. It's where pediatric oncologists see their new patients. Pediatric oncologists are doctors who deal with childhood cancer. My vocabulary is growing by the minute.

Inside, it's overwhelming, full of shiny floors and signs pointing to places where people get treated for lots of scarily named stuff that I didn't even know you could get. In the corridors, smiling staff in colorful uniforms bustle past gray-faced families looking just like Mum and Ava did when they first got the news. Like we all do, in fact. Looking lost.

It takes us twenty minutes to find the corridor where Ava's consultant, Dr. Christodoulou, is seeing his outpatients. Despite the fact that Dad is a highly trained academic, we can't seem to follow simple directions.

We sit in the waiting room, avoiding the eyes of the other families. Automatically, Mum and Dad look around to find something to read. You don't get to be a French translator and an ex-history professor without reading pretty much everything you can get your hands on, all your life. Mum grabs the only newspaper. Dad goes for the magazine with the largest amount of writing, which turns out to be *Good Housekeeping*. He reads it anyway. Maybe he'll pick up some laundry tips. Ava's already got her nose buried in an old copy of *Marie Claire*. That only leaves *Hello!* for me. I soon know more about the beautiful homes and failed love lives of B-list celebrities than I ever wanted or needed to. Luckily, the consultant is running five minutes ahead of schedule. A nurse pops her head round the door of the waiting room to show us into his office.

The consultation goes by in a blur. Dr. Christodoulou is not as old as I was expecting — younger than Dad, in fact, with a smooth, unlined face and black, wavy hair. He must have done all his training very fast. I wonder if he can really be a "highly respected expert" already. But for Ava's sake, he has to be.

He explains that her type of lymphoma is called Hodgkin's disease. The lump in her neck is not a tumor — or not the way I imagined it, anyway — it's a swelling of the lymph nodes. I didn't know you had lymph nodes, but now I do, and Ava's have got cancer. Once they've found out how far it's spread, they'll start treating it with chemotherapy, which is basically lots of powerful drugs that they'll be flooding into her bloodstream over several weeks until they've got rid of it. And if that doesn't work, they'll try radiotherapy.

Great. Not remotely frightening, then.

"But you look fit, Ava," he says to her with a smile. "That's a good start."

He's not the first person to tell Ava she looks "fit." Not by a long way. It's just not usually in these circumstances. She still smiles coyly, though, as if she's forgotten why we're here. I think she's struggling to concentrate. And he's not bad himself, as pediatric oncologists go. I really should stop noticing stuff like this.

"My secretary will book you in for the other tests you need, OK? It'll only take a few days. We like to move these things along."

Mum blows into a tissue; she's already gone through most of the box thoughtfully placed next to her. I think we're all very slightly in love with Dr. Christodoulou. Even Dad looks a bit less gray than he did five minutes ago.

"And you can make her completely better?" he asks, with a cough.

The consultant hesitates slightly. "I can't make any promises. But I can tell you that the treatment is very effective these days. Over ninety percent of our patients are completely cured." Then he turns his attention back to Ava. "Now, while you're here, I'd like our phlebotomist to take some samples." He smiles at our blank faces. "Blood samples. It won't take long."

Next thing we know, we're back in the corridor. Ava and Mum are being taken to wherever the phlebotomists hang out — in the basement, somewhere — and Dad and I are shown back into the waiting room.

I want to talk to Dad about the last bit of the conversation — about curing the disease. A ninety percent success rate is great, of course. It's an A in pretty much any subject. But I have a math exam coming up and I'm fairly sure that if you take ninety percent away from a hundred percent, it still means that ten percent of people don't necessarily get cured. What happens to them? However, Dad has already got his head buried in *Good Housekeeping* again. He's not avoiding me exactly, but I can tell he's not ready to talk. The thought might have occurred to him, too.

Instead, I pick up the abandoned *Marie Claire* from beside Ava's old seat and flick through it. It contains well over a hundred pages of perfect, impossible bodies in bikinis and high-heeled shoes. Whoopee. But I need distractions. Any distractions. So I decide to read my way through it, page by page, until Mum and Ava get back, or until my brain melts — whichever comes first.

There are a remarkable number of lipstick ads in *Marie Claire*. More than you'd think possible. And foundation ads. And perfume ads. And handbag ads. I'm starting to wonder how I've got through fifteen years of my life without owning a proper lipstick (I wear gloss if I remember; usually I don't), or foundation, or perfume (I borrow Mum's or Ava's, when I can get away with it), or a handbag. Yes, I really don't own a bag. I have a small canvas backpack that works perfectly well. Or at least I thought it did. Maybe I should own *one* handbag. I'm starting to feel I'm letting the handbag industry down.

Mum and Ava still aren't back. I plow on.

There's an article on "how to get a beach body." Another on whether bikinis or one-piece swimsuits are more flattering. And a very long piece on some aging blonde woman going through her walk-in closet of designer outfits, explaining which ones are special to her and why. I bet she owns a lot of handbags and not a single canvas backpack.

"What are you reading?" Dad asks me.

I look up. "Oh, this thing about some woman with a lot of clothes."

"Why?"

"Why what?"

"Why does she have a lot of clothes?"

This is a fair question, especially from a man who lives in the same three shirts and two pairs of trousers. I'm not sure of the answer, though, so I go back to the beginning of the article and read the opening blurb more carefully: "My love affair with fashion — Cassandra Spoke, founder of Model City, gives us an intimate tour of an über-agent's über-wardrobe."

There's a picture of Cassandra Spoke in her office. She has piercing blue eyes, tanned skin, and silky blonde hair, perfectly parted in the middle. She's wearing a black silk dress and very high heels. Behind her is the logo that represents her über-agency. It's a jagged black *M* inside a pale blue circle. The circle matches the color of her eyes, and is actually a *C*, for "City."

Oh.

This logo, I'm sure, is the same as the one on the card that Simon the scammer gave me on Carnaby Street.

Except . . . maybe he wasn't.

"Ted, are you OK?" Dad asks, frowning.

I nod dumbly and try to ignore the increasingly familiar sound of buzzing in my ears.

I think I got scouted by a legitimate model agency, owned by a fashion star. And my sister's having blood tests to see why her neck's got cancer. It feels as though the world has turned upside down. I'm not sure I'm ready for this.

SEVEN

The rest of the weekend goes by in a blur of phone calls, missed meals, forgotten homework, and sleepless nights. Back at school on Monday, Daisy helps me try to adjust to the news.

"Why don't we go outside?" she says at first break. "It's such a nice day. We could sit on the grassy knoll."

The grassy knoll is part of the landscaping outside the school's new cafeteria. I follow her out there to chat. Normally we sit by ourselves, but today we're constantly interrupted by a stream of gorgeous male students, who suddenly all want to talk to me. Me! Mind you, I quickly come back to Earth when I realize why.

"Are you Ava's sister?"

"I heard she got some bad news, right?"

"Is she in today? I haven't seen her. I'm kind of freaked out, to be honest."

"Tell her I said hi, OK? Here's my number, in case she doesn't have it."

Daisy sits with her eyes on stalks, watching them all troop by.

"I can't believe that Shane Matthews is trying to hit on Ava at a time like this," she mutters, disgusted. "Doesn't he know she has a boyfriend? What did the consultant say, by the way? She is coming back to school, isn't she?"

I nod. "She's just taking a few days out to get used to it and have some tests. He said to keep living as normally as possible."

"Like you feel so normal right now," Daisy says, oozing with sarcasm.

She's right. I can't even remember what normal's supposed to feel like. All I feel now is empty, as we wait for the next piece of information, so we can figure out what to do.

In class this morning our homeroom teacher, Mr. Willis, told everyone what had happened while I was taken to the guidance counselor for a chat about my feelings, which was a bit of a waste of time for us both, because emptiness is a difficult feeling to describe. However, it added a new one — which was guilt about feeling empty, instead of whatever feelings I'm supposed to have. I could have talked about that, but I didn't, because by then it was time to go back to class, where everyone stared at me with their mouths literally hanging open. It wasn't the best start to the day.

Meanwhile, more cute boys pass by the grassy knoll to pay their respects. Thank goodness I'm sitting here in Ava's borrowed skirt and not my micro-mini. I feel like a walking condolence-book-cum-dating-site. I suppose I could try and describe that to the guidance counselor next time, but I don't think it's the kind of feeling she was looking for.

The bell rings. Daisy and I get up. We have a math exam any minute. Why they take the month of June, the most glorious in the whole English calendar, and fill it with exams every year of your school life, I can't begin to imagine.

"How's Ava coping, by the way?" she asks.

I shrug. "I don't know. She's pretty quiet. She seems so calm but she must be feeling so . . . It's like she's avoiding it. I heard her telling Jesse how much she'll miss the beach this summer, but that's all. Mum's in tears every five minutes, though. And Dad accidentally broke his watch."

"And you?"

I use the fact that we've arrived at our math room as an excuse not to answer. Because when we got back from the hospital on Saturday, I was distracted. Perhaps I just didn't want to think about the bad news conversation, but I couldn't help remembering that logo in *Marie Claire*, and Simon the not-a-scammer-after-all, and what he said to me on Carnaby Street.

I keep trying to make sense of the whole "have you thought about being a model" thing, and I still can't do it. Mum caught me staring at myself in the bathroom mirror, and wondered if I was getting a zit. I said I was, because it was easier than explaining that I was trying to find any passing resemblance between me and Kate Moss. Or the girl on the cover of *Marie Claire*. Or indeed anyone in a magazine who's not there as the "before" picture in a cosmetic surgery ad.

I know it's selfish and irrelevant, but I just wish I knew what Simon meant, and why he picked me of all people to say it to.

At night, Ava can't sleep. Neither can I. I hear her constantly changing position in bed on the other side of the room. Her skin itches and makes her uncomfortable. One of the symptoms we didn't pay enough attention to, like the fevers and night sweats. Her body has been trying to tell her something for a long time.

"Are you hot?" I whisper.

"A little."

There's silence for a while.

"Ava?"

Nothing.

"Are you OK?"

Long sigh. "What do you think?"

More silence, while I make a mental note not to ask my sister if she's OK. Ever. Again. Idiot.

"Is there anything I can do?"

She shifts about to face the closet next to her bed. "Just don't talk to me about it, OK? Talk to me about something else. Tree hugging? Daisy's latest band obsession? I don't know — anything."

Oh, right. Fine. I wasn't going to mention it, but since she asked . . .

"Er, actually, there was something. Ava, what if that Simon guy turned out to be for real?"

"Simon who?" she grunts crossly.

I lean up on one elbow and whisper more loudly.

"Simon from Carnaby Street. The scout. What if he actually meant it — that stuff about me? What if it wasn't a scam?"

There's a sudden rustle, then a click. The bedside light comes on. Ava's sitting bolt upright in bed and staring straight at me.

"Are you sure?"

"No. I mean, he might have been having a joke or something. But his agency's real — Model City. I checked out their website.

It's got this famous girl called Isabelle Carruthers who's on loads of magazines and . . . I dunno . . . not Lily Cole, but other people you've heard of."

"What? Really? That never occurred to me."

"Thanks a lot."

"Sorry. It's just . . . Holly went on about those scammers last year. And I just assumed . . ."

"I know," I sigh. I don't blame her. Of course, if he'd picked on Ava, we'd both have assumed he was real.

"I guess every once in a while they must be genuine," she goes on. "Or how would they find people? I used to dream about modeling, you know. A bit. Secretly. Before I met Jesse."

"Really?"

"Yeah." Her smile widens. "Me and Louise. Imagine the clothes . . . The makeup. Looking your best all the time. Getting your hair done. Meeting celebrities. Traveling on private jets. Practically living in Paris. The clothes . . ."

"You said the clothes."

"I know. Practically living in Milan. Practically living in New York. The money. The clothes . . ."

It sounds exhausting. All that changing outfits, apart from anything else.

"So what happened?"

"Well, first of all, I discovered surfing. After you've had that rush, nothing else compares."

She pauses, clearly thinking back to last summer and remembering the rush.

"And?"

"Oh, and Jesse said he'd never date a model in a million years."

"Why?"

She ponders for a minute. "He never said. I didn't ask him. He just seemed pretty certain about it. Besides, he said that although I'm perfect in every way — for him — I'd be too short for anything top-modelish. You have to be at least five foot nine or something, and I'm five seven."

This is odd. Jesse is a surf dude who lives in Cornwall. "How does he even know?"

She shrugs again. "No idea. He knows lots of weird stuff."

Her goofy smile returns. Now she's thinking about the surfing rush *and* the Jesse rush. Then her expression changes again and she looks at me, head cocked, thoughtfully.

"Anyway, we're not talking about me. We're talking about you. Come to think of it, it all adds up. I watched a program about models once, and they said the girls they pick aren't necessarily the ones you'd think of. They need people who are . . . unusual. They have to have a special look. And they did mention the minimum height thing. You must be five eleven by now."

"So Simon picked me because I'm freakishly tall."

"And freakishly thin. And didn't he say he thought you looked gorgeous?"

"No. He said 'amazing.' "

"Whatever. Get over yourself, T!"

"You were just saying I could be a model!"

There's silence again. Ava's plotting something while she examines one of her perfect fingernails.

"Yeah, actually," she says eventually, with rising excitement in her voice. "If that guy *was* for real, you could! It would be SO COOL. You could get lots of free stuff and give me some of it.

You could tell me about the celebrities, what they're like behind the scenes, the tricks of the trade —"

"And take drugs and get anorexia," I remind her, thinking of Mum.

She snorts. "They can't *all* do it. Besides, Mum would never let you get anorexia. She practically force-feeds us as it is. Anyway, you eat like a horse. If you had to go more than twenty minutes without a cookie, you'd keel over."

This is true. However, Ava has put her finger on the other flaw in her plan, apart from the fact that I am neither beautiful nor clinically insane: Mum. She'd totally forbid me to even try. I point this out.

"I'm sure I could persuade her," Ava says, worrying at her fingernail. "Think of the money, Ted. Linda Evangelista didn't get out of bed for less than ten thousand dollars a day."

"Who's Linda Evangelista?"

"Oh, for God's sake! Anyway, imagine what Mum could do with ten thousand dollars."

I can't. I can imagine what *I* could do with ten thousand dollars, though — converted to pounds, obviously. I'd get our old cottage in Richmond back. The garden. My own space . . . I didn't appreciate it enough while we were there, not nearly. Oh, and I'd buy a couple of school skirts. Long ones. And lots of new underwear.

"But there is another option," Ava suggests. I'm not sure she really believes Mum would be won over by the money argument.

"Oh. What?"

"Not tell her. Not to start with, anyway. Not until you were super-successful. Nobody minds when you're super-successful."

"Brilliant. Genius," I say. I'm not often sarcastic with my sister, but honestly. Of all the rubbish ideas I've ever heard . . .

"Listen." She sits up again, with her arms clasped around her knees and her head resting against them. She looks exhausted. Those dark circles under her eyes were another clue. It seems impossible that someone you live with every day can have cancer and you don't even see it. And here we are talking about modeling: We must both be crazy. "I'm going to be . . . busy this summer. Lots of hospital appointments and . . . you remember Nan. Chemo is tough. You need something fun to think about. We both do. You can't rely on me to provide your entertainment."

This is true. I know I rely on her too much, but she's always been there — thinking up mad stuff to do — and I guess I'm just used to it. Sure it's annoying sometimes, but I don't want anything to be different. Certainly not like this. If the guidance counselor were to ask me how I was feeling right now, I'd say I was upset: upset and frightened.

Finally, Ava turns out the light and I lie there in the darkness, wondering. About Ava, about me, about Simon. About having your whole summer taken away because your dad noticed a lump in your neck. About earning ten thousand dollars a day. Is that honestly possible? And who *is* Linda Evangelista, anyway?

EIGHT

As soon as I can on Tuesday morning, I tell Daisy about my conversation with Ava.

"She wants you to do *what*?" she asks, dropping her backpack on her desk with a thump.

"I know. It doesn't make sense."

"So what was her argument?" Daisy asks. "Why did she think you'd be interested?"

"Something about life being precious," I mumble. "*Carpe*-ing the *diem*, I suppose."

"Whiching the who?"

"Seizing the day. It's something that Dad says."

"By standing around in your undies?"

"I know. But Ava says you get to go on planes and stuff. And you get paid loads of money. And it would keep her happy."

"When have you ever wanted to keep your sister happy?" Daisy scoffs.

"Since she got lymphoma?"

"Good point."

As we unpack our bags, I wait for Daisy to remind me about the drugs and anorexia. She feels the same way about fashion and modeling as I do — which is that there are fashion victims and there are real people like us, with better things to think about, like who is cooler out of The Kills and The Vaccines, or passing math.

But she doesn't. People tend to clam up when you mention cancer. I must remember that. It's a bit of a conversation stopper.

"Actually, I thought I might as well," I say, as casually as I can.

"What?"

"Apply."

"Where?"

"To Model City. You know, as a laugh."

Daisy jerks her head up in shock and spills her books all over her desk. I help her pick them up and pile them neatly.

"As a laugh?"

"Yes," I say defensively. "They have a form on their website. I could just fill it in and see what they say. Ava'll be pleased. If they say no, then that's fine. I'll stop thinking about what that guy said on Carnaby Street. If they say yes, then it means . . ."

I pause. Daisy watches me, curious to see what I'm going to say next. I'm not sure myself.

". . . It means . . . Well, it's just a laugh, really. It's mostly about humoring Ava."

Daisy says nothing, but her expression says *Oh yeah?* She's right, of course. It's true that it's *mostly* about humoring Ava, but another reason has crept up on me — one that I simply can't mention out loud.

If they say yes, it means I won't feel so bad the next time Dean thinks of a nickname for me. It means that just once, somebody, somewhere, thought the freak with the unibrow looked OK. It would be a little secret I could hug to myself.

Daisy can stare at me like that all she likes, but her dad plays bass in a Blondie tribute band and she's got Debbie Harry's autograph. I have . . . a pressed leaf collection. Besides, I wouldn't actually *do* any modeling, because that would be crazy. And anyway, Mum wouldn't let me. And I'd look really stupid in my undies.

"It's post-traumatic stress," Daisy says, patting me on the arm. "You've gone a bit gaga. It'll pass. Are you sure you're up to school today?"

She doesn't get it, but I don't care. Ava will help me with the photos for the form when I get home. It'll be fun and silly and exactly what we need right now. All I have to do is send two snapshots and some basic details about myself. How hard can it be?

Harder than I thought.

After half an hour of rummaging through my half of the closet, Ava looks around at me in despair.

"I thought this would be fun," she complains. "I thought it would be like dressing Barbie. But my Barbie didn't have a whole closet of nothing but hiking shorts and baggy cargo pants and . . . ugh! What's this?"

She pulls out a crumpled, green, tentlike thing.

"It's my Woodland Trust supporters T-shirt," I say defensively. "I had to get the big size, because the others only came down to my —"

"It's offensive. Throw it away."

"It's saving the planet!"

She sighs. "You can wear that blue tank top you use to sleep in. It's the least hideous thing I've seen. And what about skinny jeans?"

I shudder. She sighs again.

"What if they want to see your legs?" she asks.

"Believe me, they don't want to see my legs."

"But what if it matters?"

I shrug. "That only makes it worse."

We settle on my least baggy cargo pants and the blue tank top. Which leaves us with the hair problem. Ava spends ten minutes "styling" the bird's nest until it looks like a tornado's passed through it, then gives up.

"Let's just take the pictures. Sit on your bed. The website says we have to do one full-face photo and one side-on. Ow!"

She briefly squeezes her right hand into a fist. After several hours of scans and tests at the hospital, the backs of both her hands are punctured and bruised from all the needles that have gone in. But we're not thinking about that. Mum's spending most of her time on the phone to well-wishers, telling them we don't know any details yet, and it gets very boring. Making me look like a supermodel is much more entertaining. Making me look like a supermodel is all we've got.

Ava points her phone at me and I stare into the tiny lens, trying not to laugh.

"You look like a serial killer, T. Smile slightly."

"They said not to."

"Well, try not to look as if you've just been arrested for something disgusting."

"Like this?"

She takes a picture and shows it to me. Not only do I have more than a hint of serial killer about me, I also have an ash tree growing out of my head.

"I can't sit in front of the window. How about if I move around? Like this?"

I now have Snoopy lying on my bird's nest, thanks to the poster above my bed. I used to have it in my bedroom in Richmond and somehow I can't bear to replace it with anything more age-appropriate.

"And you look blurry," Ava says, examining the pictures more closely. "I don't think my phone can cope with these light levels. Let me find my proper camera."

After a five-minute search in three drawers, two keepsake boxes, and four old handbags, she finds it in the pocket of her winter jacket. I shift around our bedroom, perching on every bit of furniture and trying to look casual. But there doesn't seem to be a single spot that provides the blank background we need.

It's a relief when Mum goes out, so we can try other places in the flat. We try to keep our voices down, though, because Dad's still busy in their bedroom, working on the latest draft of his Civil War novel. It's called *Leather and Lace*, and Dad reads bits of it to us occasionally. I'm not sure he's the next Stephenie Meyer, plus Ava says that the title sounds like a 1970s porno, but hopefully someone will like it.

"How about if you balance on the back of the sofa?" Ava asks. "We can take down that seaside print. Then you've just got white space. Well, green space, anyway."

She takes a picture. I now have a dark gray shadow beside my jawline and blinding white light from the camera flash bouncing off my cheek. Alternatively, when I stand with my back to the kitchen door, its avocado paintwork makes me look vaguely purple. How does anyone who doesn't live in a palace ever manage to look good?

Ava scowls at the pictures, then at me. "They've already seen you. Why don't you just call them?"

Oh, dear. I was hoping she wouldn't ask this. The simple reason is that I have some pride. I don't want to be told over the phone that Simon was having an off day when he found me, or that they have no idea who I am after all, and will I please stop bothering them? I'd much rather hear it by e-mail.

"Because they say to use the form," I tell her tetchily.

Dad comes out of the bedroom, en route to the kitchen to make himself a cup of tea.

"What are you up to, girls? I keep hearing a lot of giggling. Are you all right, Ted? You look a bit odd. And are you wearing your pajamas?"

It's that avocado background. And my stupid outfit.

This is ridiculous. I totally give up.

"We're not up to anything," I snap. "Shall I just make the tea?"

"Would you, love?"

Ava looks disappointed. It was a nice idea. We tried. But my supermodel days (or, to be strictly accurate, forty-five deeply frustrating minutes) are most definitely over.

NINE

For the next week, the sun gets hotter by the day. At school, the grassy knoll fills up with people sunbathing between exams. At home, the leaves have turned pale on the ash tree and it looks almost as pretty as the trees in Richmond. When she's not working, Mum has her head buried in recipe books for nutritious summer salads using red fruits and green leaves. Apparently the dark colors are full of antioxidants and they'll help Ava get better — along with the vat-loads of chemicals they're about to start injecting into her. Personally, I don't see how a few raspberries are going to compete with chemotherapy, but Mum's prepared to give anything a try. This seems to be her way of coping.

Dad's way is researching Hodgkin's disease on the internet, in between manic bouts of writing and trying to get his watch fixed. Mine is . . . staring out the window, mostly. Often Daisy has to prod me at school because I haven't heard what she's just said.

Of us all, Ava is the most relaxed. Her biggest concern is that Jesse has two more A-level exams and a big sailing race to train for, so he can't come and visit her yet. Other than that, she seems to be coping amazingly well. Perhaps it's Dr. Christodoulou's reassuring attitude. Perhaps it's having most of the hot boys in her grade asking after her whenever she's out of school for more tests. Perhaps it's just that she's not very good at math. (I still can't help remembering about the ten percent, but maybe she didn't notice.) Above all, she just wants to carry on as normal.

I come home from school a week after our snapshot fiasco, and she's in the middle of a raging argument with Mum.

"I refuse to let you come with me!"

"But you can't go on your own, darling. You're very *ill*!"

"I don't feel it. And you'll just cry everywhere. I *hate* it!"

"I promise not to cry."

"You're doing it now!"

Mum rubs her nose. 'I'm not. Look, darling, this is a very important appointment."

"It's totally routine!" Ava sighs loudly and sees me standing in the living room doorway. "Tell her, Ted. I've just got to pop into the hospital on Saturday to check everything's working properly. I can do it in a couple of hours by myself. She's turning it into a major expedition."

By "everything," I assume she means the thin plastic tube she had inserted into her chest yesterday, called a Hickman line. One end sticks out so it can feed the chemo into her bloodstream when it starts on Monday. Ew. Disgusting. Actually, when she showed me last night it looked rather neat. Not as bad as I was expecting — a bit like earphones for a mega-iPod taped to her skin. But still . . . No wonder Mum wants to go with her to check it's working.

"Er . . ."

"I can walk, Mum. I can take the Underground. These things don't weigh anything. Besides, you need to work. Tell you what, Ted can come with me. How about it, T?"

"Well, actually, Daisy invited me round to . . ."

Ava puts on a hangdog expression. It's a fake hangdog expression, I know, not even designed to make me feel that guilty, but when your sister has lymphoma . . .

"OK. I'll come."

Mum sniffs. "All right, then. If you're sure. I know you don't like me fussing, darling."

Ava sighs. "Exactly."

When Ava got the diagnosis, all we wanted was news, details, and explanations. Then the test results came in and they just seemed to make things more confusing. Apparently, the disease has reached Stage 2B, which enables them to know what type of chemo to give her and how long for. But why are they starting next week, for example, and not this minute?

Dad instantly pounced with the inevitable "2B or not 2B" joke from *Hamlet*. His face was like granite when he said it, but Ava and I laughed anyway. Mum didn't. Sometimes, I sit beside him at the computer so we can try and make sense of it all. The stage refers to how much the disease has spread. It seems Stage 2 is worse than Stage 1, but a lot better than Stage 3 or 4. The B means Ava gets night sweats. They have a letter for it and we have a washing machine for it. Whatever.

Stage 2B. To me, it sounds like a venue at a music festival. Staring at Dad's computer screen that evening, the words circled around my head until they meant nothing at all.

Ava seems to be right about this latest appointment being routine, though. When we get to the hospital on Saturday, it's a totally different experience from the last time I was here. Ava knows her way around the shiny corridors pretty well by now, and a nurse only takes a few seconds to fiddle with her Hickman line and check that the insertion point is OK. Everything's set for Monday, when they'll hook her up for the first bout of life-saving chemicals. That's it. We're done.

Outside, the sky is still wrong: It's blue and cloudless. It hasn't rained for three weeks now. There's a sort of café-style, Mediterranean feel to the city and the streets are full of tanned legs and smiling faces.

"Come on," she says. "Let's go for a wander. We could check out the British Museum."

"We co-ould . . ."

"Only joking. There are some nice shops on the Tottenham Court Road. We could walk down to Oxford Street."

This is Ava's part of town, not mine. I tend to go where there are gardens and trees, like Kew, or art galleries, like Trafalgar Square. But it's nice to wander around in the summer sun with Ava, checking out the window displays. In the end, it gets so hot that we decide to walk down one of the side streets, where it's shadier.

I'm in the middle of admiring a selection of French pastries in a bakery window, arranged by color in a rainbow of edible perfection, when suddenly Ava stops dead and grabs me.

"Oh my God!"

She points across the road. We're opposite one of the uglier buildings on the street. Plain brick walls. Small windows. No shop fronts. Two people outside on their iPhones, sharing a cigarette.

"What?"

"See the logo?"

Above the plain front door is a sign: a jagged black *M* inside a pale blue *C*. Ava recognizes it from the website I showed her. I recognize it from Simon's card, and from *Marie Claire*: Model City.

"We could just go in, you know," she says.

I am having a cold flush. I didn't know you could get them, but you can, and I've got one.

"No, we couldn't."

"We're right here, T. You never sent in that form. Why don't you just walk inside and ask them?"

The girl is bonkers.

"And then they can tell me *to my face*," I point out, "that I must be joking."

"They would," she says, standing her ground, "except one of their scouts said you looked amazing."

She's remembered the exact word. *Amazing*. All I know is that I'm *freezing*, despite the sun. I've got actual goose bumps on my forearms.

"I'm going home."

But Ava's still holding my wrist. "Please? For me? You said you'd give it a go, T, remember?"

A brief image of Dean Daniels flashes in front of my eyes. Not a pretty one. But it would be so cool to be able to tell him I was a model. She senses my hesitation.

"Look, we'll just go in and ask them if you've got potential. We'll mention that scout guy and stay for five minutes, OK?

Then we'll go home. And I promise I won't bug you about it again."

"Promise?"

"Promise."

Since her diagnosis, I would swear Ava's brain has gone wonky. There's a dangerous glitter in her eyes. It's as if she's heard the worst, and now only good things can happen. I hope this is true in her case, but I'm pretty sure bad things can still happen to me. She looks so excited, though, that I can't bring myself to say no.

"Oh, all right, then."

I know, absolutely, that it is the wrong thing to do, but this is the effect Ava has on me. I'm about to enter Buzz Lightyear territory all over again.

She opens the door and I follow.

"Wow!" she mutters under her breath. "How gorgeous is *this*?"

If by "gorgeous" she means "terrifying," then this is utterly gorgeous.

We are in a luxury reception area, with black-and-white wallpaper, a shiny modern desk, a black leather sofa, and a coffee table smothered in glossy magazines. The ceiling is sprinkled with spotlights. The walls are plastered with photos of superstunning men and women, most of them underdressed. On the desk there's an arrangement of blue hothouse flowers the size of a baby elephant. Everything is fresh and gleaming and glamorous and intimidating.

Behind the desk, a bored-looking girl with long brown hair and heavy bangs is typing on her computer. She totally ignores us. Ava and I stand there, not sure what to do. Moments later, the smokers from outside come back in and whisk past us, heading for a door at the back, without giving us a second glance. I've never felt so invisible. Ava, meanwhile, plucks up the courage to speak.

"We're here to see someone about . . . modeling."

The girl at the desk glances briefly at Ava from under her bangs.

"Oh, yeah?"

"My sister's interested."

This is *so* not true after the snapshot disaster. The girl flicks her eyes to me for half a second. Then she picks up the phone, mumbles into it for a moment, and goes back to ignoring us.

Ava looks at me, and smiles encouragingly.

"Let's go," I say.

"In a minute. Let's see what happens."

She sits on the sofa, leaning forward to grab a glossy magazine from the table in front of her. I perch next to her and hear a grunt from the floor beside me. A small black dog looks up at me from his curled-up position in a brown leather dog bed with Ls and Vs printed on it. I reach down to stroke his nose.

"Don't touch Mario," the receptionist says, without looking up. "He doesn't like it."

"Sorry?"

"The labradoodle? He's called Mario? After Mario Testino?" Now she's staring at me from under her bangs as if I'm mentally challenged. "Like, the photographer?"

"Oh, right."

She can see I have no idea what she's talking about. It's Linda Evangelista all over again. I decide to leave the dog alone. I'm just about to suggest to Ava — for one last time — that we leave, when the front door swings open and a new guy walks in, complaining loudly about the heat.

I recognize him instantly, partly because of the orange backpack slung over his shoulder. To my surprise, he smiles as soon as he sees me.

"Tambourine Girl? Hi! It's Simon."

Ava's looking up from her magazine now, smiling her movie-star smile. Simon ignores her. She frowns. I get up and shake his outstretched hand. "Yes . . . I remember."

"So — you're here! Are you seeing Frankie?"

"I don't think so," I whisper. "We just popped in —"

He calls across to the receptionist. "Is she booked in for Frankie, Shell?"

Bangs Girl pouts and flaps her hands. "I called her, but she was busy."

So basically, she was happy to let us sit on that sofa indefinitely, while nobody in the office knew that we were here. Thanks, Bangs Girl. I am so not enjoying this moment.

"Frankie does New Faces," Simon explains. "Come with me." He spots Ava at last and remembers her from last time. "D'you want to come in, too? Loving the hairstyle, darling. Very retro."

Ava blushes and puts a hand to her shoulder-length curls. We follow Simon through the door at the back, into a large, open-plan office, where about twenty men and women look around to stare at us. It's as if our invisibility shields have suddenly disappeared. In modeling, you obviously have to know the right people, and I suppose that means people like Simon.

The only ones to ignore us now are a blonde-haired woman sitting at a large desk in the far corner of the room, and the slim-backed boy sitting opposite her, leaning forward intently. They seem to be busy arguing about something. Everyone else is openly staring at us. I am a walking bundle of nerves.

"Frankie!"

Simon grins across at a pixie-haired girl with a patchwork of Polaroid pictures arranged in neat rows on the wall behind her. She looks up from her computer and grins back. She doesn't look much older than Ava, but even though her desk is the messiest I've ever seen and you can only just see her above all the paperwork, she somehow seems more organized than we'll ever be. Perhaps it's because she's on the phone, talking fluently in some language that isn't French while simultaneously typing, fast, on her computer keyboard. Perhaps it's because she can do this and also flirt with Simon, making funny faces and batting her eyelashes at him.

She puts the phone down. "Two secs." She smiles, flicking her eyes back to her screen. "Just e-mailing Milan. Nightmare. There. We're done. Who's this?"

She eyes me up and down and I can feel everyone else do the same. Frankie's eyes come to rest on my pale spaghetti legs. Oh, why couldn't I have worn cutoffs, like Ava? Why did I have to pick today to wear my trusty hiking shorts? Perfect for visiting old battlefield sites with Dad. Less perfect in a roomful of designer T-shirts and skinny jeans.

"It's Tambourine Girl," Simon explains. "Remember I told you about her? What do we think?"

Frankie tips her head to one side, half-closes her eyes, and nods. "We think interesting. Nice bone structure. Unusual features. How old are you, er . . . ?"

"Ted. Ted Trout."

"*Seriously?* Anyway — how old?"

"Fifteen and a half," I mutter.

"And a half! You're so sweet! And so you want to be a model?"

"I'm not sure," I say, which is a polite lie for "No — frankly I would rather be a skydiver." I look to Ava for reassurance, but she's distracted by a large photo of a guy in skimpy underpants next to the door where we came in.

"How about we take some pictures and see what you've got?"

How about we *don't*? This was all so much easier when it was just about filling in a form. But Frankie has poked around under her paperwork and is holding a Polaroid camera like Simon's, ready to go.

I suppose now that I'm here, we might as well get this over with. Actually, it should be educational for her. Just wait till she sees how terrible I look in pictures — even the simplest snapshots. Then she can have a good old laugh and Ava and I, and my shorts, can all go home and recover in private.

Ava tears her eyes away from the guy in his underpants and squeezes my arm excitedly. By now, luckily, most of the office people have lost interest in me and are watching the whispered argument going on at the desk in the corner. Frankie gets up and leads us through to a smaller room next door. It has a row of filing cabinets at one end and a white screen next to some freestanding spotlights at the other. She checks out my shorts and gray tank top.

"That's fine. You'll do, angel," she decides. "No makeup, which is great. Just stand over there, would you?"

By "over there," she means in front of the screen, with lights shining at me. Please not. I stay rooted to the spot.

"Go on," Ava whispers. "It's fine, trust me. You just have to stand there."

That's easy for her to say. What if I'm supposed to pose and pout like those models in all the pictures? What if other people poke their heads around the door and start watching? What if I self-combust with humiliation?

She gives me a gentle shove, and I somehow shuffle over to the screen and wait while Frankie fiddles with a shiny, round silver reflector attached to another stand. Luckily, Simon followed us in and Frankie's too busy chatting with him to pay me much attention.

"He's on his final warning at school. He's driving her insane. He's supposed to be in these study periods, but he won't go because he says he 'needs visual stimulation.'"

Simon laughs. "Cheeky so-and-so."

"So she brought him into the office today to keep an eye on him. But he keeps using office phones to call this friend of his in Tasmania. He's a nightmare. Total nightmare. Last week he ran up fifty pounds on her cab account to visit the White Cube gallery."

"Is that the boy talking to the woman at the big desk?" Ava interrupts. My sister has no shame.

"Yeah," Frankie laughs. "She's Cassandra. She owns this place. And he's her son. Total nightmare. We pretend not to listen, but of course you can hear every word." She looks up at me. "There you go. I think we're ready. Relax! Think gorgeous, OK?"

Simon hands her the camera and she takes the first picture.

Of course. Cassandra Spoke. I remember the silky hair from the *Marie Claire* article.

"It's since Sheherezade, isn't it?" Simon asks. "She messed him up big-time."

"You wouldn't believe," Frankie agrees. *Click.* "Don't get involved with the girls. Rule One."

She throws her head back and laughs as if it's the stupidest rule ever invented — or at least the one least likely to be obeyed.

Which girls? Who's Sheherezade?

"There you go, angel. All done," Frankie says to me. "Let's see what we've got, shall we?"

But how can we be all done? I haven't posed or stuck my chest out or anything. I just stood there while she chatted with Simon and moved around, taking pictures from a couple of different angles. I thought she was testing the camera.

"Done?"

"Yep," Frankie says, as she and Simon examine the Polaroids. Ava crowds in, too. "And they're not bad. I've taken worse."

"Really?"

She laughs at my surprise. "See for yourself."

The photos are very plain — just my face and top half — but compared with Ava's efforts at home, they're mini-masterpieces. It's amazing what a white background and some decent lighting can do.

"So, can you walk for me?"

I must have misheard her. I thought she said "walk." Of course I can walk. But when she explains it to me, it's worse than I could possibly have imagined. It *is* walking, but it's across the office next door, in front of the twenty staring people.

"I — I don't think so," I stutter.

"Don't be silly," Frankie says with a hint of a sigh. I suppose she must be used to people who can talk in foreign languages while typing and flirting. I found "just standing there" enough of a challenge. "It's walking. Up and down. It'll only take a moment."

Ava does her pleading face. Simon smiles encouragingly. I'm still about to say no, but when he opens the door back into the main office, I realize that everyone is still mesmerized by what's going on between Cassandra Spoke and Nightmare Boy. Frankie nods in their direction and, without thinking, I set off. I'm curious to get a clearer view of him and see what all the fuss is about. It's quite nice to have an excuse to go closer, actually.

Nightmare Boy is sitting hunched over, with his back to me, so all I can see is rumpled hair, a faded pink T-shirt, paint-spattered jeans, and dirty sneakers with holes in them. His voice is a low, insistent growl, but he must hear me approaching, because he stops talking to scowl at me. Black-rimmed glasses. His mother's blue eyes. Pale face. Cute lips. Nice hair. I *wish* I wasn't wearing hiking shorts.

As I near the desk, Cassandra looks up, too. Oh my goodness. The über-agent of über-agents is staring straight at me. I turn around quickly and head in the opposite direction.

Back where I started, Frankie grins. "Cute walk," she says cheerfully. "It's coltish. Don't lose it."

I promise not to, and breathe a sigh of relief. The ordeal is over. There are no further humiliations they can put me through.

But it turns out that yes, there *are* more humiliations.

"We just need to measure you now," Frankie says, rummaging in her desk and pulling out a tape measure. She wraps it around my nonexistent chest and calls out my measurements to a guy three desks away, so that everyone can hear them.

Ava giggles. I glare at her. She had better be grateful for this. Buzz Lightyear has now paled into insignificance in the catalog of mortifying moments she has subjected me to.

Frankie has a quick muted conversation with Simon before taking us over to her desk and laying my Polaroids out on top of the general mess. I'm just relieved I don't have Snoopy on my head in these pictures. I must remember to ask Ava to delete the ones on her phone.

"Well, you've definitely got something," Frankie says. "And if you end up working with us, you'll have such a good time. We're a close family at Model City."

I glance across at Cassandra and her son. Really?

"But before we make any decisions we need to do a test shoot," Frankie goes on. "I've got one coming up soon that might work for you."

Ava grins, but suddenly I'm experiencing my second cold flush, and it's no more fun than the first one.

I can't believe we fell for it.

Here we were, assuming that they were the real thing, and they were just a bunch of scammers after all. I must say, they disguised it brilliantly, but how much money is it going to take to get out of here? I did google "modeling scams" like Ava suggested, and they said the scammers can be very persistent. They keep telling you that you have to spend more and more . . .

"The test shoot — how much would it cost?" I whisper.

Frankie looks at me quizzically, then smiles. "Oh, it doesn't cost you anything. We know photographers who need shots for their portfolio, same as you. They don't charge, and you don't. See? When you get a proper job, the client pays us and *we* pay *you*, minus our commission, of course. Don't worry, angel, we'll look after you. We're totally legit. It's why we'd need parental approval, by the way. Your parents are OK with you doing it, are they?"

"Oh, definitely," Ava chimes in. "They're really excited. They were just, er, busy today."

"Fine. Well, you can bring them in when you come and get your test shots. So, how was that?"

I am having an out-of-body experience.

They say they're "legit," but they're talking about signing me up. Did they not notice my legs? Or the unibrow? Or the hair? Or the fact that I'm still in school? Or that I don't know who Mario Testino is? Or that I'm sitting next to a goddess and they haven't shown the slightest interest in her? These people clearly have NO IDEA WHAT THEY'RE DOING.

"Ted? Ted? What do you think?"

But I suppose I should be polite. I put on my brightest smile. "Amazing."

TEN

"Wasn't that fantastic?" Ava says on the way to the Underground afterward. "Just let me call home."

"You're not telling them what we did?" I ask, appalled.

"Of course not. Duh!"

In a serious voice, she explains to Dad that we were badly held up at the hospital, but we're finally on our way home. She lies so brilliantly and fluently that I'm in total awe of her talent. Then she grins happily at me.

"See? Easy! Frankie loved you!"

"It was horrific!"

"You were great."

"You should have seen the way that boy looked at me. Like I was a worm."

"Ignore him. You're gorgeous, it's official. Ooh, I must call Jesse."

She whips her phone back out to tell him the news.

"He's totally impressed," she informs me afterward. "He says congratulations."

"I thought he didn't like models."

"He doesn't like his *girlfriend* to be a model. Sisters can do what they like. Aw, look, smiley face."

She shows me her phone. Jesse has sent her a bug-eyed picture of himself stretching out both sides of his mouth with his fingers, so all you can see are teeth, gums, and tonsils. He still looks better than I did in those Polaroids. I sigh quietly to myself.

"I'm not doing that test shoot, Ava. You know that, don't you?"

"Yes, you are," she says cheerfully.

I don't even bother to argue. There are a million reasons why I can't do it, from not really knowing what a test shoot is, to lack of "parental approval," to sheer terror at the very idea of it, to — hello? — my whole face and body. But Ava seems so happy right now that I can't bring myself to list them. I'll do it later, when her excitement has worn off.

It's not difficult for us to keep what happened at Model City a secret from Mum.

Monday is what Ava calls "C Day" — the day her chemo starts — and Mum's totally focused on making sure she's read all the paperwork, obeyed all the instructions on how to prepare, blown the budget on fresh, organic fruit and vegetables, and got everything ready for making Ava feel comfortable afterward, in case the chemicals make her feel as bad as Nan did, which was so awful that Mum cries whenever she thinks about it.

We spend the rest of the weekend scattered around the flat, with Mum sobbing into a tissue and Ava telling her off about it,

Dad busy trying to fix the gear shifter on his bike (and breaking it beyond repair), and me trying to take up as little space as possible.

If the guidance counselor were to ask me now, I'd say I feel guilty again. Guilty for being so healthy, while my sister has a plastic tube sticking out of her chest. If I could go halves with her and settle on a shared bad bout of chicken pox, or a broken leg each, I would. But nobody asked me. I am not a part of this equation. So I keep quiet and try not to make anybody's nerves more jangled than they already are.

On Sunday night, we both lie awake long past midnight. I can hear Ava's breathing, and she can hear mine.

"It's going to be fine, T," she says into the darkness, sensing what I'm thinking. I know I should be comforting her, but in the topsy-turvy world we've entered, she's good at trying to comfort me. "People get this all the time. I've just got to get through the chemo and I could be clear by December. You heard what Doctor Christodoulou said about me being fit. He's an expert. He's treated loads of people way worse than me. We just need to look after Mum and Dad, because they're really not taking this well."

No kidding. She seems disappointed by their reaction, but I have to say I can totally see where they're coming from on this one.

When Monday comes, Mum lets me stay at home while she and Dad take Ava in for her first session. Ava has to sit there for a few hours while the drugs run through her system, then she can come home. I wanted to go, too, but they all said no. So, I have several hours of daytime TV ahead of me. Not scintillating, but at least I get to miss our French oral exam — which was definitely beyond my powers of concentration today.

Daisy texts me afterward to say how bad it was. She follows it with a line of question marks and exclamation marks. I'm not sure if these refer to the exam, though, or our phone conversation yesterday, when I told her about Model City. Daisy thinks I'm crazy to follow my sister *anywhere*, but especially into the arms of a model agency. We both agreed that modeling is for anorexic people with no brain cells. Well, Daisy said it and I agreed. A teeny bit of me was hoping she'd be impressed that they liked my Polaroids all the same, but she completely wasn't. She kept focusing on the "being crazy" part.

I'm engrossed in a program about reintroducing the elm tree to the British countryside when my phone goes again. I assume it will be Mum, or Daisy calling back with more angst about French, but instead it's a number I don't recognize.

"Hi, angel," says a chirpy voice. "It's Frankie. About that test shoot? We've got someone fixed up for next weekend, and maybe you could join her. You don't have school on Saturday, do you?"

"Er, no, but —"

"Perfect. It's with Seb Clark. He's really lovely and gentle. I'll call you later with the details, but I just wanted you to get it on your calendar, OK? God, sorry, got to go."

I can hear the sound of another phone ringing in the background, then nothing. If Frankie had stayed on the line I could have explained about not doing the shoot, but I can't face calling her back. I start trying to figure out the best thing to do, but my brain isn't really working today. It's too distracted by what's happening at the hospital, and also — thanks to this program — what happened to the elm tree. Over twenty million of them were killed by disease in the last forty years. We need to replant the new ones as fast as we can. Soon the call has slipped from my mind, and I don't remember it again until Ava gets home and asks me about my day.

Which, if you think about it, is the wrong way around. My day was natural history programs, hers was chemo. But there's something strange about Ava. Whatever drugs they've given her, they've had the opposite effect from what I expected. Her eyes still have their dangerous glitter, she's full of energy, and you'd think she'd just been to a rave — or how she looked when she got back from Glastonbury, anyway.

"How did it go?" I ask.

"Ew, at the time," she admits, taking a bite out of a banana. "But I feel WONDERFUL now. Mum says it's the steroids. I don't care. If it's going to be like this for the next two weeks, fantastic!"

Are they sure she has cancer? Has she been massively misdiagnosed? Anyway, while Mum gets busy chopping apples, celery, and practically anything else green that isn't the kitchen door, I tell Ava quietly about the test shoot.

"Fabulous!" she says when I've finished. "Perfect! Hey! My sister's nearly a mod-el! It's so exci-ting! Go check her o-out!"

She dances round the room as she singsongs. What *did* they put in those steroids?

"I'm not going, remember?" I point out.

"Why?"

She stops dancing and pouts at me.

"Because I don't want to. Because it's silly. Because I'd need permission."

"You *do* want to. It's a test shoot! How cool is that? Lily Cole had test shoots. So did Rosie Huntington-Whiteley. You'll be like Heidi Klum."

Who *are* these people? How does she know about so many of them, when I only know Kate Moss and Claudia Something, who Dad fancies? Why would I want to be like Rosie Huntington-Whiteley anyway? OK, I can imagine how *people* might want to be like them. *Attractive* people. Just not people like me.

"Go on, T," Ava pleads. "You looked great in those Polaroids. It's just one morning. You'll have fun. Think of it as work experience."

"As what?"

"I dunno. Stylist? Hairdresser? Makeup artist? Designer? You'll meet loads of new people. It'll be good for you."

"Just because you want to be a surf instructor —"

"Cool job, huh? Better than your tree surgeon idea. Or Bob the Builder, I seem to remember. Or Oreo taster."

"Not necessarily. And I can't do it anyway," I say, playing my trump card, "because Mum would kill me."

"Aha!" Ava exclaims, playing hers. "But she won't know, will she? Because she'll be at work on Saturday, in that fabulous green uniform of hers, and Dad's researching at the library. So the flat will be empty and they'll assume you're here, doing homework, or at Daisy's. And if they ask difficult questions, I'll cover for you. You know how good I am at lying."

I do. She inherited all the lying genes, whereas whatever I'm thinking is written all over my face.

"And look, Frankie's gone to all that trouble, just for you. You can't let her down now, can you?" She does her pouty face. "I'll call and pretend to be Mum and tell them that it's all sorted. I'll help you get ready. You can tell me all about it. And I've just had *chemo*, T. How can you resist me?" Mega-pout.

But this time I'm ready. I pull myself up to my full five feet eleven inches and stare her straight in the eye. "No way ever. Not in a million years. And that's final."

She doesn't say anything back. She just points to the area in her chest where the tubes are, and smiles a wicked smile.

ELEVEN

And so, at eleven o'clock on Saturday, I find myself standing outside Highbury & Islington Underground station, watching Ava study Dad's *A-Z* map of London and wondering when I will ever learn. Probably never. When we're in our nineties, I'll be doing something stupid with my walker because my older sister made me.

And she'll be around then, obviously. Because what's happening is just a blip. Ninety percent of people are totally cured. Totally.

I'm still not sure how she talked me into it. I lasted twenty-four hours. Then I crumbled and she really got to work. First, she had to make the call pretending to be Mum, giving me permission to go on the shoot and saying that sadly she couldn't come along because she had a hospital appointment. (Untrue on all counts. The next appointment is on Monday.) Frankie hemmed and hawed, because apparently I HAVE to have a chaperone if I go to a shoot at my age, but then Ava said — as Mum — that I have an older sister who'd be happy to come along instead, and Frankie agreed. Unfortunately.

Then we had to figure out what "casual, figure-hugging clothes" were, because apparently I've got to wear some, and I don't have any. Well, I have that gray tank top that I wore to Model City's offices, which seemed to be OK, so my top half is set. But I don't possess "casual, figure-hugging" pants, and I am NOT wearing my hiking shorts again. I refuse to subject some poor photographer to my legs unless absolutely necessary. I couldn't wear Ava's jeans, even if she let me, because they're too generous around the bum and only come down to my shins. So I've borrowed a pair of Mum's yoga leggings. I couldn't look more ridiculous, but my sister insists.

Finally, we had to figure out how to get there. The address is an old post office building in North London that's been converted into studios. Ava's good at getting to shops and sports venues. I'm good at getting to public galleries, parks, and gardens. But neither of us has tried to get to a post office building in Islington before. I haven't started modeling yet, and it's already a lot more difficult than it looks.

"This way," Ava says, in a semi-confident tone. "What's the matter, Ted?"

I'm still thinking about the expression on Dad's face when she told him she felt like seeing a couple of films at the movie theater today, and that I'd agreed to go with her. He gave me an odd look and peered at me for ages before he said good-bye to us. Any minute now he's going to figure out we're up to something, and come and stop us. I wish he would. There's something seriously wrong with my sister, and it's not just lymphoma.

"Oh, come on! Aren't you excited?" she goes on. "Modeling

studios! Makeup! You're going to look gorgeous!" She grabs my arm and hurries me along.

Five minutes later, we're standing outside the sort of abandoned-looking building where bodies are found in detective series.

"This is it!" she says, checking the map for the last time. "Second floor."

She bounds ahead and I follow, cautiously. We let ourselves in through a large, unlocked door and head up a flight of concrete steps. If I thought being accosted by Simon on Carnaby Street was weird, this whole situation is positively disturbing. Doing it with a sister high on steroids isn't helping.

When we reach the second floor, Ava leads me down a long corridor until we hear the sound of voices. We poke our heads through a doorway at the end, and there we are: in a huge, light-filled room with a concrete floor and white-painted brick walls. A guy in a black T-shirt and shorts is sitting at a rickety table, with a shiny laptop in front of him, calling out instructions to someone I can't see. Ava knocks on the open door and he turns around to look at us. I gasp slightly. He has more facial hair than I would have thought possible. Bushy beard. Massive sideburns. Unusually large eyebrows. Underneath it all, he looks as if he might be quite young, but it's hard to tell.

"Hello," he calls across to us. "Are you here for the shoot?"

And the strange thing is that he says it to me, not my sister. Me, the model. The actual model. Bizarre, but wow.

We go over and introduce ourselves.

"I'm Seb," he says. "I'm the, uh . . . photographer."

I'd kind of gathered that from the enormous Nikon camera, with a very large lens, sitting next to his laptop. He looks around, at the lights, the cables, the screens and reflectors, the laptop, me.

"I'm going to be, uh . . . shooting you today."

"Great!" I say brightly. I'm thinking that if everything goes at this speed, this shoot is going to take a *looong* time.

"We're going to do it . . . uh . . . here," he adds, wandering over toward the white brick wall.

Does he mean this studio? Where else would we be doing it?

He can see my confusion. "I mean, like, uh . . . *here*." He indicates a particular spot on the wall, where the paint is slightly peeling. "Or, uh . . . here." He points at another peeling place, farther down. "The light's good. Atmospheric shadows. I might try a bit in natural daylight. See how we go. Interesting texture . . ."

He was almost going at normal speed there for a minute, when he talked about the light. Now he's come to a halt.

I look at the wall. It's true; the paint is more interesting where it's patchy and flaky. And the shadows thrown by the bars in the high windows are moody, almost spooky. My art teacher, Miss Jenkins, would agree it was very atmospheric.

"See what I mean?" he says.

I nod, because I do, and he smiles. His teeth look weird poking through all that beard, but it's a friendly smile. He seems pleased to have found a fellow wall-appreciator.

"Actually," Ava says, looking pale and woozy suddenly, "I think I might sit down. That journey was longer than I thought. Is there a chair?"

Seb shows her into a little room carved out of one corner with a couple of sofas in it, and a kitchenette at one end. She curls up on one of the sofas.

"Are you sure you're OK?" I ask, going over and stroking her hair. "I mean . . ."

Duh. "OK" is a relative term in my family now. I bite my lip.

"I'm fine," she says sleepily. "I mean it. Call me when you need me. But don't fuss, OK?"

With Seb hovering at the doorway, checking his watch, I don't have much choice.

"Is that your . . . uh . . . sister?" he asks.

I nod.

"Mine's upstairs," he says. "Doing hair and makeup. She . . . uh . . . helps me out."

Leaving Ava where she is, I follow Seb up a set of rickety stairs to a small changing area, built on top of the kitchenette. His sister is putting makeup on a girl with blonde, curly hair. They both turn around to say hi to me. The sister looks like Seb, but less hairy. The other girl looks like a fairytale princess. She has a perfect oval face and gray-green eyes. Her hair, wrapped around curlers, shines like coils of spun gold. Even with only foundation and eye makeup on she has, without a doubt, the most stunning face I've ever seen outside the pages of *Marie Claire*. Honestly! I have never been this close to anyone so mesmerizing. She even makes Ava look only mildly attractive by comparison. And I'm being photographed after her. *What* are they thinking?

"Hello," she says, smiling at me. "I'm Mireille. How're you doing?"

"Fine," I lie. Mireille. Mum let slip once that she thought about naming me Mireille, but she thought Edwina sounded more romantic. Not sure what planet she was on at the time. "I'm Ted."

Seb leaves us to it. His sister, who's named Julia, explains that she usually does freelance makeup work for theater companies.

"Normally, I like to do something a bit creative, but today Seb wants you natural. We're just highlighting the eyes and cheeks. I'm nearly finished with Mireille. Won't be a mo'."

I sit on a spare chair and watch as she carefully applies layer after layer of lipstick to Mireille's perfect mouth, blotting and adjusting as she goes. I remember what Ava said about work experience and try to understand what effect Julia's going for. According to what she just said, the lips are going to be the least important bit, but this is taking ages, and Mireille's lips are very . . . pink. Then Julia gets to work on the cheeks.

"Is that, er, natural?" I ask. I mean, I'm sure Julia knows what she's doing, but . . . well, actually, I'm *not* so sure. To me, Mireille looks as if she's about to go on stage at a nightclub.

"It will be different in front of the camera," Julia laughs. "It's shocking how the lights bleach you. Although Seb said he might work with natural light today, so I'm really underplaying it."

If this is underplaying it — goodness.

Julia takes Mireille's hair out of the curlers and brushes it. The beautiful girl checks out her gorgeous face in the mirror, gives a nod of satisfaction, and thanks Julia, before heading downstairs to be photographed. Meanwhile, I take her place. Julia herself, I notice, isn't wearing a scrap of makeup, apart from the backs of her hands, which are covered in test swipes of foundation, blusher, and blue eye shadow, and remind me a bit of Ava's hands at the moment, color-wise. They're still bruised from all the needles she's had poked into them to take endless blood samples. She doesn't talk much about what happens at the hospital, but I know it's tough, and I can understand that she'd rather be here, asleep, than at home, thinking about it. Frankly, right now, I'm glad she made me come, even if Julia can never make me look like Mireille.

For what seems like several hours, but must be about thirty minutes, Julia applies various creams and powders to my face from among a vast array she's laid out on the shelf beside us. Once I get used to a stranger touching my face, it's actually very relaxing. I can't see what she's doing, because I'm facing her, not the mirror. I just have to trust that it's OK. She also fiddles about with my hair, doing the best she can and only sighing occasionally. Her one comment is that my caterpillar unibrow is going to have to go sometime soon, but coming from the sister of a modern-day Yeti, I'm surprised she even noticed.

"There!" she says when she's finished. "Better."

I check the mirror at last. Please God, let me have turned into Linda Evangelista, whoever she is.

Hard to tell. Does Linda Evangelista look like a moonfaced geisha? That's my first thought, when I see my BIG eyes, pale skin, and bright lips. But as I get used to it, I realize that I'm still underneath there somewhere. I'm about one percent as pretty as Mireille, but a hundred percent more model-like than I was before Julia started. Even my hair looks like a nest made by a tidy bird who was quite proud of it. I feel like an actress, dressed up for a part, or like I did when I put on my *gi* in judo, ready for a grading. The makeup makes it easier, somehow — like a barrier between me and that enormous Nikon camera downstairs. I think I'm as ready as I'll ever be.

Julia follows me down to watch Mireille pose for Seb. I was worried they might have finished by now, and I wouldn't get a chance to see how to do it, but it seems they've hardly started. Taking a few photos is a lot more time-consuming than I gave it credit for.

I quickly check on Ava, who's still fast asleep on her sofa in the kitchen area and doesn't stir when I call. She is technically in charge of me and I'm sure she'd love to see what's going on, but she looks so peaceful where she is that I decide not to disturb her. I'll tell her all about it later. Then I go back to stand near Julia and see what I can learn from Miss Perfect.

Meanwhile, Seb has placed an old, battered wooden chair in front of the peeling paintwork and Mireille's sitting on it backward, with her chest leaning against the back of the chair and her legs either side of it. She constantly moves her head so he can capture her face from various angles. The air is full of pumping drum 'n' bass, coming from a speaker attached to Seb's laptop. I'd be dancing along to it, but Mireille is ignoring it entirely, focusing very much on giving Seb her smile and making sure her coils of hair are hanging perfectly around her face. Every now and again, Seb says, "Uh, can you . . . uh . . . ?" and wiggles his hand until Mireille shifts position and gives him the smile from a different direction.

Oh, no. She has a smile.

I don't have a smile. I mean, I *smile*, obviously. I do it a lot. But I don't have *a* smile, which you obviously need. Nor, needless to say, do I have coils of golden hair to arrange around my shoulders. My spaghetti legs will look daft on either side of that chair in Mum's yoga leggings. And I'll find it very hard to stop jiggling to the drum 'n' bass. Other than that, I'm good.

HELP.

I still can't quite believe that Ava talked me into this, but I'm here now, and I've got to go through with it. At least Seb will be taking pictures of Geisha Ted, not the real me. And they'll have the pictures of Mireille, so the morning won't be entirely wasted.

After a while, she goes off to change and Seb turns to me.

He gestures toward the chair. I sit on it unhappily. He checks me out through the viewfinder of his huge black camera and looks unhappy, too. First he adjusts a couple of lights, then he returns to me.

"Could you . . . uh . . . face . . . to me . . . Uh . . . hands?"

I look at him — not that I want to. That camera is so scary. Then I look down at my hands. What's wrong with my hands? They're just sort of hanging down beside me. I mean, sure, they look like dangling twigs, but what else can I do with them? I try placing them on the back of the chair and resting my chin on them to cover them up. Seb jolts like a startled bear.

"Uh . . . no. Too low. Your . . . uh . . . back. Humpy. Try . . ."

He leans back and sticks a leg out sideways to show me what he means. He looks hysterical. I grin.

"Nice," he says, looking slightly less depressed. "Nice grin."

Then Julia steps in to save me.

"Why don't we try turning the chair back around? Then you can try some different poses. I think Seb wants you to play with it a bit. Feel free. Relax. Have some fun with it."

Feel FREE? RELAX? Have FUN with it? I'm suddenly conscious of bits of my body I normally take for granted. My ankles. My elbows. What do I do with them? Where do they go? And my twig fingers — how do real models make their fingers look so *normal*? Never mind my face. I try every sort of smile I can think of until my mouth hurts, but Seb just looks increasingly depressed.

Eventually he says, "Uh . . . not the chair . . . Uh . . . try just standing?"

Aha! "Just standing" is something I can definitely do. I tried that at Model City and it worked. As long as "just standing" can also include "slightly jiggling," because Seb's speakers are playing a song I really like, and it's categorically impossible not to move. I go over to a piece of wall that Seb and I agree has great peeling texture, and "just stand" in various poses. Hands on hips. Hands not on hips. Leaning against the wall. Half leaning against it. Even standing sideways on and looking up at the high windows. Then, when I think Seb's finished, I do a bit of actual dancing, waving my hands above my head and wiggling my hips — or what would be my hips, if I had any.

"Great!" Seb says. "Hold it! I mean . . . uh . . . keep doing that."

He clicks away and I find that as long as I stare at the floor, not him, and only think about the music, I can keep going. Finally, I look up to check if he's still taking pictures and he clicks one final time and says, "Done. You can . . . uh . . . change now."

I stop moving.

"Change?"

"Into the dress? Did Julia show you the dresses?"

She didn't. Now she does. They're hanging on a rack upstairs. It turns out that after the "casual, figure-hugging clothes" shots, they want to take more pictures of us in not-so-casual, but even more figure-hugging, minidresses. Oh.

At this point, the door to the studio opens and Cassandra Spoke walks in, dressed impeccably in a white silk shirt, black skirt, and high-heeled sandals. Followed by her nightmare son.

Luckily, the floor opens beneath me and swallows me whole.

Except, of course, it doesn't.

Cassandra clicks across the concrete floor and gives Seb two impressively large air kisses, just skimming his beard with her golden skin.

"Seb, darling! How gorgeous to see you!" she says. "I just had to show you — they've finally published your pictures in *Dazed & Confused*. Don't they look wonderful? Nick wanted to say thank you."

Nightmare Boy sticks his hands in his jeans pockets and looks as though he doesn't want to say anything at all. His face bristles with discomfort behind his glasses. Cassandra takes a magazine out of her handbag and lays it open on the table. Her son scowls behind her, while I sneak back down the stairs and look over Seb's shoulder to see what the fuss is about.

There's a double-page black-and-white spread of a girl with big hair, doing headbanging poses in front of a wall-sized, swirly, spattery painting.

"Ooh, it's a bit like a Jackson Pollock," I say without thinking. Miss Jenkins would beam with pride. Jackson Pollock is one of her Top Three Abstract Painters and all our art class can recognize his style a mile off by now.

Nick coughs, and turns around to face me. "I was going more for Cy Twombly, actually. Although it's influenced by Abstract Expressionism, of course."

"Wow! *You* did that?"

His scowl cracks slightly. "Yes." Then he stiffens again. "Seb kindly offered to showcase my work. Er, thanks, Seb. Great pictures."

He forces the words out. Something about these pictures makes him super-uncomfortable.

"What Nick *forgot to mention*," Cassandra says with a smile at Seb and a quick glare at her son, "is that he just might get a place at art school on the back of these. It's exactly the exposure he needs. You do me the nicest favors, Seb darling."

She air-kisses Seb again, making sure to avoid the beard, while Nick does the "please swallow me up" look at the floor that I was just doing.

Poor Nick. He's trying to be cool and artistic and his mother is organizing his life for him. I'm starting to get why she drives him crazy. He looks up, catches me grinning at him, and smiles for a moment, before glancing down to fiddle with a fleck of paint on his T-shirt. It's interesting that he doesn't seem to possess any clothes that aren't worn, torn, and paint-spattered, despite his mother having a magazine-worthy über-wardrobe. He's cute when he's embarrassed. Still out of my league, though. Actually, I don't even have a league.

"Oh, hello."

We all look around. Mireille is standing on the staircase, freshly changed. She is drop-dead gorgeous in a tight pink minidress from Julia's rack, but a bit flushed at the sight of the über-agent in person.

Cassandra gives her a gracious smile. "Don't you look lovely? Actually, why don't I see how you've been getting on?"

To my surprise, Nick doesn't seem that interested in Mireille. Maybe, after years of traveling around with his mum, models bore him. He wanders off, as Seb offers to show Cassandra the photos he's taken so far. Mireille joins us at the computer and Cassandra quickly scrolls through shot after shot of her looking fantastic, until she gets to the ones of me. She sighs. I can't bear to watch.

"These ones are getting better," Cassandra says. They're the shots of me looking at the windows. Then, "Ah." These are the ones of me dancing. "Shame she's not looking into the . . . Oh."

They've got to the last picture: the one where I thought Seb had finished and he caught me with my arms in the air, looking straight at him. And do you know what? I can see why Cassandra said, "Oh." It's all right, that picture. There's something about it — the way I'm moving, the look of surprise on my face, my gangly arms waving — that's quite interesting. The girl in that picture looks . . . OK. Not like Lily Cole, or Kate Moss, and not like Mireille, but OK.

"Well," Cassandra says decisively, "either way, I think we've got what we need. Good job, Seb, darling. I don't think we need to bother with the dresses." She doesn't sound entirely happy, and I don't blame her. I only produced one good shot out of about a million — well, over a hundred, anyway, and poor Seb's been working for hours.

But that one shot is good enough for me. I can't wait to show Ava. I excuse myself and rush off to the kitchen area to see if she's awake yet.

She's just sitting up and stretching when I get there, looking tons better after her nap.

"Sorry!" she says, yawning. "Did I miss the whole thing?"

"You did. But guess what? Seb actually managed to take a decent picture of me. Only one, but it's really quite nice. It's, like, the first one *ever*. It must be that camera. I think I might save up for a Nikon one day . . ."

I trail off. Nikon cameras are so out of my price range. I was definitely getting a bit carried away there.

"It's more the lens than the camera," says a voice behind me. I whip around. "But it's a load of other things, too. The light. The background. The composition. Mostly the light, though. You could do it on your phone if you tried hard enough."

It's Nightmare Boy again. I wondered where he'd got to. He's been busy getting himself a Coke from a vending machine in the kitchenette.

"Really?" I say. "I noticed that the brickwork in the background was good. Seb chose this great, peeling bit. And it's true: He didn't use many lights in the end. It was mostly daylight."

"The best shots are," he says. He looks up at me and gives me another quick smile. "You should check out the style blogs. They mostly use natural light. I'm Nick, by the way."

"I'm guessing you're a photographer," Ava says, stretching and coming over.

He peers at her. "You look familiar. Have we met?"

"Not exactly," she says. "You were in your mum's office when we came round."

"Oh." He frowns. "Anyway, no. I'm an artist, really, but I dabble in photography. Not this sort of thing, though." He waves a dismissive hand toward the studio.

"What sort of thing, then?" Ava asks, looking hurt on my behalf.

Nick considers. "Experimental. Documentary. Pictures with a purpose. I'm still working it out. Look, I use this website — a group of us do." He pulls out a tiny notebook from his pocket, tears out a page, and scribbles on it. "If you want some ideas, look here."

He hands it to me. The paper is thick and creamy: sketchbook paper. It's still warm from his body heat.

Ava's phone goes off in her bag as Cassandra's voice wafts through the door.

"Darling? I'm going. Are you ready?"

He sighs, rolls his eyes, and walks out without another word.

"Huh: 'dabble,'" Ava says, making a face at me.

I'm not really listening. I'm looking at the piece of paper. There's a brilliant little pen-and-ink drawing of Mario the labradoodle on the back. Nick may be a nightmare, but he's talented. The spattery painting in the background of the fashion photo was fab, too.

Ava finds her phone. "Oh, hi, Dad. Which theater are we at, did you say? I suppose it has been a long time, hasn't it? We

89

decided to see three films after all. Are you sure you want to pick us up?"

She gestures at me helplessly, but I just stare straight back at her. She got us into this mess, and she can get us out of it.

TWELVE

You can fool a lot of people a lot of the time, but you can't fool an academic historian forever — or even, as it turns out, for more than about six hours on a Saturday. Dad got back ages ago from his research trip to the library and he's had a long time to pick holes in our movie story. When Ava can't actually name any of the films currently showing at our local multiplex, he insists on coming to pick us up from wherever we are, and when he finds out exactly where that is, I seriously wonder how his cell phone is going to survive the power of his reaction.

"WHAT? In a POST OFFICE BUILDING?"

"Not exactly —" Ava says.

"In NORTH LONDON? Who's with you?"

Ava doesn't have the phone on speaker. She doesn't need to. She tells him about Seb and Cassandra.

"THOSE SCAMMERS? ARE YOU OK? Have they kept you hostage? Stay exactly where you are. I'm on my way."

It takes a very long time on the Underground to get from South London to Highbury & Islington. Long enough for Julia to help me take off most of my geisha makeup, and for Seb to get going on Mireille's photographs on his laptop, choosing which to keep and using a clever program to adjust the lighting and bring out the incredible luster of her hair.

"When your dad gets here I'll, uh . . . go," he says.

Great. I shall be forever known as "the would-be model that kept the photographer hanging around while she waited for her dad."

The waiting is bad, but Dad actually arriving is worse.

"Oh, thank God you're safe," he mutters, glaring at us. Then he thanks Seb, very formally, for staying behind to look after us — as if we're about four years old — and tells us off loudly and repeatedly for twenty minutes, until we find a café where he can get some food into us.

By now his panic has solidified into colder, more organized anger.

"I don't know who to be more ashamed of," he says. "The one who's supposed to be looking after herself, or the one who should know better."

"But they said to keep living normally, Dad!" Ava complains.

"You call this *normal*?"

"And they're not scammers. I got it wrong. They're a top model agency and they like Ted a lot."

"Well, they did," I mutter, spitting crumbs from my large blueberry muffin, "until I —"

"And you thought you'd just take her along to some ABAN-DONED BUILDING to meet a TOTAL STRANGER, without anyone knowing where you were?"

Ava pouts. "Converted, not abandoned. And Louise knew," she says quietly.

"Louise?" Dad throws his hands up. Ava's friend Louise, though brilliant at volleyball, is not affectionately known as Ditz for nothing. If anything had gone wrong, she might not even have noticed we were missing for days. And she'd probably have deleted the text saying where we were. He sighs. "Ted, love, I thought you had more sense."

I *do* have more sense. I absolutely have more sense. I'm tempted to say, "But she made me!" — except that's what I've been saying since I was three, and I promised myself when I turned fifteen that I wouldn't say it anymore.

"Anyway, I'd better get you back," Dad says. "Ava, have you taken your pills?"

She bites her lip and looks guilty. Dad sighs again and, worse, closes his eyes and wipes a hand across them. Ava's supposed to be taking a cocktail of pills this week: a combination of chemo, steroids, and other scary blue things that mop up some of the side effects of the other two. I don't blame her for "forgetting." Dad does, though.

"We promised, love," he says, not angry now but verging on upset. "I know it's hard, but if you don't take them . . ."

He's thinking about the ninety percent, and apparently she's not going to be in it unless she's positively rattling with pharmaceuticals.

"Fine, whatever," Ava says grumpily. She preferred it when she was lounging on a sofa, with me dancing in front of brick walls for a hairy bloke with a camera.

"Your mother must never find out," Dad grumbles. "I left her a note to say I'd taken you out for a walk by the river, OK? And if she asks, that's what we were doing."

Ava smiles gratefully. It takes me a second longer to catch on, and even then, I still don't get it. Normally Mum and Dad present a united front in the face of misbehavior. Mum is *much* scarier than Dad, so it's great that he doesn't want to tell on us, but why?

On the way home we sit side by side on the Tube, all looking at bits of the newspaper that Dad has brought along and not talking. I can't help remembering the way the light fell on the paint-peeling bricks, and how perfect Mireille looked in every single picture, and how that last one of me was . . . surprisingly less awful than it might have been. And how Seb somehow got us to do what he wanted, even though I've never known anyone less talkative. I'd love to tell Daisy about it, but she wouldn't be interested. At least Ava and I can talk about it after lights-out, when we're supposed to be asleep.

When we get in, Mum's back from work and still in her green polo shirt, reading Dad's note.

"Did you have a nice time?" she asks in a tired voice. "Were there lots of boats out?"

"Hundreds," Dad lies confidently. I can see where Ava gets it from.

Mum smiles a sad little smile that reaches halfway up her face and stops dead. Her eyes are dull and wrinkled, and haven't gleamed since Ava's first diagnosis. Now I realize why Dad didn't want to tell her what we were up to. She's like a satellite, spinning out of orbit, and it's as if any jolt might send her into outer space. I assumed Dad was out there, spinning beside her, but he's not. He's watching as helplessly as I am, just trying not to make things worse.

Dad's right to protect her. I promise myself I will never enter an abandoned building to meet a stranger with only my sick sister for company again. It wasn't our most genius idea. I guess, looking back, something could have gone wrong — apart from my total inability to even sit on a chair backward without looking like a complete idiot.

Then I realize Mum's staring at me.

"What?" I ask.

"Oh, Ted," she sighs. "Look at you. Those shoes are falling apart. We're going to have to get you new ones. And why are you wearing those bizarre black leggings?"

THIRTEEN

Seb spent ages working on those pictures of Mireille before Dad came to pick us up. I wonder how long he'll have to spend on the ones of me. Sunday's supposed to be for studying, but I spend most of it picturing Seb working on his computer, then sending the results off to Model City for inspection. I wonder what they'll all think.

On Monday, Mum takes Ava to the hospital for a new dose of chemo through her Hickman line.

"Tell me the minute you hear anything," Ava says.

All day, I illicitly check my phone for messages. Nothing. There's no news on Tuesday or Wednesday. By Thursday it's obvious that they've decided to spare me by not telling me directly. I'd love to get a copy of that last photo, but I don't think I can face asking Frankie for it. Ava said just to call her and get it over with, but for once, I'm not doing what my big sister tells me. I shall just get on with my life and pretend this mad detour into modeling never happened. I find that usually works, eventually.

On Friday after school, I'm shopping for shoes with Mum in one of the local thrift shops when my phone goes off in my backpack.

"Er . . . hello?" I say, scrambling to get to it in time.

"Is that Edwina?" The voice is smooth, posh, and confident. "It's Cassandra Spoke. We got your test shots back yesterday and we've been having a good look. I try to call all our new girls myself. How do you feel?"

"Who is it?" Mum asks, waving a pair of hideous purple sandals at me. How come she always manages to emerge from these places looking like Audrey Hepburn, but the only things we can ever find to fit me look like they were designed for Shrek and Princess Fiona?

"Daisy. Homework problem. Excuse me?"

This last bit is to Cassandra Spoke. How do I feel about what exactly? About how much of a laugh they've all been having at my photos? What?

"We're taking you on, darling! I always like to be the bearer of good news. We really only pick the girls we think can make it to the top. Are you thrilled? We're so excited about you."

"Can you tell her to call back later?" Mum says in exasperation. "I don't want to be long here — I still need to get those eggplants."

"Er, thrilled," I whisper to keep Cassandra happy, although actually I'm just numb. I go over to a rack of lace-ups, far away from Mum, and pretend to be interested in men's formal footwear.

"I must say, you don't sound it!" Cassandra laughs. "I know the news can be a bit of a shock but, really, the world is open to you now. Frankie will arrange some lovely castings and go-sees for you, so you can build up your book. And who knows? One day you could be doing a campaign!"

"What? *That?*" Mum says.

I nearly jump out of my skin. She must have sneaked up behind me. I look at my hands, which happen to be clutching a man's oxford wingtip the size of a supertanker.

"It looks a bit large, even for you. What about this?"

She shows me something beige and cloglike, with a thick sole and a sensible leather strap around the back. Whatever. I sink onto a plastic chair and slip off my falling-apart sandals so I can try it on.

"Edwina? Are you there?"

"Yup, that sounds fine," I say. "Great. I'm really sorry, but — *shshshshshshshsh* . . ." I try to make a sound like a dodgy signal, or like I'm on a train going into a tunnel, and press the button to end the call.

That probably doesn't happen to über-agents very often. I wonder if she'll ever talk to me again.

"Goodness, Ted, you're pink," Mum says. "It is hot in here, isn't it? Did she get what she wanted?"

"Who?"

"Daisy."

"Oh, yes. It was something confusing about . . . French."

I'm quite proud of myself for making that up on the spur of the moment, especially under the circumstances. I think it's because I didn't understand about a quarter of what Cassandra was saying.

That evening, when we're alone together, Ava perches on the edge of her bed and asks me to describe exactly what happened during the call.

"Well, actually," I admit, "a lot of it was confusing. It's like learning a new language."

"Tell me about it," she sighs. "Hickman line. Phlebotomist. Prednisone."

"Ha! How about go-see? Book? Campaign? I think they mean an ad, but it sounds like a war."

"How about bloods? Meaning my blood. Lots of it, in little bottles."

I can't help giggling.

"Mario Testino."

"Kyrillos Christodoulou."

"Kyrillos?"

"His first name," she says. "It's Greek."

"Linda Evangelista."

"See! You *do* know who she is."

"No, I don't. Who is she?"

"God, T! She's a supermodel from the eighties. Canadian. She was superfamous."

"Oh. Then what happened to her?"

"No idea. She might still be doing it."

I wonder — what does happen to models, usually? You hardly ever see pictures of old ones. Maybe they end up on yachts in the Bahamas, drinking tea with designers and going out with rock stars. What else would they do?

"So?" Ava asks teasingly.

"So?" I answer, pretending I don't know what she means.

"Why are you blushing? Why won't you catch my eye? Why aren't you stomping around the room, telling me how crazy they are? What are you thinking?"

I've been thinking a lot since that call — partly about my shoes. Ava says models wear nice clothes, which means their footwear doesn't come from the thrift shop. Also, I'm thinking about Dean Daniels and Cally Harvest. Cally, who's wanted to be a model since she was ten. Imagine if I actually was one. She'd probably explode.

I have *no idea* why Model City picked me. I don't understand it. But the fact is, they did, and it all feels different now. If I tried modeling over summer vacation, I need never be "the girl with the knickers" again. In fact, that would make up for a whole summer stuck in London, posing in front of brick walls and lying to my parents.

Oh, yeah. Forgot about that bit. Ava's still watching me, waiting for a reply.

"I'm thinking about permission," I sigh. "I'd need actual, real approval from Mum and Dad, not just you pretending over the phone."

"True," Ava agrees. "So, you've changed your mind? You want to go ahead with it?"

I nod. I'm so easy to persuade. I'd like to be more cool and decisive, but I'm more a "swim with the tide, see where it takes you" sort of person, and it's taking me in an interesting direction. Or rather it would be, if Mum and Dad weren't like a dam at the end, waiting to stop me.

"Don't worry about them," Ava says confidently. "I have it all worked out. Trust me."

And yet again, despite everything, I do.

FOURTEEN

The weak point in the dam, according to my sister, is Dad. On Saturday morning, as soon as Mum's gone out to work, we set to work on him together. I go first.

"Er, Dad," I say, wandering into the kitchen where he's washing dishes. "I may need your help."

He looks around and smiles. "What is it, love? If it's math again, I don't think there's much I can do. Those statistics are way beyond me now."

"It's not math, it's modeling."

I explain about Cassandra's call. He swears loudly, his fingers fumbling in his ridiculous yellow rubber gloves, and drops a plate. It breaks. We decide to continue the conversation at the dining table, out of range of fragile china. Ava joins us, looking pale and woozy this morning, but determined to back me all the way.

"But listen, my loves, are you *sure* they're real?" Dad asks suspiciously.

Ava steps in. "Model City are the best, Dad. I know Ted's not your . . . typical beauty queen, but she's got what it takes for modeling. She's just lucky that way."

He smiles and takes my hand. "We could do with some luck in this family. But your mum would never let you, of course. You know what she thinks about models."

"Yes," I admit, "but she doesn't actually know any. I met one last week, and she was lovely. She didn't take a single drug the whole time we were there."

He laughs.

"We were thinking . . . er, I was thinking . . . that I could try it out. Maybe do a few jobs — small ones. Earn some money. See for myself if it's OK, *then* tell Mum."

I see him falter for a moment, and look at him pleadingly. It was when I mentioned earning some money that he wobbled. Dad hates the fact that Ava and I don't have an allowance anymore, and he still tries to slip me a five occasionally. Simply breathing in a city like London seems to cost money. My original plan was to apply for a waitressing job over the summer, but they're hard to get around here because everyone wants one and even if you get one, you have to work a whole day to earn enough for one meal out with your friends. Dad knows this.

Ava gives him a winning smile. "It would keep Ted busy."

He nods, still faltering.

"And it would be safe, I promise," I tell him. "They sent me an e-mail about it this morning. I'll show you. It says I have to have a chaperone at all times until I'm sixteen. Either you could do it, or they'll provide one. And I'd always tell you exactly where I was going, and give you contact numbers and everything."

He sighs and doodles absentmindedly in the margin of the newspaper.

"When I was your age, Ava," he says, "I needed some vacation money. A friend's dad had a farm. He offered me and some mates free board and lodging and a little money if we could help pick lettuce. We took a look around the farm: nice, rolling countryside, friendly farmer's wife. The town was famous for its summer music festival. So we said yes." He turns to us with haunted eyes. "And, girls, I have never worked so hard, for so little money, in my life. It's backbreaking, pulling up lettuce, and it never ends. Hours and hours and hours of it. Those fields just went on and on . . ." He doodles some more and says grimly, "I hate lettuce. Don't tell your mother, but I can't abide the stuff . . . So, Ted, you'd just be wearing nice clothes, like a proper fashion model?"

I nod.

"I've always been partial to Claudia Schiffer, you know."

I do know. Schiffer: *That's* the name of the Claudia girl who's the other model I've heard of, apart from Kate Moss. She's German and has blonde hair and also lives in London. I know all of this because if ever Dad sees a picture of her he gives a happy sigh and Mum punches him affectionately — well, *quite* affectionately — on the shoulder.

"It would be just like that," Ava says confidently, with a hidden wink to me.

"And how do you propose to do all this without Mum finding out?"

"By telling her that Ted *has* got a waitressing job. At that hotel near Daisy's. Just until she works everything out. Then she can show Mum it's safe, and that she's enjoying it."

"And I only want to do a few jobs anyway," I add. "*Please?*"

He runs a hand through his mad-professor hair.

"What exactly would I have to do?"

"Well, Stephen, if you can just sign *there* . . . and *there*. That's lovely. I must say, we're thrilled Ted said yes. She's going to be a real star. And she takes after you, doesn't she?"

"I suppose." Dad smiles in a confused sort of way, looking around the Model City offices and wondering what two wild-haired, caterpillar-browed freaks like us are doing in the middle of them, signing permission forms.

As if she's reading his mind, Frankie says, "We'll book her in for hair and beauty before she starts. She needs to lose the . . . you know."

She draws a finger across her forehead, and I wonder exactly how they're going to get rid of my facial fuzz. I'm not sure I want to know. The last time Ava tried to tweeze it, years ago, it was agony and I paid her to stop.

"Has Mireille been in yet?" I ask to take my mind off it.

Frankie looks embarrassed. "Actually, no. She was very commercial, but she didn't have what we were looking for."

"But I don't understand . . ."

Mireille was categorically the prettiest girl I've ever seen.

"We need girls with an edge. Something fresh, to catch people's attention," Frankie explains. "She'll do very well. But not in high-fashion editorial."

"Where, then?" I can't stop myself from asking.

"Underwear catalogs?" Frankie suggests. "Anyway, let me show you your book."

I've been wondering about this. Cassandra Spoke mentioned my book, too, and it sounded really important. Do they expect me to read a particular novel? Is it a textbook about modeling? That would be great, as I keep discovering there's a lot I don't understand. How to avoid modeling in underwear catalogs, for a start — I'm trying to get *away* from being "the girl with the knickers."

Instead, what Frankie pulls out from under a pile of paperwork isn't a book at all — it's a large black binder with the Model City logo stamped on the front, and clear plastic pockets inside, most of which are empty. She turns it around to face us and opens it up. Inside the first pocket is the last picture of me that Seb took: the one with my arms above my head and the surprised look on my face.

"What do you think?"

Oh. O-kaaaay. Despite all the time he took over it, Seb hasn't magically morphed me into Kate Moss, or Linda Evangelista, or Claudia Schiffer for that matter. It's still just me and my brick wall. And Mum was right: Her yoga pants do look ridiculous on my spindly legs. But it's an interesting picture. Seb's good. Behind it are two more photos of me from the shoot where I would say the brick wall definitely outshines me. Frankie seems happy, though.

"We have lots to talk about," she says.

Dad looks at his watch. It's after school and we are technically at the hotel in Richmond, talking about waitressing. Mum will be expecting us home for supper soon, and after that I have a mountain of homework to catch up on. But I'm starting to enjoy myself. I keep glancing at Dad's signature on the permission forms and it looks so official, somehow — like I'm really supposed to be here.

"I'll book in some time for you to come in and discuss

nutrition and finance," Frankie continues, sensing this visit needs to be short.

"Finance?" Dad asks. Math is not his favorite subject.

"Taxes, savings, and a retirement plan," she says. "Ted will be self-employed, but obviously we'll help explain what she needs to do."

I'll need a retirement plan? I might be earning so much I need to *pay taxes*? This is so exciting!

"Meanwhile," Frankie is saying, "here's the plan, angel. I'm going to line you up for go-sees during the first few weeks of the summer, while things are still busy. Don't worry about the book being small at first. Once you get a few tear sheets under your belt it'll start looking healthy. You'll need a comp card as well, but that's fine, because we'll sort it out for you, OK?"

"Right," I agree. "Great."

I can tell I still have some major vocabulary issues to address. I have no idea what she just said, but it sounded like the kind of thing you pay tax on, which is SO COOL.

FIFTEEN

After this, it's quite difficult to concentrate at school. But at least I'm not the only one. With exams over, almost everybody starts thinking about their vacation plans, including most of the teachers. Sadly, there are a couple of exceptions who still insist on following the curriculum. Even more sadly, one of them is Miss Jenkins, our art teacher, who is generally my favorite, but possibly takes her subject just a little bit too seriously.

The last art teacher wore swirly skirts, crocheted vests, and mismatched earrings, and went on about the Renaissance. Miss Jenkins is different: She wears crimson lipstick and pencil skirts, with her hair in a bun held together with a drawing pencil, and she takes us on outings to the biggest exhibitions at the Tate Modern museum and makes us have opinions about conceptual art and stuff. Her style is interesting, for a teacher. In a rare (for me) moment of fashion forwardness, I did try adapting my (pre-shrunken) school skirt once, with safety pins, to make it look more pencil-ish, but I could hardly walk. Anyway, I've always been a fan of Miss Jenkins — until now. She seems to have this mad idea that we all want to spend our vacation thinking about our school certification exams.

"As you know," she says at the end of our final class before summer break, "you have to submit three projects next year. They all have to be thought through, with full illustrations of your working process. The biggest one's due by Christmas, but I'm going to let you choose your subject now so you can do plenty of preparation over vacation. Even so, you'll be stretched, believe me. Here are the subjects to pick from."

She writes them on the whiteboard in blue marker:

Still Life
Interior/Exterior
Self Portrait

Beside me, Daisy sighs disappointedly. In a society where pop stars go to awards ceremonies dressed in raw meat, how can exam boards be so utterly devoid of imagination? Across the room, Dean Daniels yawns loudly, stretches his arms out, and then collapses on his desk in a mock coma. This is one of those moments when I have to agree with him. Miss Jenkins pretends she hasn't noticed the general reaction.

"You need to think deeply about what your chosen subject represents. Go to galleries — get inspiration. Read books. Use the internet. Find artists who've played with the genre. Remember *some* of the stuff I've taught you. Consider the media you're going to use, how you're going to combine them . . . There's more to it than drawing a couple of apples and a glass of water."

Daisy nudges me. She's read my mind. I've already picked my subject — Still Life — and a couple of apples and a glass of water is *exactly* what I'm planning to do.

"She won't be happy if you just do a lot of shading," Daisy mutters.

I shrug. "But I'm really good at shading. It's my favorite thing. And besides, I might be too busy to do . . . all that other stuff."

"What, sitting around in your undies all summer?"

The bell rings, and we start to pack up.

"I would not be in my undies!" I tell her, offended.

"Sorry, someone else's undies." She does the frown. She is still not remotely convinced by my vacation plans.

"That's underwear catalog modeling and it's commercial," I explain. "I'm high-fashion editorial."

"Just listen to yourself, Ted!"

I do. I sound ridiculous. I shut up.

"Anyway," she says, changing the subject, "did I tell you about Hamburg?"

"No," I sigh.

Daisy's dad's tribute band is going on tour to Germany in August. Daisy and her mum are joining them so Daisy can practice her German. Every day they seem to add a new date and Daisy will be away for longer. Today, she seems particularly excited about Hamburg, for some reason. Maybe it's the tribute-band touring equivalent of "high-fashion editorial." At least now I'll be busy while she's away.

On the way back to our homeroom, we nearly crash into Cally Harvest rushing along the corridor, hair flying, accompanied by some of her "glossy posse" friends.

"Is it true you're going to Germany?" she asks Daisy. "On tour?"

Daisy nods and fills in the details about Hamburg. Cally looks even more impressed. She thinks Daisy's so cool. They've been hanging out together more since . . . well, since I started staring out the window a lot and not answering Daisy's questions. I guess I haven't been such a brilliant friend recently.

"And what about you, Friday? Any plans for summer break?" Cally asks. Every tiny scintilla of impressed-ness has vanished from her face. The glossy posse hang around behind her, arms folded, looking equally bored. What could Freaky Friday possibly be up to that was interesting?

"Well, actually, I'm going to be a model."

Silence.

Cally stares at me for five seconds. Nobody in the glossy posse even breathes. This is possibly about to be the best moment OF MY LIFE.

Then Cally cracks up laughing. "Oh, yeah? Prove it."

And of course I can't. So I stand there looking stupid, as usual.

Cally turns on her heel and walks off, trailing glossy posse members in her wake, still laughing. Daisy shrugs.

I can feel a tear forming. "At least you could be happy for me," I say bitterly.

She turns to me with a surprised frown, then laughs.

"*Happy* for you? There you are, with your perfect skin, never a zit, and legs up to your armpits . . . You just stand around and people make you into a *model*. And I'm supposed to be *happy* for you?"

She walks off, shaking her head and leaving me in shock. I hardly recognize the girl she was talking about. I'm Freaky Friday, remember? Her best friend? The one Cally just laughed at? This is not how it was supposed to work out at all.

SIXTEEN

"She's just jealous," Ava assures me back at home. "You may not think so, but she is. You have to be kind and gracious. It's a trick you'll pick up."

Me? Gracious? I can't picture it somehow. Queens and princesses are gracious. Field hockey–playing, gorgeous Ava is gracious. Gawky, accidental panty-flashing freaks don't have the luxury of being gracious. Or at least I didn't think so, but maybe the girls who sign with Model City do have to, regardless of how they feel. Thank goodness I've got my sister, because I think I might be losing my best friend.

However, Ava isn't feeling so great, either. After two weeks' rest, she's back on the chemo again, and this time it's harder. More dizziness, more tiredness, and a body that's remembering it didn't really like it last time, apart from the steroid rush, and please can it not have to do it again? Except it does have to. Two weeks on, two weeks off. This is the second cycle of six.

The good news is that Jesse has finally finished his A-level exams, as well as the big sailing race he'd been training for, and he can finally come up and visit. In our old cottage in Richmond, the sofa folded out into a bed and he could have stayed with us, but here that just isn't possible, so he's staying with a friend. He's only in town for the weekend and Ava is planning it like a . . . well, like a military campaign: what she will be wearing at every moment of each day, what makeup she'll be using, which perfume, where they'll go, what they'll eat, whether there will be any snogging opportunities, and, if so, how she will snuggle up to him in such a way that he won't be put off by the tubes sticking out of her chest.

When she finds out my plans for the weekend she even factors me in, which is just another symptom of her Jesse-related good mood. Despite the chemo, Ava has a sort of sparkle about her whenever she thinks about him. It reminds me of the way she was when they gave her the steroids. Hormones, Mum says. Very similar to steroids, but with fewer side effects. However, whereas the steroids are supposed to help her eat, the hormones seem to have put her off her food almost entirely. She can't face anything more than mozzarella and tomato salad, which is her new comfort food. Meanwhile, all Mum's exotic fruits are piling up in the corner of the kitchen, slowly changing shape and color in a way I don't like the look of at all, like they're about to melt into some sort of Salvador Dalí Surrealist heap.

Jesse arrives the Friday before school ends. Although it cuts out a couple of hours of potential snogging time, Mum and Dad insist on having him over for dinner. As soon as he walks through the door, it is perfectly clear how Ava has managed to withstand a whole year of Shane Matthews's persistent attempts to date her at school. He's changed from last summer and is, if anything, even more beautiful. His hair is bleached blonder by the sun, his eyes dance and twinkle, his body is still tall and slim but filled out to become solid and reassuring. He is utterly, meltingly gorgeous.

Even Mum can't help batting her eyelashes as she offers him pre-dinner chips and peanuts. I don't pretend I'm not impressed, too, because it's pointless. He must know how amazing he is, but unlike the cool boys at school, he doesn't show it. Whereas Shane Matthews always wears his rugby scarf or jersey to remind you he's on the school team, there's nothing to indicate that Jesse is a top-class sailor. Maybe his tan and his super-antiglare sunglasses would give him away — but Ava had to point the glasses out to me on the last photo he sent. You'd probably assume he was an actor. In fact, he's planning to be an accountant when he graduates university. The hottest accountant in the southwest of England, as Ava often points out with a sigh, but an accountant nevertheless. Ava loves how multitalented he is.

He's good at conversation, too. Knowing what Ava's going through and not knowing how to talk about it, most people struggle to know what to say in our house at the moment, but Jesse's full of tales about his sailing competition, how his boat nearly capsized, and how they won despite massive cheating by the opposing teams. Dad asks him lots of technical questions about race tactics, and Mum and I join Ava in simply admiring his face. Altogether, he copes with it pretty well.

"Are you sure about tomorrow, darling?" Mum asks Ava eventually, dragging her eyes away from Jesse for a moment. "Taking Ted, I mean. I'm sure you two have better things to do than babysit your sister."

"No, that's fine." Ava smiles. "We're just going to do some window-shopping. It'll be nice."

Mum shakes her head. She knows about dates and boyfriends, and that younger sisters aren't usually invited. "Well, you're very kind."

"It's nothing," Ava says modestly.

Actually, it's subterfuge — but Mum's right, it's still very kind. This weekend, Ava's pretending to take me with her so I can secretly go and have the hair and beauty sessions that Frankie has booked for me in central London. Meanwhile, Ava doesn't want me anywhere near her during her snog-fest with Jesse, but they've arranged to meet up with me afterward, so we can all agree what we supposedly did together and get our stories straight.

As planned, at half past ten on Saturday, they bid me good-bye at the Covent Garden Underground station. Ava and Jesse head for the shops, while I follow Frankie's careful instructions to a hairdresser's called Locks, Stock, and Barrel, where I'm supposed to have the bird's nest seen to. My castings, or go-sees, or whatever they are, start next week, and Frankie wants me to look my best.

The place seems normal from the outside — a little boutique with a black door. So far, so good. But once through the door, it opens into something strange and modern and unexpected.

After weeks of school, homework, and exams, I have to take a deep breath and tell myself I'm *supposed* to be here. It doesn't look like a hairdresser's — more like a giant spaceship with hair dryers. It's all polished steel, white floors, bright lights, and shiny surfaces. The staff look cool and trendy, and the customers are rich, confident, and . . . old. All of them seem to be in their thirties, at least.

Frankie has told me to call her if I have any problems, and I'm tempted to do it now and explain that I really don't think teenagers belong here. I even get my phone out of my backpack to do it. But Ava would tell me not to be so pathetic, so I go up to the desk and introduce myself.

Sure enough, they're expecting me. After a shampoo and head massage, a girl called Hannah fiddles about with scissors to bring out "texture" and "interest." Personally, I can't see much difference when she's finished: I'd say it looks like a smaller nest, made by a bird who likes really shiny twigs. But this may be a good thing, as it means that with any luck when I get home, Mum won't even notice what she's done.

Down the street from Locks, Stock, and Barrel is a little beauty salon, which is also on Frankie's list. I've never been into one before, but the warmth and pervading smells of rose and lavender might tempt me in again. Just when I'm starting to think that this place is infinitely nicer than the hairdresser's, a woman called Nirmala in a white coat sets to work removing the middle of my caterpillar.

How wrong can a girl be? All Ava's previous tweezer attacks on my forehead pale in comparison.

Nirmala starts off by waxing the area above my nose, which is bad but quick. Then, to complete the look, she gets a long piece of cotton thread and starts pulling out each hair individually. This is called threading, apparently, as I learn between ouches. Forget the rose and lavender: If threading had existed during the Civil War, it would definitely have been used for torture.

Just as she's finishing, Ava and Jesse arrive to pick me up. Ava opens the treatment room door, with Jesse looking over her shoulder. She doesn't seem to mind that for only the third time her gorgeous boyfriend has seen me in a year, I'm lying back with a bib around my neck, my face hot and prickly from its recent sufferings.

"Hi again, Jesse," I mutter.

He smiles awkwardly. "Having fun?"

"Not exactly."

"But check out the results, T," Ava insists, as Nirmala kindly hands me a mirror.

I examine my face. It's still pink and flustered, but for the first time in my life, I have two normal eyebrows. Nirmala smiles as I grin at her gratefully. Suddenly, the pain doesn't seem so bad. I will, frankly, go through it as many times as it takes.

Jesse takes us to a nearby café to celebrate.

"OK," Ava says, peering at the bridge of my nose once Jesse is in line at the counter. "You definitely look like you've done *something*." She considers for a moment. "We'll tell Mum we got home early and I gave you a beauty session at home while she was still working. I could probably do that stuff to your eyebrows if I tried —"

"You're not coming near me again!"

Ava sighs. "I don't have to. It's *pretend*, remember? We'll just say I did it all with tweezers."

"Ow!"

She's right, though. Mum's so busy with work and anticancer remedies that she's not going to pay much attention to the relative hairlessness of my face.

Jesse joins us, armed with a Coke and two coffees.

"Congratulations, by the way," he says. "On the new job. I didn't get to say it to you directly before."

But he still has a strange awkwardness about him. I assume that it's because he doesn't really approve of modeling. However, when he sits down next to Ava, she turns away from him. Now that I look closely, something's wrong with Ava, too — the Jesse sparkle has gone from her eyes. It was still there at breakfast, so something must have happened while I was at the hairdresser's. Something not good. I look at them both, confused, and don't know what to say.

Ava breaks the silence with brittle brightness. "Jesse needs congratulations, too," she says, fixing on a smile. "He did so well in that sailing competition that he's been asked to crew a boat around the Mediterranean. All summer. And maybe the autumn, too. He's just been telling me about it."

"Wow. Sounds great," I mumble. But it's not what I'm thinking, which is that this is *tragic*. No wonder the sparkle's gone. How is Ava going to cope without him for so long?

Jesse sighs and shakes his head. "I don't have to go. I'm supposed to be teaching surfing this summer anyway. It's just that the money's much better on the boat and it would help pay for school. But —"

"But nothing," Ava says sharply. "It's the Mediterranean! Just think of all the places you'll go. Ibiza, Majorca, Sardinia . . . And on a yacht! A luxury sailing yacht! And they're paying you. If someone asked me, I'd go. Anyway, I'm going to be so busy with my treatment I won't have time to see you, and I'd be no fun if I did. It's much better this way. It's a really good idea."

She stares into her coffee.

Jesse looks at me helplessly. "I've told her I'll stay if she wants me to."

"Well, I don't," she says with the same grimness Mum generally uses when the argument is over.

We spend another agonizing ten minutes hardly talking to each other, and then I leave to go home on my own, so they can ignore each other without me.

I was all set to go with my "Ava gave me a makeover" story, but Mum doesn't notice a thing.

When Ava gets in — hours earlier than she was supposed to — she doesn't want to talk. The second round of chemo is making her feel dizzy and weak, but I know that's not the problem. Jesse is.

"It's a stupid idea. You'll miss him," I insist from the bottom of my side of the closet, where I'm trying to find a pair of sandals to wear next week that fit me and don't make me look like a troll.

"I'll be fine," she snaps. "Do you think I want him to see me all pasty and exhausted, with my hair falling out and God knows what, when he's constantly surrounded by beach babes? It's so much better this way. Anyway, it's your first day at work soon. That's much more important."

She sits on her bed for a moment, holding her head in her hands. I know she's thinking about her hair. She's terrified of losing it. I don't know why, exactly, but it's the thing she worries about the most. Every now and again she likes to reassure herself that it's still there — thick and dark and lovely — her crowning glory. Then she steadies herself and starts rummaging around in her side of the closet, flicking hangers aside and then rummaging some more. Eventually she finds what she's looking for.

"Aha! I want you to have this. You'll need it."

She's holding out a little gathered white-and-blue striped skirt — about four inches shorter than anything I'd be seen dead in, but very cute.

"Why?" I ask. This is, after all, the girl who has vowed never to let me borrow any of her stuff EVER.

"Because you go out looking like a bag lady, and I'm embarrassed at the thought of you meeting all those fashion people in your usual getup."

"Really?"

"Yes. You look terrible," she sighs.

"I mean — really about the skirt? You never lend me stuff."

"I'm not lending, I'm giving it to you," she says crossly. "When Jesse's not around all I can face wearing at the moment is sweatpants and old T-shirts. You might as well get some wear out of this."

She holds it out to me, and her face is bleak and resolute. My sister is so strong, so stubborn and determined, that I can feel a stray tear forming in the corner of my eye and I have to blink it away quickly. I know how annoyed she gets by Mum.

"OK. Thanks."

I take the skirt. Ava holds my eyes for a grim moment, then smiles gratefully. Even though she's the one doing the giving, I think she's glad that I'm not still arguing with her about Jesse and her stupid decision to let him crew this yacht. She's putting all her fight into battling lymphoma and she hasn't got any left for me.

In that moment, we form a sort of truce. We've always argued, because that's what sisters are for, but I silently agree to let her make her own stupid decisions in her own stupid way for as long as this disease has got a hold of her. She's all I've got, and I need her.

In her gratitude her shoulders relax and the tension seeps out of her body.

"Ya-ay," she says weakly. "My si-ister is going to be a mo-odel!"

Apparently.

SEVENTEEN

Five days later. Day one of my "waitressing job."

I'm sitting in a damp room in a warehouse in Bermondsey, East London. There are about thirty of us altogether, all waiting to be seen by a couple of designers who run a trendy style blog. Almost everyone in the room is tall, thin, young, female, nervous, and holding a plastic folder like mine. Most aren't wearing much makeup, but quite a few are in skintight jeans, or almost identical miniskirts and tank tops. Thank goodness Ava convinced me to wear her skirt and not cargo pants, like I planned. Is this some sort of modeling uniform I didn't know about? There really is so much I don't know.

In fact, I've decided to ask the girl sitting beside me to at least help sort out some of my vocabulary issues. Her name is Sabrina, she's from Model City, too, and we're sharing a chaperone because Sabrina's family live in Newcastle and she's staying in the model apartment that the agency runs in West London. Sabrina isn't up for this job — she's hanging around for me and in a couple of hours I'll be hanging around for her somewhere else.

"This is a go-see, OK?" she says. "You *go* and *see* the people who need to hire a model for a particular job. That means it's a casting."

"Wait — a casting or a go-see? That's what I don't understand."

She sighs. "Both. But sometimes, you go and see a designer or a photographer just to show them your face so they remember you. That's a go-see but *not* a casting. See?"

"Yes."

No. I totally get why there's a magazine out there called *Dazed & Confused*, and why it's so popular with models.

Sabrina plows on. "But, if it *is* a casting and not just a go-see, and they *like* you, then they option you, which means they want you, and if you get first option and you're available, then you do the job. It's pretty straightforward."

Help! She lost me at "option." I get her to explain it again. She does, and it still sounds like "Blah blah blah blah *option*. Blah blah blah blah *straightforward*." However, I get the vague impression that an option is a good thing and that's what I want to get from this casting. Or go-see, or whatever it is. Trouble is, that's what we all need to get, and there's a roomful of us, and they only need two girls.

Gradually, the room starts to empty. Girls troop regularly back past us on their way to other appointments. Most of them seem to be on their own, although some of the younger ones like me have their mothers with them. This part would be pretty lonely if I didn't have people like Sabrina for company.

The next name is called.

"Ted Richmond. Hey, Ted Richmond, anyone?"

The voice is already agitated. You have to be quick around here, or they just move on to the next person. Sabrina jabs me in the shoulder.

"That's you, remember?"

Oh, yes. Frankie decided that "Ted Trout" wouldn't look so great on my comp card (which is like a big business card for models with photos on it), so we had to come up with another surname, quick. Dad was pretty upset. He didn't go through ten years of being called Fishface at school just to have the family name abandoned at the first opportunity. But Frankie and I overruled him. I thought for a bit while Dad suggested various other surnames. I couldn't help thinking about our old house, for some reason. I still miss it so much. Eventually I settled on "Richmond," and Frankie agreed.

It was a really great idea, except I can never remember that's what I'm supposed to be called. Thank goodness for Sabrina.

I grab my folder out of my bag and rush through the studio doors.

Ahead of me are a couple of desks, pushed together, with three people sitting behind them. It couldn't look more like a nightmare vision of an oral exam if it tried. In fact, it also reminds me of one of Dad's favorite paintings about the English Civil War, which shows a Cavalier boy being questioned by some scary-looking Cromwellian soldiers. It's titled *And When Did You Last See Your Father?* That poor little boy looks a lot braver than I'm feeling right now.

I feel my way across the floor toward them and hand them my book. They flip through it. With only three pictures to look at, it doesn't take them long.

"Ted Richmond?"

"Yes." I have mastered my own name. Hooray.

"Model City?"

"That's right."

"Hmm. Can you turn round for us, please?"

I turn. Quite an elegant pirouette, considering.

"Back view. Just the back view, please."

So I face the door and try not to feel intimidated. I can feel my muscles tensing up. My shoulders are up around my ears. Should I try and relax, or would that look too slouchy? I'm not sure if I . . .

"That's fine. You can go now."

Oh, no. All I had to do was "just stand there" and I managed to mess even that up.

"Miss Richmond? Miss *Richmond*?"

Help. That's me. I haven't mastered my own name after all. I turn back.

"Your book."

The man in the middle is holding my folder out to me. I half expect him to be wearing a leather jerkin and a big, Cromwellian hat circa 1645. It's almost a surprise to see the black T-shirt and stubble.

"Don't worry, I'm sure you were fine," Sabrina tells me when we're back out on the street. "If they didn't want you, it's just because you haven't got the right look. I hardly got any jobs in my first six months of New Faces."

"Useful," I say. "Thanks."

This is *not* how it happened for Lily Cole.

Day Two is the same as Day One — with the exception that I'm not concentrating when I get out of the Underground and I get lost on the way to the model apartment to meet Sabrina.

By Day Three, there's a definite pattern emerging. My alarm goes off under my pillow so I don't wake Ava too badly. I change into the closest thing I've got to the model uniform, which is Ava's skirt, if it's clean, and a T-shirt of some description (not my Woodland Trust one, although when I get brave enough I might try and wear it as a dress). I go to a café near the model flat, where I'm supposed to meet up with the latest agency chaperone and whoever else she's accompanying today, so we can travel together to our first destination. We go to castings and/or go-sees. There is some form of minor disaster — usually due to the fact that I've forgotten something or don't understand what they want me to do. I check with Frankie later, to see if I've been optioned for a job. I haven't. I travel home alone, trying not to take it personally.

I take it personally.

At least I'm starting to make friends. I keep bumping into the same girls as we compete for the same jobs. If Dean Daniels could see us all — a roomful of tall, skinny freaks all lining up together — he'd go into shock. The thought always makes me smile.

Sabrina is my favorite. Whenever we meet up, she makes sure to continue my fashion education. She's still horrified by how little I knew when I started.

"So, what's Rule One?" she quizzes me while we wait in the line for a job for a newspaper feature.

"Don't go out with a model." I grin, remembering Frankie that first time she took my Polaroids.

Sabrina laughs. "Where did you get *that* from? That's, like, the *last* rule! What's the real one?"

"Be professional," I recite dutifully.

"Which means . . . ?"

I run through the list of things Frankie told me before I started. Being professional means being on time, with clean hair and nails, wearing appropriate clothes and shoes, including underwear (appropriate underwear, not *any* underwear — of *course* you'd be wearing underwear), remaining polite, not taking your top off (ew), not complaining, and doing whatever you are asked, however painful, tiring, or downright peculiar (except taking your top off — see above). There is nothing about Paris, Milan, or any of the stuff that Ava first mentioned, but maybe that comes later.

Then I add the things I'm learning for myself. Being professional means carrying an enormous bag around with you everywhere (borrowed, after much pleading, from your sister), which contains a load of stuff I never knew you could possibly need: your *A-Z* map of London, to find wherever it is you're supposed to go; your book; your spare, recently purchased, thrift shop high heels, in case they want to see how you walk in them; gel insoles for when they rub; a change of clothes; and something to read while you're waiting around. It means concentrating during all fashion-related conversations, so you don't look completely clueless when somebody mentions prêt-à-porter (ready-to-wear clothes) or Karl Lagerfeld (design guru for Chanel) or boho chic (dressing like a trendy gypsy), and you can seem suitably awed if anyone talks about Anna Wintour (editor-in-chief of *Vogue*). It includes sometimes being able to tell your sister fashion-related stuff she didn't already know. Ava enjoys those bits nearly as much as I do.

It doesn't include getting an actual job, though. Or not yet, anyway.

July turns into August and Daisy heads off to Germany, leaving her phone behind, so I couldn't stay in touch even if I wanted to — which I'm not sure I would, because Daisy's sympathy for my disasters is pretty much zero, as expected.

Ava gets her first set of results after two months of treatment and they're not as great as we'd hoped. Of course, we wanted the scans to say that the chemo was doing a great job and the cancer was disappearing. But it's not as simple as that. Dr. Christodoulou thinks she'll need radiation treatment after the chemotherapy, to make sure. That means the full treatment won't be over until nearly Christmas, and it will involve Ava being zapped with X-rays on top of the toxic chemicals. Somehow, it feels like she just failed a final exam and has to take it all over again. But this time, it's a life-or-death final. We make a silent pact not to talk about it.

Meanwhile, my dreams of becoming an instant supermodel still aren't going to plan, either, which is a shame, because if they were, it would really cheer my sister up.

I am utterly not Kate Moss. In fact, I'm starting to wonder if it's too late to find a summer job that pays actual, reliable money and doesn't involve being rejected on a daily basis by people who want someone taller or shorter or curvier or darker or blonder or just overall prettier or without — as one stylist for a shoe feature put it — "the fattest ankles I've seen all day."

"You haven't got fat ankles," Ava assures me when I get back from that particularly stressful go-see. "You haven't got fat anything. She must have had wonky glasses."

"They were very thick lenses," I agree, to reassure myself, but make a mental note never to try and get any work for Manolo Blahnik or Jimmy Choo (big-deal shoe designers). "And Frankie says not to worry. She's booked me for three more test shoots to build up my book. She says that'll help."

"What?" Ava asks. "Not more brick walls, I hope?"

"The wall was the best bit," I remind her. "But no. There's a beach shoot — that sounds good. And some artist Frankie knows who needs someone with a long neck and a lot of patience. Not sure what that's about. And a new designer who needs some pictures for his lookbook."

"Hey!" she says, smiling. "You said lookbook without flinching, like you knew what one was. You're talking fashion, T! And just think about the beach, OK? You'll love it. It'll be gorgeous."

Good point. Soon I'll be *modeling* on a *beach*. Wow! She's right: Even if I'm not getting paid, surely it doesn't get much better than that?

EIGHTEEN

Wrong AGAIN.

The "beach" in question turns out to be a gritty strip of mud beside the River Thames, not far from St. Paul's Cathedral. For once this summer, the sky is drizzly and overcast. My job is to wear a black jumpsuit secretly pinned and taped into place so it fits me properly, and make it look interesting for a stylist called Linda Lucinda and her friend Greta, who's testing a new lens for her camera. I spend a morning cartwheeling across wet, slimy pebbles while Greta plays around with "aperture sizes" and perfects her "depth of field." Good news: When it's all over, Greta shows me how her focusing gizmos photograph me in sharp definition while the "beach" in the background is vague and blurry. Bad news: My hands really hurt from all those cartwheels, and although the pictures are very arty, they mostly make me look like a demented spider.

The artist project is very different. No cartwheels this time: Instead I have to sit extremely still for four hours while she glues pink tissue-paper petals to my tank top, arms, neck, and face, including my closed eyelids, and takes pictures of the results. This shoot could have been fabulous and relaxing, except that I had a large Coke before we started, and so I spend three hours and twenty-seven minutes desperately wanting to pee. And the results, though beautiful, aren't ideal for my book, because the only part of me you can really see properly is my knees. They're a lot better than my "fat ankles," I suppose, but not necessarily my best feature. Although, to be honest, I'm still not sure what is.

By the time I get to the new designer, my expectations are so low they're scraping the floor. It's not helped by the fact that the man in question, Azar Sadiq, doesn't speak much English and relies mostly on hand gestures and some form of Arabic to explain what he wants.

We meet in a studio on Curtain Road, which seems appropriate somehow, in the Shoreditch neighborhood of East London. My chaperone today is a woman named Beth, who settles herself down with a chick-lit novel, while various friends of the designer set about doing my hair and makeup and translating Azar's hand gestures for me.

At this point, the day starts to get more interesting. It turns out that Azar's first collection involves transforming severe gray suit jackets by incorporating colorful old kite tails from Kabul, Afghanistan. They are absolutely lovely — completely original and unique. I can understand why he's so excited about them.

Gradually, as the shoot progresses, I forget that for some reason he wants my hair and face to be painted pale blue, and that

I can't understand half of what he's saying. Using sheer enthusiasm, he manages to communicate his passion to bring Afghan culture into western tailoring. And the clothes are so enchanting that by the end I feel like one of those kites myself, floating high above the city, carried away by the power of his imagination. For a few moments, I even forget about how worried I am for Ava — all I can think of is telling her how I was Kite Girl later tonight.

Afterward, we all examine the photos together on-screen. By some of my more awkward poses, you can tell I'm still learning what to do with my hands and feet, but the jackets look stunning. So do the billowing silk skirts I'm wearing underneath them. These pictures will look fabulous in my book, finally.

The fun of that shoot carries me through yet another week of lining up and rejection, and in fact I'm trying harder now because I realize I'd love to be a part of something beautiful. If models could choose the work they did, I would work with people like Azar and his friends every day. Although it would help, of course, if they paid enough money to cover some decent sandwiches. Mum's getting very suspicious about the amount of fruit I'm stealing from home to take with me, especially since I'm supposedly working in a restaurant. I'm not sure she believes my story that I need to draw it for art.

By now, August is well underway and "the Italians are on holiday," to quote Frankie, which means that most of the rest of the fashion world has to go on holiday, too. The flood of go-sees peters out to a drizzle. Of course, I'm supposed to be "at work," so I still have to leave the flat every morning and go somewhere.

I like art galleries because they're free, and so is the local library. The librarian's getting used to ordering in glamorous books on photography for me, so I can learn about the fashion greats and pick up posing tips. When I'm not reading them, I'm often outside with Ava's camera — which, incredibly, she let me borrow — learning how to find interesting locations and make use of the light. Nightmare Boy was right: It's amazing what you can do when you try.

When I was bored one evening, I looked up the website he gave me. It's full of useful info. I'm still a beginner photographer, but I'm getting way beyond the Snoopy-on-head stage. Ava thinks my picture of a spiral staircase, looking like a seashell, is surprisingly good. In fact, she stuck a copy inside the closet door, next to her pictures of Jesse and Louise, and one of me posing for Azar. I don't think she strokes and kisses it, unlike Jesse, but even so.

Messing around with photography also takes my mind off the fact that more often than not, I'm hungry. There's only so much fruit you can steal. I would have done much better financially if I actually had been waitressing.

"Don't lose faith," Frankie says over the phone. "We might try you again at Christmas. You'll be sixteen then. There's a lot more we can do with you."

But I don't want to be doing this at Christmas. I literally can't afford to spend every holiday having my ankles criticized by women in ridiculous glasses, whose handbags cost more than my whole wardrobe put together.

✯

After five weeks of total failure, Ava persuades me to give it one last try. She does so from the bathroom floor, while waiting to throw up. Sometimes the drugs she's taking to counteract the side effects of the chemo aren't as powerful as the chemo itself. But still she carries on. When I see what she's putting herself through, another week of go-sees seems only fair.

This time Frankie sends me to a casting in a studio in Battersea for a stylist called Sandy McShand, who's been asked to create high-fashion looks on a budget for a daytime TV talk show. I do my usual lining up. I remember my name, which is a step forward, but other than that, nothing's different. Nobody smiles. Nobody nods. Nobody says anything much beyond "Hi," "Turn around please," and "Can you walk?" I go home as disillusioned as ever.

But when I call Frankie in the evening, she says the magic word: *option*. Sandy wants me for fittings tomorrow! Somehow, without knowing it, I did something right.

NINETEEN

"Think glamour. Think hot. Think sexy. Think vamp. Think fabulous."

This is it. The start of my new career.

It's quarter past nine in the morning and I'm in a TV studio in West London where, in ten minutes, I will be seen by thousands of people who like watching fashion segments on daytime TV shows. OK, so it's scary. After all those go-sees I got a bit carried away with the *idea* of doing it. The *experience* of doing it is slightly different.

Sandy McShand is giving us his last-minute pep talk before he goes out to sit on the sofa and describe the looks he's put together, based on the latest knitwear collections. It's all very well, but I'm thinking: *Five-inch red platforms. Wobble. Early start. Knitted bathing suit with detachable shorts and suspenders. Spaghetti legs.* Where are Afghan jackets and billowing skirts when you need them? Not to mention the blue face paint, which made me practically unrecognizable.

Dad gives me the thumbs-up from the corner of the green room. He offered to be my chaperone today because he's always been interested in how TV programs are made. In fact, a pretty, blonde production assistant has offered to give him a tour of the studios. He looks really excited. He wouldn't be looking like that if *he* were wearing five-inch red platforms.

I'm standing next to Sheherezade Scott. She joined Model City last year and has already done more jobs than she can remember. Whatever it is you're supposed to have at go-sees, Sheherezade's obviously got it in bucket-loads. She is all angles — angular bones, angular hair, angular eyes. Her skin is so pale it's almost translucent, her eyes are golden, and her hair is almost waist length, frizzy and brown, cut to resemble a series of cascading triangles. She looks busy and distracted — she has two other jobs scheduled today — but she was brilliant during our run-through. I plan to copy her as closely as I can.

She adjusts her suspenders.

"Are you ready to vamp?"

"As I'll ever be."

It would help if I knew what vamping was. I get most of my vocab from Dad, and he's never mentioned it. Is it something to do with vampires? Am I supposed to look bloodthirsty? Is it even possible to look bloodthirsty in knitted shorts? In the run-through, I was concentrating on walking, stopping, turning, and not falling over. Also not staring into the camera, because we're supposed to pretend it's not there. Sandy McShand kept calling things out in such a strong Scottish accent that I couldn't understand most of them. "Stop shaking" was one, definitely. But right now, I feel as though I have no control over my body at all.

"Relax," Sheherezade says. "It's fun. Go for it."

Her name is familiar and suddenly I remember why. She must be the girl that Nick Spoke broke Rule One for, by getting involved with her. Model City can't represent two Sheherezades, surely? I seem to remember Frankie saying she "messed him up." How? He certainly seems messed up: resentful, surly, and anti-modeling. Well, it certainly wasn't because she was ugly.

At this moment, she gets a nod from a man in headphones, someone pats her on the shoulder blades, and off she goes. I watch her on a monitor as she does her walk, then hangs around for a couple of minutes while Sandy explains about the inspiration behind her outfit. It's not Victorian bathing machines, as I'd imagined, but Diaghilev, an impresario from the 1900s who founded the Ballets Russes. I've never seen anyone try to do ballet in knitwear, but the talk-show hosts nod seriously and look impressed.

Sheherezade thrusts out one hip, making sure she's diagonal to the camera. She told me that if you face it head-on it makes you look loads wider. She looks cool and distant. Is that vamping? I decide to try it anyway.

With a minute to go, they position me just out of shot. I wonder what Sheherezade would be like as a girlfriend for a would-be artist. Did she pose for him? Was she the girl in the magazine pictures Cassandra showed us at my first test shoot? She was head-banging, so you couldn't really see her face, but the hair was similar. It crosses my mind that if Nick Spoke likes girls with waist-length hair, I'd never stand a chance. Not that I did anyway, of course.

The man in headphones nods to me. Sheherezade saunters off and gives me a cool smile. Another man with a clipboard shoves me in the back, a lot harder than I was expecting. I start my wobbly walk and head for the blue X on the floor where I'm supposed to stop and turn. When I'm halfway there, one of the hosts calls out.

"And the shoes, Sandy. Tell us about the incredible shoes."

What am I supposed to do? Do I keep walking like I was supposed to, or start hanging around so they can admire the platforms? I stop dead and swing myself forward with one hip, like Sheherezade did, twisting my body around so the camera doesn't make me look enormous. What was it Sandy said? I remember vamping, but there was other stuff, too. "Hot" was possibly one of them. I'm increasingly hot under the studio lights, so that's not difficult. I think of Kristen Stewart — she was a great vampire. Maybe I could look like her: pale and sulky. I give it a go.

Sandy's saying something. I'm so busy doing my Kristen Stewart impression and trying not to wobble that I can't hear him properly. He does a gesture, swirling his hand around. He wants me to do the twirl. So I do. Then I remember I'm in the wrong place, so I walk forward to the mark and do it again. Pretty well, I think. Now a different man with a clipboard is waving at me. He's waving me backward. Wow, that went quickly. I breathe in, and try to do my coltish saunter off the set.

Five minutes later, after a superfast change that took a lot of rehearsing very early this morning, we do it all over again, side by side. By now, I think I'm getting the hang of it. Apart from one major wobble on the platforms, I'm pretty sure I'm vampish all the way through. It's even starting to be fun. I can hardly understand a word Sandy McShand is saying, but it doesn't seem to matter. I look *Twilight*-ish and vaguely undead. Sheherezade links her arm through mine and smiles a dazzling smile. I grin as happily as I can. It's almost a shame when I realize it's over.

"Not too bad, was it?" Sheherezade asks, already slipping carefully out of her suspenders as we reach the changing area.

"No, actually. It was —"

Her phone chimes and she cuts me off.

"Hi, Sam," she says, changing rapidly. Somehow she manages to strip, get dressed, and hold a conversation with her booker at Model City about whether to take a job in New York or go to a party in Dubai. I'd been hoping to talk to her about it all, but there isn't a chance. As soon as she's dressed, she's gone.

With no other jobs to dash off to, I take my time getting changed. In my head, I'm replaying my final coltish walk and wondering if it looked as good as it felt. When I'm ready, I sling my bag over my shoulder and try to locate Dad again so I can ask him. Somebody says he might be outside, getting some air with that production assistant he made friends with. They point to a door at the end of the corridor and the next thing I know, I'm standing outside, in a parking lot. Dad's nowhere to be seen, but Sandy McShand is wandering up and down with his back to me and talking very loudly into his phone.

"She was fabulous! Amazing! She had this stop-start walk. Perfect to open Christopher's show. I can't remember her name, but can you get her for him? He needs to see her. Seriously."

I stop dead, stunned. He said "amazing." And "stop-start walk." Is that coltish? I can't quite bring myself to believe I was that good, but maybe . . .

Sandy's still facing into the parking lot, listening intently now.

Of course, if this Christopher person (Christopher Bailey at Burberry? Christopher Kane the Scottish designer?) wanted me for a catwalk show, I couldn't do it because I'm not old enough yet, but I would be soon. And designers need models for other things. He could use me for a lookbook for fashion buyers if he wanted to. Or for an advertising campaign. I mean, normally I wouldn't be seen dead in stuff like knitted suspenders, but for an *advertising campaign* I'd be prepared to make an exception.

"There were two of them. Yes, that's right. Oh, you saw it? No, not her. She was very nothing. The other one. Long name. Frizzy hair. Yes, her."

He ends the call and turns around to go back into the building. I'm in his way, because even though I want to disappear, I'm stuck to the spot. He looks at me for a split second, then right through me. He doesn't register me at all, and why should he? I'm not amazing after all. I'm "not her." I'm the one who was "very nothing."

When I finally get back inside, Dad's waiting for me in the hall.

"All done, love? Ready to go?"

I nod. I'm *so* ready to go.

The job came with a chauffeur-driven car. It seemed so glamorous at six o'clock this morning when it arrived to pick us up. (Dad told Mum he had to meet a friend at the airport; I sneaked out with him.) Now I feel all wrong sitting in a limo. As it wends its way slowly back home through the morning traffic, Dad's phone rings. It's Mum.

"Ah," Dad says. "Really? Are you sure, love? I don't think it could have been, because she's waitressing, isn't she?"

There's a lot of shouting down the phone. Dad winces and holds it away from his ear. Now he knows how it felt for Ava when he called her after my first test shoot.

"Actually I am. Sorry, Mandy," he says. "We'll explain when we get in."

He turns to me.

"Your granny phoned her. *She'd* got a call from a neighbor who was watching. Didn't think of that. Mum said I'd better be with you, or we're both in more trouble than we could ever imagine."

TWENTY

This was not how I imagined telling Mum.

"I can't believe it," she says, gasping for breath, as soon as we get in.

She's sitting on the sofa, with the TV still on the same channel that featured Sandy McShand. Ava must have brought her the glass of water sitting beside her, because it's clear she hasn't moved for ages.

"Wasn't she grand?" Dad says, still hoping for a miracle.

Mum doesn't even look at him. She's staring at me.

"How long?" she asks, her face drained and pale. "All summer?"

I nod.

"All by yourself? Oh my God — what have we done?"

"Well, not by myself," I point out. "I had chaperones. There were lots of people around."

"Every day, you've been doing this?"

I stare at the carpet. "Most days. But not working. Just trying to get work."

Mum looks helplessly to Dad, then back to me. "When were you going to tell me?"

"When I got a job. A good one."

"And appearing on *national TV* didn't count as a good one?"

"Well . . . when you put it like that . . ."

She sighs so deeply it sounds as though all the breath is coming out of her. I was expecting her to blaze with fury, but she's beyond blazing. This is almost worse, because there's panic in her eyes. Poor Mum — spinning further out of orbit, and I've put her there.

"I can't believe I didn't realize," she says, squeezing her eyes closed and pressing her hands to her head. "My little girl . . . out there, surrounded by sharks . . ."

"They weren't *sharks* exactly . . ."

"Come. Sit here." She pats the sofa beside her. When I sit down, she looks at me wonderingly and reaches up to stroke my hair — which is a bit stiff and sticky because it's still full of about a million hair products. She strokes my arm instead. Her voice is surprisingly gentle, now that the panic's subsiding. "How was it? Really?"

"Really?"

The tenderness in her voice catches me off guard. For the first time since Ava got her diagnosis, she's looking at *me* — really looking at me and wanting to know how *I* am — and this is *so* not a good time to ask. I wish she'd asked me after the day Cassandra called, or Kite-Tail Day, or the day Nirmala removed the caterpillar. I wish I wasn't starting to cry.

"It's been OK," I sniff, moving into her open arms. "Well, nobody likes me, and I only got one job, and they said I was very nothing, and my ankles are fat, and all the other girls seem better at it than me . . ."

I'm crying quite a lot now. I can't help myself. Mum passes me a tissue. She always has them on hand now, just in case.

"I bet they aren't," she says with a dawning smile. "Just so you know, darling, I thought you looked fabulous in those" — she starts shaking — "really, really silly platforms. And those *suspenders*! What was that stylist *on*?"

The smile creeps across her face. The panic has gone and instead there's her old, familiar twinkle. She gets the craziness of Sandy McShand! And she thought I looked fabulous. I snuggle into her as closely as I can. Oh, I've missed my mum. It's funny how you can share a flat with someone and still miss them so much.

"And I ought to say, Mandy —" Dad pipes up.

Mum glares at him to cut him off and remind him this is all partly his fault, but he stands his ground.

"— your daughter has been getting up on time, every day, and finding her way to God-knows-where around London, and sticking with it despite all the rejections, and never complaining. And she's been poring over fashion books and learning about photography. You'd hardly recognize her."

Thanks, Dad. I think that was supposed to be a compliment.

Mum pulls me even closer. "Just don't do it again, darling, promise. Not without me there, anyway."

I promise. Not that I stand much chance of doing it again — not after today.

Ava comes in from our room, where I guess she's been hiding.

"Sorry," she says to me sheepishly. "She switched channels when Gran called and I couldn't stop her. How did it go?"

"Oh," I sigh, just glad the whole thing is finally over, "it was nothing."

Later, at the library, they find me last month's copy of *Dazed & Confused*. I want to check if the head-banging girl with the extraordinary hair was Sheherezade. It's not surprising Nightmare Boy felt uncomfortable that day in Seb's studio if he was being forced to look at pictures of his ex-girlfriend. Was she really as stunning in the pictures as I remember?

I find the feature. And yes. Yes, it was her; and yes, she was stunning. Wearing painted silk hot pants and a tight cotton jacket, Sheherezade has an energy in her photos that's electric. She hasn't just mastered her fingers, feet, and elbows; she can fling her body in five different directions at once and still look amazing. No wonder he went out with her.

Amazing. Not my word anymore. Someone else's.

What was I thinking? I could never, simply *never*, be this girl.

Ava blames herself. But I tell her not to worry. As Dad said — good things happened as well as bad this summer. I made friends with Sabrina. I know who Karl Lagerfeld is, and what brush to use for what type of blusher application. I can find my way around the weirdest corners of London. If nothing else, I could always get a job as a local tour guide now.

Meanwhile, there are less than two weeks left of vacation, and I've got my Still Life project to get on with before the start of term. Things are about to get serious at school. It's better not to have any more summer distractions.

I call Frankie to let her know that I'm not available for go-sees anymore.

"Oh, are you sure, angel? It was just starting to go somewhere."

"Not really," I point out. "Sandy McShand didn't like me."

"Hmm. Did he tell you that? Well, that's just an opinion. You're gorgeous! Don't let one little Scottish stylist get you down. Anyway, are you off somewhere nice?"

"What?"

"On your vacation?" she insists. "Isn't that why you're stopping the go-sees? Then you've got school, of course, but we can pick things up at fall break or Christmas —"

I see. That's why she's so relaxed about it. She assumes I'm jetting off somewhere glamorous for a few days, not giving up entirely.

"Well, actually, Frankie —"

"Oh, God, Rio. VIP." I can hear her other phone ringing insistently in the background. "Sorry, angel, got to dash this minute. No problem about the go-sees. Call me when you're back, OK? Have fun!"

I would so love to be the girl Frankie obviously thinks I am. The one who mixes modeling with posh vacations. The one whose school friends beg for details of her glamorous life. The one who thinks Freaky Friday is Lindsay Lohan's finest moment, not a term of abuse.

"Yeah, right. Thanks," I say. But she's already hung up the phone. She's talking to some VIP in Rio.

And I have a whole bunch of bananas to shade in this morning.

★

I'm on my third banana (having made the bunch smaller by eating two of them) when I hear an angry growl from the sofa. Ava's watching the classic movie channel, which has become a recent favorite of ours. I assume that Spencer Tracy has said something deeply irritating to Katharine Hepburn.

"Idiot!" Ava calls out.

"What's he done this time?"

"He's invited me to a party."

"Who? Spencer Tracy?"

"No, T. Honestly. He died decades ago. Jesse."

I look around. She's furious.

"Wait a minute. Your boyfriend has invited you to a party?"

"Yes," she seethes. "Idiot."

I'm not totally following this. I go over to the sofa to join her, so she can explain it to me.

"So what's the problem?"

She rolls her eyes. "He's planning a barbecue on the beach in Cornwall for when he gets back from that yacht in October. He wants to know if I'll be well enough to go. Look at me. He still doesn't get it."

"Well, that's because you don't tell him," I point out.

Ava has gradually cut herself off from all of her friends except Louise. She doesn't want them to see her on her bad days, when she's sick and exhausted from the treatment. She doesn't want to hear the pity in their voices when they ask how she's feeling. She doesn't even like me knowing how bad it is a lot of the time, which is why I normally pretend not to notice.

"He doesn't want to picture me like this. Think about it, T. He's surrounded by cool sailor girls all day, with highlights and toned abs and red bikinis."

"You've been checking out his friends on Facebook, haven't you?"

She looks guilty.

"There's one in particular who's like a walking Barbie doll . . . He works with her every day, T. He says he misses me, but he's just being nice. Long-distance relationships never work. Three Hollywood couples split last week because of it."

I make a mental note to tell Mum to confiscate her celebrity magazines.

"And he always said I looked like a movie star. Well, I don't anymore."

In a familiar gesture, she puts a hand to her patchy hair. It's lasted very well, but she's on her third cycle now and the chemo is getting to it. She hasn't cut it yet, which means long strands on the pillow, in her hairbrush, in the shower . . . What's left on her head is lank and tired, like the rest of her.

"You don't *at the moment,*" I correct her. "Actually, you do at the moment. You look like Anne Hathaway doing an Oscar-winning performance of a girl bravely fighting cancer. Slam-dunk award. Promise."

She looks at me with hollow eyes. Then her lower lip starts to wobble. Her upper lip joins it. They tilt up. I think she's giggling. She IS giggling. Anne Hathaway did it. Finally.

"You're sweet, T," she says, "but the drugs have made me blow up like a balloon. Anne Hathaway never looked this pale and puffy."

"You forget that you made me watch *The Devil Wears Prada* for fashion research," I point out. "Pale, yes. Bony, rather than puffy. But even then, she still looked like a movie star, same as you do. Look, I'll prove it to you."

I go into the hall, where my modeling bag has been sitting untouched for the last few days, and come back holding Ava's camera.

"We'll turn our room into a studio. I know how to do that now. We just need to hang up a couple of white sheets to create a background and get the lighting right. I'll make you look glamorous. You can do the makeup, because you're better at that than me, but I can get you to do some cool poses. You saw what they did to me: You can turn *anyone* into *anything* with enough lipstick and mascara."

She looks up at me, not angry now, but frail and confused, and really not like my big sister at all.

"But . . . why?"

"To show Jesse, if you insist on not seeing him in person. So he can be thinking about you instead of Barbie Girl."

Actually, that's not it exactly. It's to show Ava herself that she doesn't look as bad as she thinks. Different, yes. Patchy-haired, possibly. But still basically gorgeous. Some things you just don't lose.

"Really?" She sounds almost convinced. "Not now, though. Honestly, T. Give me a couple of days. Right now I feel . . . Excuse me."

She drags herself off to the bathroom again.

She may have a point. Just after a fresh bout of chemo is not her best time. Even in *The Devil Wears Prada* they never made Anne Hathaway look *that* bad.

Ava's brave, but I can see now that she's struggling more than I'd realized. She needs something to keep her going while Jesse's away. Something fun. Something to take her mind off her body, and how everything's gone out of control.

What's Ava's idea of the most fun thing you can do without a boyfriend? Then it occurs to me. Shopping.

More specifically, shopping for cute little tops, new handbags, and skinny jeans. She tried to cheer herself up by giving me a skirt, but it would be even better if I could get her one. Much more effective than the endless blueberry and nasturtium concoctions that Mum keeps feeding her.

I call Frankie again and ask if she can advance me some of my "very nothing" TV money. After all, I earned every penny of it wobbling about on those red platforms for Sandy McShand. Normally it can take months for the money to come through, but when I tell Frankie about Ava, she agrees to put some in my bank account straightaway.

"Give her a hug from me, OK?" she says.

I promise I will. Actually, I won't, because hugging hurts Ava at the moment, but I know what she means. I'll give Ava a spoonful of ice cream from her instead.

TWENTY-ONE

What we're up to isn't exactly illegal, but it isn't encouraged by Ava's doctors. Or technically *allowed* by Ava's doctors. They don't want her out and about in major public places so soon after her latest session of chemo, in case she gets an infection.

Does Constantine & Reed count as a major public place? Since opening in July, it's now officially the coolest store in Knightsbridge, with bouncers at the door, like a nightclub, and lines of teenagers waiting to get in. It probably counts as a *bit* public. But it's *so* amazing that I'm sure the doctors wouldn't mind if they could see us drawing up outside in our taxi. Meanwhile, Mum thinks we've gone to the library, and Dad didn't ask *where* we were going, which was perfect.

Inside, the store is exactly how Ava's friend Louise described it: huge, dark spaces with spotlights in the ceiling, colored lights in the floors, and loud music pumping through the sound system. The good-looking staff wander about in shorts, high heels, and tans, and there's a strong sense that if you went back outside you'd be on the beach in Miami or somewhere glamorous in LA, and the bouncers would be making space for J-Lo and Jay-Z.

I can't believe I never took shops like this seriously before. I've always gone for places that sell things cheaply, on racks, in simple displays that I can quickly flick through. I could never understand Ava's passion for wandering around, soaking up the atmosphere. Here, things are draped on quirky pieces of futuristic furniture. It takes ages to figure out what's what, but as soon as you find something you like, you discover something even more desirable right next to it. It's not about finding your size; it's about being cool and fitting in. And I want to. Suddenly, I really want to. I wouldn't mind a job here myself next year. I wonder if they hire ex-almost-models with TV issues.

Ava is happier than I've seen her for weeks. For half an hour, she wanders from room to room, with Louise in tow, picking out things to try on. There's a massive line for the changing rooms, but this is when it helps to have your best friend working there. Louise has reserved the best room for us, so we just waft right up to it when Ava's ready. There's even space for me to sit down and admire her as she tries things on.

"Call me if you need me," Louise says. "I won't be far away."

Once Ava's inside, Louise catches me for a moment outside the curtain, puts a hand on my shoulder, her eyes wide with shock. She's been so busy working recently that she hasn't seen Ava for a little while and she obviously wasn't expecting her to look so different. I suppose I'm used to it, because I've seen it happen gradually, day by day. I put my arms around Louise and give her a quick squeeze. I'm just grateful that she didn't say anything. Ava hates people commenting on her new appearance, and Louise is a good friend for respecting that.

Inside the dressing room, Ava is struggling to undo a fussy top without interfering with the tubes in her chest. I help her out of it, then turn to admire the huge pile of other things she's brought to try on.

"Pass me that dress, would you?" she asks.

It's a stretchy floral number that slides over your head. No fussy buttons. I do as I'm told, then check out what else she's chosen. There are lots of skinny jeans in different colors and styles, a few simple tops, some pretty dresses with ribbons for decoration, and lacy cobweb cardigans. Interesting: They're all very much Ava's style and they'll look gorgeous on her, but I happen to know that they're not the latest trend — as modeled at every go-see — which is more voluminous and luxurious and out there. I always assumed Ava was a fashionista, but really, she's just a girl who's comfortable with her own look. I love her confidence. I still haven't got around to wearing my Woodland Trust T-shirt as a dress yet, and there's a part of me that really wishes I would.

Suddenly, there's a noise behind me. A sort of strangled shriek from Ava. It's definitely not pleasure caused by the loveliness of the cardigans. I look up and catch her reflection in the mirror. Her face is drained and gasping. It's poking out of the neck of the floral dress she's got on, which has strange, dangly embroidery around the neckline that I don't remember seeing before.

"Help me. Help me. Get it *off*!"

I stand up quickly and reach forward to help her. Which is when I spot it. The embroidery around the neckline isn't embroidery at all. It's *hair*. Ava's hair. Lots of it. Pulling the dress over her head must have dragged it out, not in strands, but clumps.

We stay there for a moment, breathing fast, not talking. I didn't know hair could *do* this. I can feel my panic rising, especially when I see the exposed patches on Ava's scalp. This is exactly what she feared the most, and the sudden appearance of her pale, exposed skin is shocking. I wonder if I'm going to be sick. Why did we stupidly go out without Mum? But the fact is, we did, and Ava's only got me. Somehow, I'll have to deal with this.

I calm my breathing and think. This is just one more surprise in a summer full of surprises. I have recently dealt with fat ankles, cartwheeling on wet pebbles, and looking like an idiot on daytime TV. Ava has coped with far worse. Of course I can deal with this.

"It's OK," I tell her gently, putting my hands on her quivering shoulders. "Close your eyes. Put your arms up. I'll get it off. Don't worry, I've got you."

Her breathing calms a tiny bit, too, and she does as she's told. For once, it's useful being so much taller than her. It makes it easier to pull the dress back over her head. I quickly brush as much hair off her shoulders as I can and wrap one of the cardigans around her.

"Get rid of it!" she whimpers.

I pick up the dress and I'm about to take it away when she squeaks, "The hair! I mean the hair." Then, with a sob, she slumps slowly to the floor.

So, carefully I remove the hair, strand by strand, until the dress is back to its old state, ready to give back to Louise. Trust Ava to worry about the clothes. As I work, I steal glances at her head with its patches of bare scalp and remaining tufts of hair lying limply against the skin.

"You need to cut the rest off," I say gently. "Before it gets any worse."

"I know," she says, biting her lip and shivering. "I was going to get it shaved soon. But I'm scared, T. I'll look like a Buddhist nun. Or an *alien*. A big, fat, ugly alien."

"A gorgeous alien. We could do it now. I'll come with you."

"I just want to stay here."

She can't stay here, in this dressing room. The longer she stays, the harder it will be to move.

"I'll hold your hand," I reassure her.

"Will you?"

"Yes." Then I think of something. "And I know somewhere we can do it. You'll be fine."

She looks lost and uncertain. "And you promise you'll hold my hand?"

"Every minute," I tell her. "Trust me."

Louise is standing outside the curtain. She heard the shrieking. I ask her to get us a taxi and she goes off straightaway to find one, without staring, or saying anything to Ava, or asking why. Not remotely ditzy in any way. I like Louise.

TWENTY-TWO

Twenty minutes later we're in Covent Garden, standing in the reception of Locks, Stock, and Barrel. It's the only posh hair salon I know. It reminded me of a spaceship the moment I walked through the door to have my hair cut. The perfect place to become an alien.

The girl at reception looks through her book to see if she can fit Ava in.

"What was it you wanted done?" she asks. "Cut and blow-dry?"

"No, we need it all cut off," I say.

Louise lent Ava a straw trilby to wear, but she's hot and she's fanning her face with the hat.

The receptionist catches sight of Ava's head and gasps.

"Excuse me."

She disappears. When she comes back, she's with a young, rangy man dressed in black with a studded belt and several earrings.

"This is Sergio. He'll look after you," she says, flushing with embarrassment. I hope Ava didn't see the expression on her face.

We follow Sergio through to a chair at the back of the salon. He puts a gown over Ava's shoulders and sits her down. Then we all look at her patchy head in the mirror, and her patchy cheeks, still red from crying in the taxi. I do as I promised and keep hold of her hand. Sergio doesn't look very sure about this.

"How short do you want it?"

The message hasn't gotten through. As calmly as I can, I explain again about shaving Ava's head. There's not much else we can do at this stage. Leaving any hair behind will just look patchy and silly. Sergio's eyes widen, but he nods. He goes off to get clippers and whatever else he needs. Meanwhile Ava grips my hand tightly.

"Stay with me."

I look at her in the mirror, where her frightened eyes seem huge. "Of course I'll stay with you."

Without letting go of her hand, I pull up the seat beside her and sit in it. It feels so wrong that she should be losing what's left of her lovely hair, whereas my rubbish bird's nest is still sitting there on my head, looking as hopeless as ever. I've never liked my hair.

Which gives me another idea.

"I'll do it with you."

"What?"

"We'll do it together. It'll be easier if we do it together."

"Don't be silly," she says. But I can see something new in her face. Curiosity, besides the fear. Curiosity is a much better look. And I'm curious, too. And strangely excited.

"Come on! It'll be an adventure."

So when Sergio comes back, we send him off for another hairdresser and more clippers. He looks even more doubtful. The salon's very busy. He disappears for quite a while and I can see lots of whispering going on among the staff. Other customers start looking around, wondering what's going on. Then an older man appears behind us. He smiles at us both in the mirror. He's huge — like a grizzly bear in a silk print shirt and gold jewelry. But his smile is pure honey and when he opens his mouth, his voice is rich and warm: like an American soul singer about to launch into a big number.

"Hi, I'm Vince," he says in an accent that is pure South London. "I'm the head stylist. Now, I understand you two beautiful ladies need my help."

Calmly and confidently, he places his hands on Ava's shoulders, looking as though he deals with patchy-headed teenagers every day of his life. Sergio returns, clippers in hand, to stand behind me. He looks a lot more comfortable now that Vince is here.

"Shaving a head is an art form. It's a ritual," Vince explains. "We should have incense and flower ceremonies. Instead we have coffee and this month's *Vogue*. Anyway, let me show you what we can do."

He puts the clippers in front of us and shows us the difference between shaving the head completely, and leaving a millimeter or two of hair. I'm about to go for the gentler option, but Ava grips my hand and says firmly that she wants hers shaved off completely.

"I hate it now. Get rid of it, please?"

Vince can see the blackness in her eyes. He doesn't argue.

"I'll have what she's having," I say. He smiles and nods. There's a pause while we're given drinks and magazines to take our minds off it. Then Vince flourishes his clippers like castanets.

"Ready, beautiful girls?"

We say yes together. We hold hands tightly. We're ready.

The clippers get going and our magazines sit untouched on our laps. Our drinks go cold. We're mesmerized by what's going on in the mirror. Slowly, our heads and faces start to change in ways we couldn't imagine.

The first thing that happens is that I notice how alike we suddenly look. Without our hair as a distraction, our features seem stronger. Our eyes are similar: different color, same shape. Our chins have the same dimple. And I have slightly nicer ears than Ava. Cool! As it gradually appears, I'm fascinated by my scalp. I'd always assumed it was smooth as an egg, but it's actually bumpy. It's a whole part of me I had no idea about. I know I'm going to spend ages examining it in the mirror at home.

Ava looks down to see what's left of the curls landing in her lap, on her shoulders, and on the floor.

I squeeze her hand again. "Watch your face. Watch mine."

She looks at me gratefully. "Wow, T! You're like something out of *Star Trek*."

I am, but I rather like it. "Actually, I remind myself of Megamind," I say, admiring my domed forehead.

She stares at me. Then at herself. She smiles.

"I look like a boy!"

"A boy with cheekbones to die for," Vince cuts in. "And the back of your head is *divine*. I'll show you."

He picks up a handheld mirror and adjusts it so Ava can admire her profile. He's right: It's magnificent. She just needs loads of chokers and jewelry to show it off.

We can't take our eyes off ourselves. It's as if we're looking at different people. These girls somehow manage to be strange and scary, but also powerful and strong. I wouldn't mess with the person I see in the mirror. But I'd want to know more about her. And I thought Ava would be fragile once all her beautiful hair was gone. Instead, she's the opposite.

"You look like a warrior princess," I tell her.

She grins. "I know! I look like you."

"Uh-huh. Two warrior princesses."

"Oh!" Vince exclaims. "Xena and Gabrielle. I *adored* those girls on TV. Did you ever watch that show? They were so *crazy* and *strong* and *hot*! You can be Xena," he says to Ava, "and you can be Gabrielle. I see you now, fighting the gods, casting bolts of lightning. Add a bit of gold armor and you're *smokin'*."

I love it. I'm Gabrielle — whoever she is. No, I think I'll be Xena, too. And I'm storming across the . . . wherever they storm — I'll have to get the DVDs — causing havoc and fighting with gods. It's just how I feel.

Once the hair is gone, Vince and Sergio go over our heads again with the clippers at their lowest setting, paying attention to every bump and hollow.

Ava lets go of my hand to feel her scalp. She does it gingerly at first, then with growing confidence.

"It's so smooth and soft! It's like stroking a baby."

So much better than the fluffy patches that were there before. She looks healthier now that they're gone.

I stroke my own head. My hair was tougher than Ava's, and what's left feels like sandpaper. There's a shadow on my scalp where it used to be. It looks as if someone has drawn my hairline in light pencil. And I have a cute hairline. I never knew this.

Vince and Sergio rub lotion into our skin. It smells of pears and sweet spring flowers. I can't help twisting my neck, adjusting to the new freedom. I had no idea how heavy my bird's nest was. My head moves differently now that it's not there. I could swear my neck's grown longer.

Vince pats Ava's shoulders. "Come on, Xena, we're done now," he says. "I *love* that look on you."

She looks at herself seriously in the mirror and nods. "It looks a lot better than it did."

I'm glad she thinks so, too. She looks very elegant now. Her Elizabeth Taylor eyes shine through.

We take off our gowns and head for the reception desk. I reach for my wallet in my bag. Which is when I catch sight of the price list propped up beside a space-age flower arrangement. I didn't pay for my last haircut here — Frankie arranged everything. So I didn't know that an average stylist charges £75 for a cut and blow-dry. Vince charges £150 — *each*. Mum complains when a haircut costs £50, or at least she did. Now Dad cuts hers for her. I didn't know you even *could* spend this much.

Oh, goodness. I've done one measly modeling job and already I'm over £200 in debt. Ted would crumple at this point, but Xena just assumes that something will sort itself out, because warrior princesses are not defeated by mere hairdressing.

And Xena is right. Vince follows us and has a quiet word with the receptionist before greeting his next customer.

"That'll be twenty pounds," she says, surprised, punching numbers into the computer. "Vince says it was a simple job."

I try to look sophisticated and relaxed, not pathetically relieved, as I pay her with my debit card. But when I've finished, I look over to catch Vince's eye so I can say thank you. He's back at work, but he sees me in the mirror and gives me a flash of a smile. A sad one. I think he knew why we were here today, but he never let on to Ava. Vince is a hero.

The two Xenas make their way out into the legendary landscape of Covent Garden. They are proud and brave (and not in debt), and all they need is some golden armor to complete the look. And leather bikinis, but frankly, there are limits. Wherever we go, people turn and stare. Normally I hate this, but today I think it's only natural. Who wouldn't stare at a couple of warrior princesses, striding through their domain and acknowledging the loyalty of their subjects? We smile at them regally. A few of them smile back.

I may — to some people — look like an alien life-form. But I know how I feel. Even aliens can be hot.

TWENTY-THREE

As soon as we get home, we rush into the kitchen to tell Mum what we've been up to. She takes one look and gives a sudden shriek of her own. Her knees buckle underneath her. Oh, no. I hadn't thought about this. To have one bald daughter might seem like carelessness, but two . . .

Dad comes out of the bedroom, where he's been writing, and turns pale. He goes to Mum to hold her up, glaring at me. He's shocked by what I've done and angry at the effect it's had on Mum. But already she's pulling herself together.

"Ava, darling! You look wonderful! Ted, too. Well done. Come and give me a hug."

She hugs both of us to her, tight. I think it took her a second to work out what had happened, but she's our mum: A second was all it needed. She sniffs and takes a deep breath.

"I knew this moment would come and I've been saving things up. Come into my room. I'll show you."

For a minute, I felt more Megamind than warrior princess, but thanks to Mum, the moment has passed. She may be tired and cranky at the moment, but when we really need her to be amazing she summons it up from somewhere.

We follow her into her bedroom, where she pulls a box out from under the bed. It's an old boot box, from the days when she could afford to buy boots. And in it are silk scarves, folded between layers of tissue paper.

"I used to have quite a collection. I'm sure there are enough for both of you. Why don't you pick out the ones you like? I don't want your heads getting cold."

We sit side by side on the edge of her bed, in front of her dresser, and check ourselves out in her mirror. We pile the scarves wherever we can and try different methods of tying them around our heads.

Ava finds some long turquoise and violet scarves in the softest, most delicate Indian silk, and winds them into a knot to one side of her neck. Their tassels hang past her shoulder. Now she looks more gypsy princess than warrior princess. Mum uses an eyebrow pencil to beef up Ava's eyebrows. Somehow she's kept most of her eyelashes, and with a bit of soft eye shadow and some eyeliner, she's back to Jesse-ready total glamour again.

I try out all sorts of looks, from "the Queen out riding" to "crazy Victorian palm reader." The key is to look cool and abandoned, not like Grace Kelly on a shopping trip. The scarves feel fabulously smooth and soft against my head, but they slip around and nothing's quite right. I miss the simple, bold shape I had before. In the end I settle for a couple of Mum's dangly earrings and nothing else.

Throughout supper, Mum keeps staring at me, and she can't help looking anxious, bordering on freaked out. I sense she really wants me to go with the scarf option. Dad can hardly look at me at all. I've never done anything that my parents didn't like before — at least, not that I can remember. But something has changed, and it feels good.

It's not as if I'm breaking any laws or anything. I'm just being who I am. This is me. I am bold; I am scary; I am strong. I am a rebel and a warrior, like my brave and beautiful sister sitting here beside me. A warrior who *really* likes the cassoulet Mum's made tonight and can't get enough of it. Also, two helpings of blackberry-and-apple crumble for dessert.

I am Xena. Deal with it.

After breakfast the next day, I borrow one of Mum's berets and Dad's bike, and go for a long ride as far as Richmond Park. It feels exhilarating to be out in the fresh air, surrounded by my favorite greenery, with the wind in my face and the sun on my skin. I could have done this before — Dad wouldn't have minded — but for some reason it never occurred to me. Apart from cartwheeling on the "beach," I haven't had enough exercise recently. Over the last few weeks, life seemed increasingly complicated. Now I can't believe I ever worried about my fat ankles.

Just as I'm freewheeling down the longest hill, my left hip starts vibrating. I pause and get my phone out of the pocket of my shorts. It's Ava, sounding wistful.

"Hi, T. You've been gone for a while. Is everything OK?"

I tell her about the fresh air feeling and the faintest hint of autumn in the whispering leaves this morning. I love the changing seasons. Even the breeze seems to know that summer is nearly over.

"Jesse just texted," she says. "I sent him one last night, telling him what we did yesterday, but I didn't think he'd get it for ages. He's in Saint-Tropez, by the way." Long sigh. Like me, she's probably imagining the endless selection of ripped-abs, Red-Bikini Babes in Saint-Tropez. "Now he wants to know all about my hair. He knew it would be a big deal."

"And?"

"And . . . I'm not sure what to say."

She sounds back to being timid and nervous, not her old self at all. Also, her old self would have called Louise, not me. Ava and I have been talking more ever since . . . well, ever since everything that's happened this summer. But I've never known her go out of her way to call me.

"I'll come home now," I tell her.

"Except . . . I liked what you said about the breeze, T. I need to get out, too. Shall I meet you in Wandsworth Park?"

I agree. Wandsworth Park is nothing like Richmond Park, despite the name. One is a glorious expanse of countryside in the city. The other is a little patch of green beside the river, not too far from our flat, where I've been practicing photography recently. But it's much easier for Ava to get to, so I race back there on the bike, as fast as I can.

When I get there fifteen minutes later, panting, she is sitting elegantly on a bench by a long, wide stretch of grass, wearing a simple cotton summer dress, delicate makeup, and one of Mum's blue silk scarves wound expertly around her head like a turban, with the ends trailing over her shoulder.

"You look wonderful!" I say before I can stop myself, because it might sound corny, but she does.

She smiles and looks embarrassed — but not incredulous, which is a good start.

"What you said that time about the photo for Jesse . . . can you take one now?" she asks. "While I'm feeling brave enough? It's easier than trying to explain to him."

"I'd love to. Except I don't have the camera on me." I shrug apologetically.

She looks even more embarrassed. "I do. I brought it with me. Just in case. I know you said that thing about making our room into a studio, but to be honest, I hate our room right now. I hate everything about that flat. Just because . . . bad associations. You know."

I do. I hate it, too, a lot of the time. I bet she hates the bathroom the most.

"Outside is good," I agree. "I've been practicing here quite a bit. And Nick — that boy, you probably don't remember — anyway, this guy, he said that outdoor light is good. Style bloggers use it all the time."

She grins at me. "I remember Nick," she says. Then she grins at me some more.

I go pink. I can't imagine why she's looking at me like that. He's just some boy who mentioned interesting types of photography. No big deal. I haven't heard from him all summer, and I didn't expect to. What does she mean? I thought we were talking about style bloggers.

"Hand me the camera," I demand. "I'll see what I can do."

If my test shoots have taught me anything, it's that you rarely get a great picture by just waving the camera around and pressing the button. If Jesse's going to see Ava at her best, the background has to be right, and I have to capture the best angle of her face, with the most flattering light and shadows, and she has to be smiling just enough, but not too much, and not doing that stupid thing with her fingernail.

I put myself in Xena mode and explain to Ava how I need her to sit. I wish I could fiddle with depth of field, like Greta did on the pebbly beach, but Ava's camera isn't that hi-tech. Instead, I concentrate on getting her in a decent pose and composing the picture so she's surrounded by green, with the blue of her scarf showing up brightly against it. Certain angles make her face look too round, thanks to the steroid regime, so I avoid those. Others bring out her lovely cheekbones and her pretty nose. It's looking OK, but it's only when I do an impression of Vince — "A bit of gold armor and you're *smokin'*!" — that her face comes alive, her violet eyes sparkle, and I get the shot that will compete with the Red-Bikini Babes.

"There!" I tell her. "What did I tell you?"

She checks the camera screen and pouts. "I look like an egg dressed as a pirate."

"You do not. Look at your smile."

"OK. I look like Anne Hathaway doing an impression of an egg dressed as a pirate."

"That I'll accept," I agree, grinning and putting away the camera.

But I notice that she sends the picture to Jesse as soon as she gets home, and that by lunchtime, Mum has it as the new wallpaper on her phone. It shows it pays to think about what you're doing. It's not up to Seb standards, I admit, but it's definitely the best picture I've taken so far.

Over lunch, Dad still keeps staring at us, and me in particular. He's trying to be as enthusiastic about our new appearance as we are, but the effort shows.

"I've been doing some research," he says. "There's a very good wig shop in Notting Hill, apparently. I'll book a cab to take you there."

"I don't need one," Ava says. "The hospital will give me one, remember?"

"I do," Dad says, "but those are pretty basic. Your mum and I — we want you to have something that's very natural and realistic. I mean, you look great now" — he coughs — "obviously. But your nan . . . well, when she had chemo . . . she said a good wig made all the difference. For . . . public occasions. We can afford it if we're careful. And, Ted, you'll need one, too."

"Sure, Dad," Ava says obediently. "That's very kind."

I realize she's in keep-the-parents-happy mode. Poor Ava. It's really tiring, being ill. Then it occurs to me: I may be happy with my bald head at home, but school starts in a few days. Dad may have a point.

So Mum accompanies us to the wig shop and we spend ages in front of the mirror, turning ourselves into different people. It's great. First, I'm Marilyn Monroe, then Fergie. Ava is Elizabeth Taylor (easy), then Katy Perry, then our old nan. Honestly — our nan. In a shaggy, short, blonde-streaked crop, just like she always used to wear. Creepy.

I fall in love with a short, dark, slinky wig with ruler-straight bangs that makes me look like Louise Brooks from the 1920s. (It's amazing what you learn from watching the classic movie channel with your sister.) I'd love to get it, but it's super-obviously a wig. I know I'm going to have to settle for something that looks vaguely like the bird's nest. Although when I describe it to the lady in the shop, she seems slightly horrified.

Eventually, Ava goes for something shoulder-length and wavy. It's called the Scarlett Johansson. Who wouldn't buy a wig called the Scarlett Johansson? Even so, she puts it in a bag to take it home, rather than wearing it right now.

"It makes my head hot," she complains.

The woman nods. "A lot of my customers say that. I wish they'd invent them with air-conditioning. You looked great in it, though. You could be a model, you know."

Ava smiles and catches my eye.

My wig, in the end, is called the Robert Pattinson. Says it all.

TWENTY-FOUR

"It looks as though it's about to eat a bit of lettuce," Daisy says pensively.

Fresh back from Germany, she's come over to hear my news and check out my new hairpiece. On my head, she admits it's very hard to tell the Pattinson from the real thing. But on my dresser, where it is now, she says it reminds her very much of a long-haired guinea pig.

"I wish you'd put it away."

"I can put it back on," I offer. "I need to attach it with wig tape, though, if I'm going to do it properly."

"No, I like your head like that. It's very nineties Sinéad O'Connor. She sings this song by Prince called 'Nothing Compares 2 U.' Have you seen the video? It's incredible. I'll have to show you."

With Daisy, it always comes back to music. In fact, she's not that interested in most of my modeling stories, apart from the one about the kite tails. She doesn't actually say "I told you so," but transmits it in sheer brainwaves. Then she goes on about her dad's gig in Düsseldorf and how much she missed Marmite. Basically, she's just glad that things are back to normal.

Except they aren't, exactly. Not for me. I may look the same — with the R-Patz on, anyway — but I feel different somehow. I have an urge to stride through ancient domains, dominating my kingdom, and there's no denying the fact that under the R-Patz, I am bald. If anyone finds out, how's that going to go down at Richmond Academy?

However, I've learned one thing from those endless, hopeless castings, and it's that you just have to hold your head high and keep walking. So, despite my nervousness, when I show up in class on the first day of the fall term, I try to act as if nothing has happened. And the strange thing is — it seems to work. The R-Patz is hot and itchy. But after everything I've been through this summer, nobody notices anything at all.

Strangest of all, I have Cally Harvest to thank. It turns out that after a couple of Jell-O shots one evening in Magaluf, she had Dean Daniels's initials tattooed on the back of her neck. It's the talk of the class and makes her the center of attention. Dean's thrilled. Personally, I'm not convinced it was such a great idea. She's going to need to wear turtlenecks a lot if it doesn't work out. Or else she's going to have to be very careful in her choice of future boyfriends.

Soon, we're back into the swing of the school day. The final period is art, which is the one I've been looking forward to. Miss Jenkins is keen to know how we got on with our projects over the summer, and I can't wait to show her. When it comes to my turn, I unveil all my sketches of shaded fruit with a flourish.

"Really, Ted? Is that it?" she says, with a general lack of appreciation bordering on disappointment.

I look at my bananas, and back at Miss Jenkins, shocked. I also did a glass of water.

"I worked really hard on it!" I protest. And I did. I shaded those bananas for *ages*.

"But did you *think* about it? At all? Which artists inspired you? Oh, Ted — that manga drawing you did of Daisy last year was really good. It captured her softness and her spikiness. I was hoping for something more . . . original from you."

I bite my lip. I would so love to be original.

Miss Jenkins sees my lip tremble slightly. She's not as harsh as her crimson lipstick might suggest.

"Did you do *anything* artistic over the summer?"

Does wobbling up and down in five-inch platforms count as artistic, I wonder? Or having tissue-paper petals stuck to me? Or wearing a jacket made out of kite tails? The thing is, it was always the other people who were artistic. I was just there. And even then I was officially "very nothing."

"Not really," I admit. "Except . . . I took some photos, I suppose, of staircases and stuff. And of my sister."

Miss Jenkins sighs again. I'm sure she's about to say something about family photos not counting, but then she pauses, as if she's just remembered that my big sister is Ava, and that Ava is (a) beautiful and (b) fighting for her life.

"Really?" she asks. "What were those photos about?"

At which point Nathan King, who's been playing around at the back of the art room, bumps into a table and sends several tubes of poster paint flying. One explodes and covers Melanie Sanders in bright green goo, and she starts screaming hysterically.

"Sorry," Miss Jenkins groans. "I'm needed."

What did she mean "about"? I wonder. My pictures were of Ava, so they were "about" her, surely? Except, I realize as I ponder it, they were more than that: They were "about" how she still looks beautiful, even though she's changed so much this summer. They were "about" her bravery in facing up to everything the doctors are doing to fight the lymphoma . . .

And gradually, an idea begins to form. By the end of the class I know exactly what my art project — my new art project — is "about," and how I need to research it, and how right Miss Jenkins was to spot that all those endless shaded bananas were — I admit it now — a total waste of time.

TWENTY-FIVE

When I get home, Ava's sitting at the folding table, dosing up on ice cream to take away the metallic taste that chemo always leaves in her mouth.

"Ava," I ask, "you couldn't possibly do me a favor, could you?"

She looks at me suspiciously. "No, you can't."

"What?"

"Borrow my mascara. You'll only get it all gooey and forget to put the lid on. You've got some money now, T. Get your own."

"No, it wasn't that," I say. Although I was rather hoping she might relent about the mascara. Apart from that skirt, and her camera of course, she never did fully master the art of sharing. "Actually, I was wondering if you could pose for me. You know I've got to do this thing called Still Life —"

"Oh, not the stupid fruit again!"

"Yes, that. Well, I was wondering if you could pose *with* the fruit. After all, Mum keeps buying it to make you better, and hopefully it's working, and your head is such a beautiful shape . . ."

"Really?"

"Really. I think it would look interesting next to a pile of strawberries and raspberries and papayas and —"

"It would look surreal," she says with a frown.

"Yes, it would," I agree. "Very."

"Hey!" Her frown transforms to a grin. "That's not bad, T! Coming from you. Positively artistic."

I simper modestly. "So you'll do it?"

She worries at her fingernail for a while, then nods. "But this time you have to help *me* out."

"OK," I say nervously, hoping it isn't anything needle-related. "How?"

"When I was in the hospital on Monday, the nurses said I looked different." She laughs. "Apart from being bald, I mean. Different in a good way. They thought I'd be a mess after I lost my hair, but I told them about what you did, and Vince, and the whole experience. They want me to share it with some of the other girls, because they're worried about it, too. Will you come with me? The whole point was that there were two of us."

She gives me a casual smile, as if this isn't a big deal. And I give her a casual "Sure" back, because she's not into big emotion at the moment, and I don't want her to know how I feel. But I feel stunned. It *is* a big deal. This could be the first time she's ever asked me to do anything for her because I might be good at it, and not just to help her out of a hole. In fact, this time it's me that goes off to the bathroom for a while, just to be by myself and get my head around it. If the guidance counselor were to ask me how I was feeling right now, I'd say that despite everything, I was feeling . . . elated.

After supper I borrow Dad's computer and have another look at the website where Nick Spoke and his friends discuss photography. I'm sure Nick won't remember me — after all, he had other things on his mind when we met — but I want to say thank you to him for the ideas he's given me.

Actually, I don't know why I'm trying to contact him. He will be rude and busy, and he'll probably think I'm cyberstalking him. Just because he can draw, and we have a common interest in backgrounds, it hardly explains why I'm opening myself up to potential ridicule from Mr. Abstract Impressionism. Even so, I write a comment to say how much I like one of his pictures, and how I'm using photography in my school art project. Then, before I post it, I delete the bit about the school project, because he's going to art college and it makes me sound so childish.

He must have a smartphone or something, because he e-mails me back before I've shut Dad's computer down.

Thanks for the comment. How did the test shoot go, by the way?

Oh my goodness: He does remember me. He remembers Seb's shoot and everything. Maybe it's because he had to look at those pictures of Sheherezade. I explain that I'm not cut out for modeling, and he sends another instant reply.

Good call. Did you see the links to Man Ray? Or Ansel Adams? Check them out.

I think we've just started an e-mail conversation. Though what did he mean by "good call"? He certainly seems anti-modeling, so I wonder what would impress him — short of having your own art show at a gallery, maybe. Meanwhile, knowing something about Man Ray and Ansel Adams might be a start.

I'm on my third biographical website when Dad finally tells me to shut down his computer and go to bed, because somehow the whole evening has disappeared in a moment. I'm not so sure about Ansel Adams — endless rolling deserts, and personally I like lots of trees with leaves on — but Man Ray's eccentric portraits and eerie lighting are exactly what I need to inspire my new project. In fact, if I ever got a puppy, I wouldn't mind calling it Man Ray. Then I could smirk knowledgably if anyone asked me why. Not that Nightmare Boy would need to ask, of course: He would just know.

TWENTY-SIX

Next day, I spend some time in the school library, poring over books on the Old Masters of painting and also on portrait photography, looking for more useful images for my art project. I have in my mind the detailed, glowing paintings of fruit and flowers that Dutch painters did in the seventeenth century, and also bold, modern portrait photographs. I want Ava's head to look strange and magnificent, the way it does to me.

I make a list of artists and photographers who might be helpful, but this is just the start. It will take a lot of research to find the perfect inspiration. Plus, I have to "illustrate my journey." The school board doesn't make it easy for you in these final-grade projects. Miss Jenkins is going to want postcards and printouts, sketches and plans. But it just so happens that the National Gallery, which is crammed with old masters, is right next door to the National Portrait Gallery, which is bursting with photos of famous people, so that's my Saturday morning taken care of. I'm really looking forward to it.

★

Ava wanted to come with me, but after a couple of trial days at school, by the weekend she's wiped out. We postpone the trip, but on Sunday she's no better. Besides, the day dawns drizzly and gray: a proper autumn morning, with even more of a nip in the air than before. Ava decides instead to catch up on some of the *Xena: Warrior Princess* DVDs we ordered on Amazon. She'll be on her own, because Mum is off to work soon at the store and Dad is off to meet with the TV researcher he made friends with on my "very nothing" day.

I'm not too thrilled to hear about this meeting. For a start, I don't like being reminded of that day, and also I think that however much Dad likes to hear about how TV shows are made, it's not very nice for Mum if he takes time off from writing to have coffee with attractive young women. Not that I'm telling Mum how attractive that production assistant was. But she was — very. If they'd put her in five-inch platforms alongside Sheherezade, she wouldn't have been "very nothing" at all.

On top of everything, I noticed Dad making a real effort with his appearance before he went out. He hasn't done that for ages. He tried on all his jackets and most of his ties, and even got out his old fedora and checked himself out in it in the hall mirror. He left the hat behind in the end, though.

On impulse, I grab it from the hall table as I head out. It might make me look suitably arty for my gallery tour. And it will be an awful lot more comfortable than the R-Patz, which is getting increasingly itchy on top of my new hair growth. With relief, I leave the wig behind. It sits peacefully on the hall table, the spitting image of a long-haired guinea pig, waiting for me to return.

I spend a happy hour in the National Gallery, examining various Dutch painters' takes on fruit, vegetables, flowers, plates, vases, and basically anything they could fit on a table. It's mostly what I was expecting, except that they seem to delight in imperfections. They love painting mottled surfaces on peaches, or apples with insect holes in them, or flowers with torn petals. Somehow, it makes them seem more alive. But the best bit is the shop, where I stock up on postcards to show Miss Jenkins my working process, as required.

After a quick walk around the corner of Trafalgar Square, I get to the National Portrait Gallery, where they happen to be holding a special exhibition of Richard Avedon photographs. The posters show stunning portraits of strong faces: exactly what I'm after. I can't afford the ticket for the exhibition, but I buy a couple of beautiful postcards. One of them shows a modern-day princess with daffodils in her hair — arranged in such a way that they seem suspended around her head, like the flowers on the wallpaper behind her. I love that effect.

I keep thinking about it as I head for the Underground at Charing Cross station. In fact, I'm just getting the postcard out of the paper bag to have another look when a sudden gust of wind whips Dad's fedora off my head and straight into the road in front of me. I rush forward to grab it, when a pair of strong arms reach out from nowhere and hold me back. An enormous, bright red London double-decker bus zooms past, missing me by millimeters.

Oh my God. I nearly died to save a hat.

I turn around to say thank you to the arms that just saved my life. They belong to a businessman in a pinstripe suit, who gives me a very odd stare. Maybe this is how people look at you when they know it's thanks to them you're alive at all. I stare back, dumbstruck, and after an awkward moment he strides off, just as another bus rolls by, squashing Dad's hat as flat as a pancake.

Suddenly, this day isn't turning out so well.

For five minutes, I wander down the street in a daze. I can't face going into the Underground quite yet. Or the thought of telling Dad about his fedora when I get home.

Gradually, I notice that lots of people are heading in the same direction as me — more than usual. I could even swear I recognize a couple of the faces, although I can't think where from. Still dazed, I follow the crowd. Then lots of the people turn through a big stone archway, which is manned by security guards. You need a pass to get through and I don't have one, so I stop.

I look beyond them. There's a large stone building on three sides of a courtyard, with a massive white tent in the middle. It's surrounded by colorful banners announcing London Fashion Week.

Oh wow. I wonder if any of the girls I did go-sees with will be there today, walking for designers. I hope so: It's such a big deal if you get a catwalk show. Meanwhile, I can't even take care of one lousy hat.

I lean against a pillar and remember the rush of wind when that bus passed me. I never did say thank you to that man in the suit. I wonder why he stared at me like that.

And then I notice someone else staring. A little woman, just a few feet away. She's the most extraordinary sight, but she's looking at me as if *I'm* the strange vision.

"JEANS E-BERK," she says loudly as soon as she catches my eye.

Is she talking to me? Is she trying to sell me jeggings? Is she deranged? Looking at her, it wouldn't be too surprising.

She is wearing a calf-length dress made out of leather patches held together with orange zippers, a gold silk Puffa jacket, a skull-print scarf so famous that even I now know it's by Alexander McQueen, and boots with four-inch metallic gold platform heels.

"Please tell me you're a model," she drawls in an exotic, American-type accent that I can't place.

"Er, well, I suppose I used to be," I say. I'm not sure I should be talking to escaped psychiatric patients in the middle of the street, but her eyes are holding me in a hypnotic grip.

"Thank God. Of course you are. Jeans E-Berk. Do you know her?"

"Personally?"

"Oh sweet mercy! Of course not personally. She was an actress. In the sixties. *Á Bout de Souffle. Breathless* to you. Jean Seberg!"

"Oh! Jean Seberg!"

"Ah! So you know her?"

"Not really."

She sighs, very, very deeply. "This is going to take a long time. You don't have a show, do you?"

"What, here? No. I don't even have a pass."

Her eyes widen. "Perfect!"

She puts a firm hand on my elbow and guides me into the doorway of a gatehouse to one side of the archway. It's quieter here. She seems slightly less crazy now.

"Delicate face. Killer hair. Jean's who you remind me of right now, but there are so many others. Sinéad, Aggy. Of course, Aggy . . . But you're unique. And so young. What are you? Fifteen — nearly sixteen? How long have you had your hair like that?"

She got my age right to the month, practically. Nobody does that.

"Er, about two weeks," I admit. "Except it wasn't this long before."

Oh sweet mercy indeed. I'm explaining the obvious about hair growth to some French-movie-obsessed, age-guessing weirdo. Why? Shut up, Ted. I wish Ava were here.

It's only at this point that I fully realize what the woman's looking at. I've been so busy thinking about the bus and the fedora, then being accosted by a lunatic, that I'd forgotten how I must look now that the hat's not there. My hair is still less than a centimeter long. I must seem a bit . . . freaky.

"You're incredible," the woman says. "Who are you signed with?"

"Model City," I say, "but —"

"Ah! Cassandra! How is she? We haven't spoken in a while. She must be ENCHANTED with you. What have you done?" She looks at me accusingly.

"Er . . . nothing?"

"Nothing? No shoots? No campaigns?"

Oh! *That* kind of "what have you done?" Not the kind Dad gets from Mum when the answer is "I didn't mean to, and anyway I can fix it."

"No," I answer. "I tried, but it didn't work out. Then I got my head shaved and school started, so —"

"Wait! Does Cassandra *know* about this? Did you tell her?"

I shrug.

"My GOD! I'm a GENIUS! I've got you all to myself, you DARLING! Don't tell anyone. Don't say a word. I'm going to tell them. No, I'm going to *show* them. Stand there. Not there — in the light. *There!*"

She shoves me around until she's got some daylight on my face, whips out the fanciest phone I've seen in my life, and takes a couple of headshots of me. I know by now not to try and pose. This is one of those "just stand there" moments. Plus, I don't really have any idea what's going on.

When she's done, she shoves her phone back in her bag, which is a vast, leather, studded affair, and holds out her hand.

"Tina di Gaggia. I make the next trends happen and, baby, YOU are the next trend. What are you doing right now?"

"Er, going home."

"Are they expecting you? Is it urgent?"

"Not exactly, but —"

"Have you ever seen a catwalk show?"

"No."

"Baby, this is Somerset House and I'm on my way to see the most DARLING show. The highlight of the week. Laslo Wiggins. You know him?"

Finally! Words that make sense to me. Laslo Wiggins is one of THE names to look out for at Fashion Week. He's responsible for the latest volume trend that Ava's missing out on.

I nod. "I know who he is."

"Well, he's huge. HUGE. And he's huge because I made him huge. People practically need oxygen equipment to scale him. And in a year, he'll be BEGGING you to walk for him. Trust me — I never lie. Come with me and see the show. It's right there."

She points over toward the tent.

"But I don't have an invitation."

"You do if you're with me."

I stare at her skeptically. Another thing I've learned is that catwalk shows are notoriously hard to get into, which is why the security guys are there. People guard their invitations like Golden Tickets to the chocolate factory. They don't just let in fifteen-year-old girls who happen to show up with some woman they met off the street. Even if she's wearing what I strongly suspect are next-season Charlotte Olympia platforms. Sabrina would have killed for those.

"Come on," Tina teases. "It's only half an hour. And it will BLOW YOU AWAY, I promise you."

"I wish I could, but . . ."

She ignores me. She's on her phone.

"Cassandra? Darling! I'm with one of yours." She turns to me. "What's your name, baby? It's Ted. Yes, her. She's had a makeover and I just want you to know I saw her first and I OWN this girl! Now — are you in the tent for Laslo? If I bring her in, can you meet us at the guest entrance and assure her I'm not some psycho? Love you, darling. LOVE. YOU." She turns back to me. "See? Perfectly safe. It'll be the best fun you'll have all year. Come and see the pretty dresses. Cassandra can't wait to see your new look, but remind her: I found you this time. I want first rights on EVERYTHING."

For a moment, I try to pretend I'm Ava. Ava would know scary stories about gold-jacket-dressed women who lure young girls into Somerset House and do strange and terrible things with them. But the thing is, I know Tina's telling the truth about Fashion Week. And the security guards are *right there* to keep out the riffraff and paparazzi, so if anything did happen I could grab one of them. If Cassandra isn't in the tent after all, I'll turn around and go straight home. But if she is . . . maybe I'll get to see a fashion show. I've heard so much about them recently. I wouldn't mind seeing just one.

TWENTY-SEVEN

When I get home, careful to avoid Dad, I catch Ava in the middle of a scarf-tying rehearsal in our bedroom — experimenting with the best fabrics and tying methods to keep them from slipping off at crucial moments. It's for her first style session at the hospital.

She looks pale, still recovering from a busy week, but when I tell her what happened at Somerset House she screams so loud with delight that Dad rushes in, terrified she's had a seizure. He sees me and I have to explain about the hat. Not good. That takes a little while. He nearly has a seizure himself. Then he leaves us to it so he can get back to his book.

I don't tell him about Crazy Tina, and I don't ask about his meeting with the TV researcher. Instead, Ava and I sit side by side on the edge of her bed, squished up in front of the mirror, checking out our bare heads.

"Did she really say you were unique?" Ava asks. She has a point: Without our very different hair, our similarities shine through.

"Yes. She says I have a Jean Shrimpton quality, combined with a Twiggy zing."

"Who's Jean Shrimpton?"

AHA! A model that Ava hasn't heard of and I have! All that research over the summer has totally paid off.

"She was a model in the sixties," I say airily. "She modeled for Bailey."

"Bailey?"

AHA AGAIN!

Ava sees the grin on my face and rolls her eyes. "OK, OK. I get the picture. So? What did Cassandra Spoke say when she saw you? And what are you going to do?"

I shrug happily. "No idea. Cassandra liked the look. She could hardly say she didn't, the way Tina went on about it. I know I said I'd never touch modeling again, but there was something about Tina . . ."

When she spotted me, it was as if she could see Xena standing there. I even told her about my warrior princess thing while we were watching the catwalk show, and she nodded, like that was perfectly normal. She got it, instantly. It was as if nothing could shock her.

"There was something so exciting about her," I say to Ava, passing her a new scarf to try. "She totally *carpes* the *diem*. And she knows *everyone*. She waved to Anna Wintour in the front row and Anna *smiled back*. I can't wait to tell Mum."

"Yeah." Ava grins. "She'll be knocked out."

Which only shows how little we know our own mother.

When she gets in from work, looking as tired and stressed as normal, I try to cheer her up by giving her the full story. From the look on Mum's face, though, I might as well be telling her I just got arrested. She doesn't scream delightedly. Instead, she drags Dad and me to the dining table for a family conference.

"So let me get this straight," she sighs. "Some stranger accosted you on the street?"

"Yes."

"And told you she *liked your hair*?"

"Pretty much."

"Because it reminded her of a French actress?"

"American actress," Ava corrects her, wandering over to join us. "Jean Seberg — you know. She acted in some French films, though. And she had totally iconic hair."

Mum doesn't look convinced. "And you followed this woman to a fashion show that just happened to be on right around the corner?"

"Well, yes, at Somerset House —"

"And now she's telling you she's going to make you a supermodel."

"Not exactly," I correct her. "She just pointed out that she's helped the careers of the last six girls to appear on the cover of *Vogue*. And of course I wouldn't believe her just like that, but Cassandra Spoke agreed. She says Tina's really famous in the fashion world. She gave Karl Lagerfeld ideas for the last Chanel collection."

Mum's stress peaks at a new level. "But I thought you'd given all that up!"

"Me, too."

"The last time we discussed this you were in tears, darling, because you said everyone was better than you."

"I did," I agree in a very small voice. "But you said I was fabulous, Mum. And Tina agrees. She's just . . . on a different level from everyone else. If she wants something to happen, she can make it happen. And she says she might never have spotted me if I had a full head of hair. It's this" — I touch my head — "that makes the difference. I'm better prepared now, Mum. It won't all be so new and confusing."

"And heartbreaking," Mum adds.

I move on quickly. I'd rather not remember the heartbreaking bits. "Before, they just sent me along for any old job. Tina says she'll only send me for things she knows I can get, and she'll tell them I'm coming."

Mum sighs. "What do you think, Stephen?"

But Dad doesn't answer. He's looking at Ava in a way that instantly reminds me of the day he first noticed the lump on her neck.

"Are you all right, love?" he asks.

Ava nods. Her face is gray and there are dark blue shadows under her eyes. Her eyelids flicker for a moment. And then she sinks sideways out of her chair and onto the floor.

Mum leaps up and rushes over to check her.

"It'll be her red-cell count," she says, sounding panicked. "The nurses said they were worried."

Dad carries Ava gently to bed while Mum grabs the phone to call the hospital. They put her on hold while they try to find a nurse from Ava's team to talk to her.

"Ted, I haven't got time for this," she says to me irritably, phone in hand. "Your father seems to think you're old enough to make up your own mind about what you do. He said something about lettuce recently that I didn't catch, and frankly I wonder about him sometimes. You're *not* old enough to make up your own mind, but I'm too tired to argue, so here's the deal: You can try doing what this woman suggests for a while, as long as it doesn't affect your schoolwork in any way. If you get a job, Dad or I will come with you to make sure you get treated properly. Hopefully you'll get at least one happy experience out of these shenanigans. Hello?"

A nurse speaks to her briefly down the line, then asks her to hold again. She sighs and forces herself to stay calm, but her shoulders are shaking and any minute now she's going to need another tissue. I'd love to go up and hug her to say thank you, but I'm worried that if I touch her, she might crack. Somehow, my mother has a way of giving me what I want and making me feel extremely bad about it.

"And if you do get any money," she continues in the same irritable tone while she holds some more, "you can use the first payment to buy your father a new fedora. In the meantime, will you please go and put a bandana on, or something, if you refuse to wear that expensive hairpiece round the house? You look disconcertingly like Uncle Bill when he joined the Royal Marines, and it's giving me a headache."

By the time Mum gets to talk to the head nurse overseeing Ava's care, Ava has come to and she's feeling weak, but OK. The hospital says to bring her in in the morning, when they'll check red-cell count. They seem to think she's better off in her own bed tonight, although I wonder. She's hot and uncomfortable, finding it hard to sleep. As do I.

At midnight, she wakes up from a fitful doze and puts the light on.

"What's the matter?" she asks.

I don't know how she can tell there's a problem. I'm lying flat in bed, with my eyes closed, but I suppose when you share a room with someone for a year, you get to know them pretty well.

"Mum."

Ava sighs. "She's got a lot on her mind. Don't take it personally."

I lie there not saying anything. Even so, Ava senses what I'm thinking.

"She's doing too much. She's trying to hold the job down, and come to the hospital with me, and . . . all the other stuff. That's why she gets so ratty. She doesn't mean it."

"I know," I sigh back.

I open my eyes and turn to Ava. She looks dreadful: pale and sweaty. Even her lips are gray. No wonder the nurses were worried.

"Maybe I shouldn't push it," I suggest. "Mum obviously doesn't want me to."

"What did she actually say?"

"She said yes, I could do some jobs. She said she wants me to get some 'happiness out of these shenanigans.'"

With difficulty, Ava leans up on one elbow and smiles at me. "Then that's what you should do. Tina di Gaggia sounds fantastic. Listen — why don't you give it until Christmas? See if she can really help you. I'll have my results by then. We can compare notes . . ."

Oh, right. I can find out if I'm a supermodel yet, and Ava can find out if she's still alive. Brilliant. In fact, the more I think about it, the crazier it seems.

"Ted? You're not crying?" she asks.

"No," I admit. "I'm giggling. I was just thinking about us comparing notes."

Ava thinks about it for a minute and giggles, too, coughing with the effort. In fact, we both keep setting each other off even after she turns the light back off and the rest of the flat goes silent. Cancer gives you a really weird sense of humor. Either that, or there's something wrong with both of us.

TWENTY-EIGHT

As if I needed further proof after our first meeting, Tina di Gaggia is like nobody else I've ever met. On Monday — less than twenty-four hours after meeting me — she leaves me a voice mail while I'm at school. I love her unusual accent: sort of Italian, sort of American, with maybe a hint of Spanish. I wish I knew where she was from. Rio, maybe? Or Rome? I feel as if I ought to know, so I don't dare ask. It's like not knowing about Mario Testino.

"OK," the message says, "so here's the deal, Teddy-girl. We HAVE to meet tomorrow, Tuesday. I've been talking about you, my hotness, and there is NEWS. I'm back to NYC Wednesday, so it's now or never, and it has to be now. I'm sending a car to pick you up at six, so dress nice, do your face, and we'll do some test shots at my hotel. Frankie and Cassandra will be there, so we'll have a ball. LOVE. YOU."

Can she possibly be serious? I call Frankie to see if she has a clue what's going on, and it turns out that everything's arranged. Tina has a suite at Claridge's, and we're going to meet there. She's told various people about me and they're keen to see pictures, but of course there aren't any decent ones of me with my new Jean Seberg hairdo.

"When she said 'dress nice,' what did she mean?"

"Oh, you know, cool and funky," Frankie says, as if those aren't two of the most unnerving words in the world.

"And 'do your face'?"

"Light makeup. Nothing OTT. Focus on the eyes. Oh, and you might want to get your brows threaded."

She's right. My caterpillar is impressively luxuriant at the moment, after a few weeks of being left alone. But I have SCHOOL tomorrow and we don't have a team of stylists on tap at Richmond Academy.

"And what's she going to do, exactly?"

"Oh, just take a few shots to show some people in New York. Let Cassandra see what she has in mind. See how things go."

"Please tell me this isn't normal."

Frankie laughs. "No, Ted. This isn't normal. Nothing to do with Tina G ever is. It's why people love working with her. They say the G is for gold, by the way, because everything she touches . . . you know."

It reminds me of King Midas. He turned his own daughter into gold and she died. It wasn't a happy ending.

"Er, I'll be all right, won't I?" I ask.

Frankie pauses for a second, but her voice is firm and bright when she answers. "Yes, angel. This is as lucky as it gets. Don't worry about a thing."

When I get home, Mum's in the hall, pulling on her coat over her green uniform.

"How's Ava?" I ask.

"They're keeping her in overnight," she says, with a tight smile and a frightened look in her eyes. "I'm just going to visit."

I feel my heart plummet.

"What's happening?"

Mum looks at her watch. "I'm not exactly sure. I think she's having the transfusion now."

"Blood transfusion?"

"Yes."

I picture wires and blood and needles, and Ava hooked up to . . . I don't know what. Ava all by herself. I feel sick. I need to see her.

"Can I come with you?"

"No need, darling," Mum says briskly. "Dad'll be home soon."

"But I want to. Please?"

She scans my face, which mirrors the fear in hers. I don't want to be here by myself, waiting for Dad, not knowing what's going on. She gives in.

"OK," she sighs. "But go and grab a banana first. I don't want you fainting on me, too."

On the way to Ava's ward, I try to ignore all the signs saying ONCOLOGY, and the fact that so many patients look thin and pale. I try to forget the image of Ava this morning, when her sleeping head on the pillow seemed so fragile that I suddenly had to lean down and make sure she was still breathing.

But I'm glad I came. When we get to Ava's ward, we find her lying peacefully in a bed by a window, with a tube of dark red blood disappearing under her pajamas, where the line goes into her chest. The blood comes from a bag hooked up to a stand behind her. It's not as bad as I imagined at all. She still looks tired, but her skin has lost its gray tinge and she opens her eyes and smiles to see us.

"You missed the best bit, T," she says quietly, with a wicked glint in her eye. "There was this enormous needle. They took my Hickman line and they —"

"Ugh! Shut up! You're teasing."

She grins.

"How's it going, darling?" Mum asks, fussing around her and plumping her pillows. "What did the doctor say?"

"No idea," Ava says, leaning back on the pillows.

Mum goes off in an anxious huff to check with the nurses.

I stand beside Ava's bed, trying to look at home here, like I don't know that all the teenagers in this ward have cancer. Like I do scary stuff like this all the time, and it's not scary at all. The glint in Ava's eye changes to something kinder.

"Why don't you pass me my phone?" she says to me. "It's been going off for ages and I can't reach it."

I dig it out of her bag, which is in the cabinet beside her, and help her check her messages, because she's not up to fiddling with phone buttons right now.

"Ooh! Jesse!" she says. "Good. Open that one."

The message turns out to be a video. I play it for her and hold the screen so we can both see it. There's her boyfriend, looking beyond gorgeous in bleached hair and red trunks, standing on deck under a cloudless blue sky, smiling at the camera and singing a silly but sweet "get well soon" song about the transfusion. It would be cute, if he didn't happen to be standing in the middle of four Red-Bikini Babes, all with their arms around each other, all singing along. How he ever thought this would cheer Ava up, I can't imagine.

"I'm sure they're just friends," I say unconvincingly.

"Yeah. Whatever."

"Which is Barbie Girl?"

"That one."

"I see what you mean."

She sighs and shoves the phone under a pillow. "So, how about you, T? Any news from Tina? I've been telling everyone you're a model."

"Hardly!"

"*So?*" she insists.

"Well, as a matter of fact, Tina did call. She wants me to go to Claridge's tomorrow evening so she can take pictures and show them to New York."

It feels absurd to be saying this here, under these circum- stances. But she asked.

"Ha! Told you!" Ava grins. Suddenly, she looks much better, but I feel sick again.

"I can't do it," I explain. "Frankie says I need to look cool and funky. And get rid of this . . ." I point to the caterpillar. "And I've got nothing to wear. And whenever I try and do smoky eyes I look like a startled panda. And I —"

"But you want to?" Ava interrupts.

"Yes. I *want* to. But I —"

"I'll be out tomorrow morning. And I'll be full of shiny red blood cells. I'll be your makeup girl and stylist when you get back from school, OK?"

"Really?"

"Of course. But," she adds sternly, "you'll have to do your own eyebrow. If we wait till tomorrow, the patch will still be pink."

"What? With *tweezers*? *By myself*?"

I realize I've raised my voice a bit at this point. I glance around the ward and notice a few faces staring back at me sympathetically.

Ava gives me a mocking smile. "They see your head and assume we're talking about your next chemo regime — not just *plucking a few hairs out*, T. Jeez."

"OK, I'll pluck them," I promise. By now I'm totally puce. Ava's really enjoying herself. "But you mean it? You'll help me?"

She leans forward with that glint in her eye. "Try and stop me. I've seen you getting ready for parties. You need me *so bad*."

TWENTY-NINE

"Just plucking a few hairs out . . . Just plucking a few hairs out . . ." That's what I keep saying to myself as I carefully attack the unibrow in the bathroom mirror that evening. It's not chemo. It's not a blood transfusion. It's not even that painful after the first twenty hairs or so. I can do this! I so want Ava to be proud of me when she gets back.

Mum hears all the initial squeaks and squeals and comes in to see what I'm doing. I'm not used to being able to tell her honestly what I'm up to when it comes to modeling, so it feels weird to explain that it's for meeting Tina. To my surprise, she smiles and offers to help. Ava's right: She doesn't mean to be mean. And wow — she's a genius at eyebrow tweezing. I wish I'd known this before.

"I just didn't offer because I didn't think you needed it, darling," she says, deftly removing yet another offender and putting her warm finger on my skin to dull the ouch.

Ah, Mum and my "inner beauty" again. That's sweet. But it's good to have her focusing on my outer beauty, too.

Ava said she'd be feeling much better the next day, and she was right: Blood transfusions rock. By the time I get home from school, she's a different person — pink-cheeked, energetic, and full of wardrobe suggestions, which are laid out on her bed for me to choose from.

She's good at this stuff, and her new energy's infectious. Ninety minutes later, I'm ready. I'm wearing Mum's best silk summer dress from years ago, made "cross-seasonal" (it's a word; you get used to it) by the addition of a velvet jacket from Boden and one of the Indian scarves Mum lent Ava. My shoes are my school ballet flats, because they're all I've got that fit right now. My eyes are smudgy and smoky, and they're my favorite part. Eyes are Ava's strong point, and she has a bag full of M·A·C eye shadows to prove it. We didn't do much else with my makeup, partly because we weren't sure what to do, and partly because once we'd added some lip gloss, it sort of looked OK.

"There!" she says, admiring her handiwork. "I am totally a fairy godmother. Can't wait to hear how it goes. Don't let Tina bully you."

"Bully me?"

"She sounds very persuasive. Just make sure you don't let her talk you into anything you don't want to do."

"Don't worry, she won't. Warrior princess, remember?"

She smiles. "Xena all the way."

I wish Ava was coming with me, but Dad is my chaperone for the evening. He's waiting for me in the living room, dressed in his best job-interview suit, polished shoes, and his smartest tie. He also smells quite strongly of Dior Pour Homme. Claridge's *must* be posh. He and Mum look at me appraisingly. Then they look at each other and shake their heads slightly.

"Bad?" I ask.

Dad smiles. "No. Good, I think. Just different. Not what we're used to. You look so *old*, love."

The doorbell rings.

Mum tuts at Dad. "He means grown-up. That must be the driver. Off you go."

I walk out of the flat on the arm of my rather dashing, if frizzy-haired, father, and feeling most definitely old. I'm off to Claridge's. To talk to a bunch of über-fashion people about über-fashion stuff. What could be more grown-up than that? Right now, all I need is heels. I used to worry that they'd make me taller than any boys I might like, but I'm starting to think that's not such a bad thing. Xena could handle them. She doesn't mind people looking up to her.

"Champagne?"

"Er, Ted doesn't drink yet," Dad says.

"Oh God, ignore me," Tina says, pouring herself a second glass. "Of course she doesn't. Which is WHY . . . this virgin berry cocktail will KILL YOU. It will literally KILL YOU. You'll love it. Try."

Tina's suite at Claridge's looks like the kind of place I imagine the Queen hanging out, except more expensive and gold-embellished — so maybe Madonna, or Victoria Beckham, or possibly even Beyoncé and Jay-Z. The bar is mirrored and vintage, and groaning with champagne bottles and amazing-looking things in jugs. Tina is pouring one of them into a glass for me. It's so intensely red it could easily be pure poison, like something out of a Disney cartoon, but I assume that when she says something will "literally kill you," she means "*not* literally kill you, but taste great."

I try it. It's fruity and gorgeous. I could drink the whole jug. Dad catches my eye and grins. I bet his champagne is delicious, too. And he's clearly delighted by Tina. I'm pretty sure he's already working on his Tina impersonations, to use later to amuse Mum and Ava. Luckily, his "I can't believe you are a real person" expression is very similar to his "oh, how delightful to meet you" look, and only his immediate family can tell the difference. I'm glad he's here, or I'd be certain I was dreaming.

Frankie is sitting on one of the gold-tasseled sofas in the living area. Cassandra Spoke is by a window, looking as elegant and perfectly groomed as ever, but frowning and trying to get a signal on her BlackBerry. Tina's moved on to arranging little plates of blinis with what must be caviar spooned on top, changing the background music from classical to hip hop, and holding an on-off conversation with Frankie about her outfit.

"OH. MY. GOD. Don't ask me who this is. Don't even ask me. He has a tiny studio in Bed-Stuy and everyone is going to be BEGGING for his leggings two years from now. He's a Lycra GENIUS. Don't even go there. His name is Andy Wong. You heard it from me. He is the ONLY leggings guy. Now thank me, because that's your leggings issues solved for the rest of your LIFE."

"Andy Wong?" Frankie checks, whipping out her iPhone and typing into it. "Fascinating. I didn't know Lycra could even do that crocodile effect. And the gilet?"

"The gilet? This is nothing. It's just a little thing Frida did for me at Gucci. It's based on a fur vest my mother had. I so love vintage, don't you? But when it's falling to pieces, you have to reimagine it. Which is why Frida did it for me in chain mail. Fur is so obvious, no? Now, Teddy-girl, my DARLING. We're here to talk about YOU. Are you ready to be a STAR?"

I perch on the edge of my sofa, trying hard not to put my berry cocktail anywhere I'm likely to knock it over by mistake. Everything in this suite looks like it was made out of silk and is completely undrycleanable.

"Er, no, I don't think so," I say, being perfectly honest. I'm not sure I'm even ready for crocodile leggings.

"Isn't she ADORABLE? I've got so many people stateside SLAVERING over you. But, let's see. It's all very well having the face, the hair, the incredible ME behind you, but you've got to *project*. Before I get too excited, I've got to see what the camera sees."

Dad catches my eye. Before she gets too excited? If this is her simply warming up for more excitement . . . I think he's worried she might go off like a firework, and it's doubtful the leggings would cope.

She cocks her head to look at me and purses her lips — a bit like she did when I didn't instantly get her Jean Seberg reference. But the expression only lasts for a moment. Before I know it, she's holding my face in her hands and giving me a flash of a smile.

"Face, fabulous; outfit, disaster. Come with me, darling. We need to get you out of the mall and into something more glamtastic."

We go into the bedroom part of the suite with Dad hopping about anxiously in our wake.

"Sure you're OK, love?" he calls.

"Fine, Dad. Don't worry," I giggle.

Tina looks thoughtfully at a vast pile of clothes spilling out of a huge Louis Vuitton suitcase in the corner. Then she pounces on something near the bottom.

"This, I think. Take off your jacket."

I do. Without another word, she unzips my dress, pulls the top part down so it's around my waist, unhooks my bra, and wraps an enormous blue silk scarf around my chest, tying it in a big knot on my right shoulder. The whole thing happens so fast I hardly have time to be shocked. Besides, I discovered on the TV job that you often have to get changed so fast that you can't afford to be prim and proper about it. At least it's over quickly and nobody's watching, thank goodness.

"Now listen, princess," she says as she works, "I've seen your test shots, and I see the problem. What were you thinking about when you were working?"

I think back to the shoot with Seb. What *was* I thinking about? My fingers? My feet? The general craziness of the whole situation? The wall?

"Well, in the best ones, I guess I was thinking about the background."

"Oh, save me!" Tina says, rolling her eyes dramatically. "You were thinking about the *background*? No wonder you look so . . . nothing."

Oh my God. Can she read Sandy McShand's mind as well?

"Listen, baby," she goes on, "camera lenses are incredible pieces of equipment. They pick up the most important thing in the picture, and you want it to be your eyes. You want it to be what's *inside* your eyes. You want it to be the story you're telling. Not the wall behind you, OK?"

Yes, I nod. OK. I understand her completely. I think.

"Er, what story?" I ask.

"That's up to the photographer," she says. "Who, this evening, is me. So don't worry, I'll tell you when we get there. Start with your eyes and your body will follow. Ready?"

If she says I am, then I am. With the scarf wrapped around me, my top half looks superglam. Tina tells me not to worry about my bottom half: It won't be in the picture, so she doesn't mind that the neck of my dress is draping around my hips and the sleeves are hanging down like a couple of spare legs.

I follow her back into the sitting room, where Dad raises an eyebrow at my strange outfit, but says nothing. I don't think anything Tina did would surprise him now. She's already picked a spot in the corner of the room with a simple gold background and arranged the lights so that they'll flatter my face. I can feel her shift into a new gear: sharp and focused. I realize that she may look totally crazy, but she's been working hard to get this right, and she knows what she's doing. She's just a whole lot more fun about doing it than anyone I've met so far.

Instead of her phone, she picks up a professional-looking camera from a side table and nimbly adjusts the settings. Frankie leans forward on her sofa. So does Dad. Cassandra puts her BlackBerry away and comes over to watch.

"Sorry about that," Cassandra says. "My son. Locked himself out, the idiot. He's coming over to collect my key. Oh, Ted, that's looking good!"

Right. So that would be Nightmare Boy. Coming over any minute. Meanwhile I'm half-dressed and posing for a crazy fashion force of nature. At least he's used to this sort of thing. Maybe I can say something clever about Surrealism when he comes. Meanwhile, I push the thought to the back of my mind and try to focus on what I'm doing.

"Looking gorgeous, my princess!"

Tina comes up to me and takes my chin in her hands, adjusting my face till it's exactly where she wants it. She talks more quietly now, and there's a different intensity to her. Before she was showing off. Now she's working. So am I. Actually, this feels good, too.

"OK, Teddy-bear. We understand each other. I want that warrior princess you told me about when we were watching the burnt-orange mini-crini come down the catwalk. That's the story. I want to *see* that girl, and I want her to be brave and hot. I know you can do it, because when I saw you at Somerset House I knew you'd just had a BAD experience, and you were super-scared, but glad to be alive. Your eyes *talk*, Ted. That's why you're so exciting. Talk to me."

Oh, wow — this woman *is* telepathic. Ava and I watched *Silence of the Lambs* recently, and Tina's the Hannibal Lecter of style gurus. Totally scary, but absolutely right. Maybe we do understand each other.

"Let's go," she says. She moves backward to her chosen spot and adjusts the lens.

I think about sitting next to Ava in Locks, Stock, and Barrel. I picture all the *Xena: Warrior Princess* episodes Ava and I have watched together since we shaved our heads. I imagine I'm in beaten gold armor and we're striding through the Elysian fields together. I try to project what I'm seeing through my gaze. It's a strange feeling, but one of the few benefits of not being able to lie properly: I know people can see what I'm thinking. I'm sure Tina can see the Elysian fields in my eyes.

"Yes, princess! Go, baby!"

I may not have gold armor on, but I have the scarf. I try to move my shoulders so the silk knot catches the light. Even my fingers feel natural today. Out of the corner of my eye, I spot Dad, Frankie, and Cassandra all watching. But it's OK. They're watching Xena, and Xena is cool, confident, and in control.

"Here, princess. Right at me," Tina says, clicking away.

I stare into the lens. I stare right down it and through it. It's not so frightening anymore. In Tina's hands, I'm pretty sure it understands me, too.

After the photographs, she gets me to do a quick video. I just have to say my name, and where I'm from, and mention Model City. Then I have to turn from left to right, to show off my profile. It feels a bit silly, so Tina suggests I do a practice version. When it's done, she grins.

"Perfect! You were so natural, princess. We got it on the first take. That's what we'll use."

Only Tina can get me to relax this way. There's no doubt: We *do* have an understanding. After a whole summer of being "very nothing," I'm starting to wonder if maybe I've got . . . something.

"That's it," she says. "You guys chat while I boot up the Mac in the bedroom and check the film."

"Is it over?" I ask. My other test shoots lasted hours.

"Could be," Frankie says with a grin. "Tina knows what she wants, and she gets it. Oh, excuse me."

She gets up to answer a knock at the door.

"Nick, hi! Come in."

She moves aside and he steps into the room. I recognize the old, faded pink T-shirt, worn under a scruffy blazer. My heart stops beating for a moment, then makes up for it by pumping like the rhythm section of a big brass band. He's glowering from behind new glasses — with cool round frames — and his fingers are stained with ink. Please let him notice that I'm wearing sky-blue silk that matches my eyes, and not that I'm half-dressed. Please let him ask me something about Man Ray, so that I can answer intelligently and show I've done my homework. Please let him at least look in my direction.

But he doesn't. He avoids checking out my side of the room entirely and heads straight for the sofa where Cassandra's sitting next to Dad.

"Look, Mum, I haven't got long. The guys are waiting downstairs."

He hasn't even seen me. This is pretty crushing. I sink into the nearest chair and pretend I wasn't expecting to say hello.

Cassandra sighs. "Wait a minute. The keys are in my bag somewhere."

Her bag is enormous — suitcase-sized handbags are in this season. While she roots around at the bottom, Tina emerges from the bedroom, beaming.

"DARLINGS, I am QUITE FABULOUS. Oh. Hello, Nick."

Even Tina seems a bit subdued by Nightmare Boy. I wouldn't have thought it possible. But from the way he glares at her, I'm guessing they have a history. She flicks her eyes away from him and gathers herself.

"It's there. It's all there. She's got the LOOK. That's all I'm saying."

Cassandra abandons her handbag search and looks up.

"Really? Can I see?"

"Of course."

The two of them go back into the bedroom to check the pictures on the computer. Frankie flashes me a grin and goes to join them. I sit like a lemon in my chair, wondering what to do. Dad, who is utterly oblivious to awkward moments, stands up and introduces himself to Nick.

"Hi. I'm Stephen Trout. Ted's dad. Pleased to meet you. Sorry to keep your mother busy on an evening like this."

Nick shakes Dad's hand at least. He shrugs.

"Don't worry. It's normal. Mum's a slave to her job." He gives a sarcastic laugh and glares in the direction of the bedroom. "But, you know, modeling comes first. That's what we always say. I mean, it's life or death, right?"

Dad coughs. He's finally picked up on the atmosphere. Dad doesn't like atmospheres. We're all embarrassed and silent for a moment.

Then Nick shakes his head.

"Hang on. Did you say Trout? Ted Trout?"

Dad smiles awkwardly and corrects himself.

"Ted Richmond. Sorry. Always forget that."

Nick waves his hand as if he's not remotely interested in my new surname. Then he finally looks in my direction, raises his eyebrows, and takes me in from head to toe: the hardly-there hair, the makeup, the makeshift top, the unzipped dress. I am not at all what he saw last time, in Seb's kitchenette, in Mum's baggy yoga pants.

"Oh, it's you," he says, surprised, staring at me for the longest time. But not only does he not look impressed, he looks thoroughly disappointed. "So they got you in the end, did they? When Mum talked about this new girl, I didn't realize it was you."

I try and force a smile. I really, really want to take off this stupid scarf and zip up my dress. I wish I could have been wearing jeans and Dad's fedora and doing something artistic. I want to tell him it isn't real — it's only an experiment and I'm just a normal teenager. But I'm in the middle of a photo shoot in a suite at Claridge's. It kind of *is* real.

"So, you're Ted *Trout*?" Nick goes on. "Ava's sister? I thought I recognized her when I saw you both that day, but I couldn't place her. I should have, though. The number of photos Jesse's shown me . . ."

"Wait," I say, getting up and holding my dress around my waist like some sort of loincloth. "You know Jesse?"

"Yeah, he's an old mate. I met him in Cornwall years ago. He's a good man, Jesse. Anyway, how's your sister? I haven't heard since he hit the Mediterranean."

Now that he's talking about Jesse and Ava, Nick's face is totally different. His scowl has softened. Behind his glasses, I get a glimmer of what he's like when he's not being angry with his mum, and her career, and everything to do with it. He looks tender and vulnerable. The kind of boy you just want to curl up with and have conversations about Man Ray. Or anything, really.

"So Jesse told you about Ava?" I ask.

Nick smiles a slow, funny smile. "All the time. We Skype. He's usually very, very boring on the subject. Her talent for surfing, her jokes, some funny, cute thing she does with her fingernail . . . God, it's endless."

Dad smiles back, and so do I. Frankie, Tina, and Cassandra return from the bedroom, chatting. They stop dead when they see Nick's new expression, and the fact that he's addressing me like a civilized human being.

"Anyway, he told me what she's going through," he says, turning serious again and ignoring them completely. "Is she still . . . on track?"

I nod, and gulp. Normally, I've got my "She's fine" line all ready when people ask about Ava, but he's taken me by surprise.

"She's finding the chemo pretty tough. She was great today, though. She helped me do my eyeliner. Sorry . . ."

The eyeliner has just started to smudge. Suddenly thinking about Ava has confused me. Nick's concerned expression makes it worse.

"Give her my . . . whatever. Fond regards," he says quietly. "And . . ."

"Yes?"

He's looking at me now as if he's about to wish me luck, or say something nice. But then his eyes drift down past my makeshift scarf, my bare midriff, and my loincloth dress, and he just looks sad.

"Nothing. Good-bye."

He sees Tina hovering behind me and gives her the full force of his nightmare glare. Cassandra hands him the house keys, and he's gone.

"Well!" she says, staring after him. "You wouldn't know it, but he's not as bad as he seems."

"He didn't seem bad," I say.

Despite everything, I'd like to meet him one day when I am not half naked, in my mother's bougie dress, or being made to "walk." I think he'd understand about Ava: the good bits and the bad bits. I think he'd understand most stuff, actually, like I get how soft he is, under that nightmare coating. Next time, if there is a next time, I promise myself I will be so . . . amazing that he'll take proper notice of me. Maybe he'll see Xena, like Tina did. Maybe he'll be impressed. You never know.

"Come and get dressed," Tina offers. "I'll help you."

When we're alone, she gives me a wry smile.

"You're wondering how he got that way, aren't you, princess? And why he blames me?"

I don't try to deny it. The woman is a mind reader, and we both know it.

"Is it to do with Sheherezade Scott?" I ask.

"Aha!" she says, handing me my bra and carefully untying the scarf, "Got it, princess. So, you know Sheherezade? She is Gor. Geous. Like you, but a different energy. They dated for a few weeks. Total love-fest. Then I sent her to Tokyo and — LIKE I'D SAID SHE WOULD — she became a big star. She did a couple of campaigns out there and one of them was with Emilio Romano. The Calvin Klein boy. No doubt you've seen him in his briefs. Oh. My. God. Anyway, she and Emilio had a little thing going on. It happens. Two beautiful people, alone in a big city — hello? Nick thinks it's my fault because I made her big in Japan, and, princess, he's TOTALLY RIGHT. But we don't have time for him now. We only have time for YOU. Cassandra agrees with me. You. Have. It. We have to manage this carefully, because it's going to go INSANE."

THIRTY

Appropriately enough, it's in choir on Monday that Dean Daniels first spots something unusual about me. Mr. Anderson has shifted us around this term and now Dean's in the row behind me. I'm not sure if it's because I'm still slightly in shock from my evening at Claridge's, or because I forgot to use wig tape this morning and the R-Patz is wonky, but Dean gives me a lingering stare when I walk up to my place.

Daisy nudges me. "I think he may be onto you," she whispers.

This term, Mr. Anderson has got us practicing Handel's *Messiah* full-on, and it's really complicated. I'm in the middle of a loud, tricky high note when I first feel something poking the back of my head. I look around sharply. Dean's standing there, acting innocent, clutching a pen. When I turn back, I can feel the pen gently nudging the R-Patz sideways and I can hear the slow bass note of Dean's gathering laughter rumbling under the music. After a good shove, the wig slips a good inch sideways, lolling at an angle over my right ear.

Before I can grab it, it topples onto my shoulder, and from there onto the bench behind me. The music stops. Mr. Anderson is staring. So is half the choir. There is a general sharp intake of breath and a few nervous giggles. Everyone is wondering what will happen first: Dean cracking a joke, or me crying.

The thing is, this may be a shock to Mr. Anderson, but it's more of a relief to me. I look at the R-Patz, curled up on the bench, and catch Daisy's eye.

"Anyone seen my guinea pig?"

There is a long pause while everyone tries to take in what's happening. Was it really me who made the joke this time, not the class comedian? Even I'm not sure for a moment, until I hear Daisy's laughter. Everybody else is too shocked by the sight of my scalp to say anything.

"Are you OK?" Dean asks, looking pale.

I smile at him. "Fine, thanks. Absolutely fine."

He looks relieved. Perhaps he wondered for a moment if I'd "caught" cancer from my sister, but he seems glad I'm OK, and now he's the one who's embarrassed. I'm not, though. Not at all. Not now that my warrior princess self is out in the open, for all to see. The others may be shocked for a while, but they'll get used to it.

Meanwhile, Dean bends down to pick up the wig and hands it to me like a gentleman. I keep smiling, because I'm grateful to him for helping me make up my mind about my hair, even if my mother really isn't going to appreciate my decision.

Finally, Mr. Anderson regains his speech.

"I see! Goodness. Edwina. Are you . . . ? That looks rather . . . Right. OK, everybody. Why don't we . . . ?" But nobody's listening, and even he can't stop staring. "Actually, are you all right, Edwina? I mean, that looks a bit . . ."

"I'm honestly fine," I tell him, stroking the smooth whorls of my real hair, which is glad not to be stuck under the sweaty wig. "It's just something I did with my sister."

"Oh, I see." He takes a deep breath, then seems to calm down a bit and smiles. "Well, that was a noble gesture. Would you like someone to help you put your . . . hair back on?"

I grin at him. "No thanks, Mr. Anderson. I'll keep it for special occasions. I don't think I really need it anymore."

Mum isn't happy, as I expected, but there's another advantage to keeping my new look on a permanent basis, apart from the slight rebel edge it gives me. When I go in with Ava to the day ward at the pediatric oncology unit over the weekend, I feel like one of the gang. We meet up with boys and girls who are worried about losing their hair, and some who've already lost it. With Ava's help, they're creating new looks for themselves: learning makeup techniques, designing scarves and hats, and sharing tips about what stays on your head most easily, looks cool, and keeps the heat and cold out.

I love it how Ava's staying in control of her life and helping other people, even during the tough times. I'm so proud of her, but of course I can't say so. I just go along. Here, I don't stand out at all. I'm just the girl with the camera, ready to take pictures of kids in various types of headgear and makeup, so they can see if it works.

I'm learning so much about faces. We all agree that, collectively, we look like half a dozen eggs in a basket. But individually, we look very different. Ava has a knack for bringing out the most in someone's eyes or smile, or finding a hat that gives them the cool vintage vibe they were after. I'm getting good at capturing it on camera, so they can appreciate the full effect.

When we're not at the hospital, Ava helps me with my new art project at home, as promised. I'm a bit behind, so there's lots of work to do. Three weeks later, I'm in the middle of taking some experimental pictures of her when Tina calls.

"Ted, BABY! You thought I'd forgotten you!"

"No! Not at all."

In fact, to be honest, in all the bustle of school and the hospital, I'd almost forgotten her. Or at least I assumed she might not get back to me until Christmas. The summer taught me that things don't necessarily happen overnight.

"You did, and you were WRONG, princess, WRONG. I've been working my gorgeous, tiny BUTT off for you, and it's all coming together. Listen. Are you listening?"

I apologize to Ava, who's currently nestling her head between an enormous pile of grapes and a pineapple, and mouth "Tina" at her. She grins at me and extracts herself from the fruit while I take the call.

"OK," Tina says in a businesslike tone. "Don't thank me yet, but there's an ad campaign for a fragrance that will LAUNCH YOU SKYWARD, baby girl. If you do it, you'll OWN New York. Not just New York, anywhere with any sense of fashion. It's so hush-hush I can't even tell you who it's for, but it's incredible, and you'll LOVE the brand. When I tell you who it is, you'll literally DIE."

"Wow," I say, ignoring the "literally."

"The casting director already has another girl in mind, but don't worry about that. She's wrong and you're better. The campaign's being shot by Rudolf Reissen and he's my FAVORITE photographer right now. He's breaking through and he's so hot you'll SIZZLE. He already wants to see you, but I want more than that. I want him to WANT you."

"Fine. Er, how will he do that?"

"His chief assistant will tell him. His name's Eric Bloch and he's in London next week, casting for a magazine job. Eric's a photographer in his own right. He'll see you, he'll use you, he'll love you. Then he'll tell his boss about you, Rudolf will go CRAZY for you, and persuade the casting director for this campaign to change his mind. That's how it works. Voilà!"

I laugh. "That sounds complicated."

"My darling, it's IMPOSSIBLE. It requires MAGIC," Tina agrees sternly. "Only I can do this. But watch me. I see the future. You just have to be fabulous, OK, princess? And you'll love Eric — he's DIVINE. But don't touch. He's engaged to a supermodel. She'll never forgive me if she loses him to my next discovery."

I promise I'll try to be fabulous and guarantee that I won't steal the divine photographer from his supermodel girlfriend. These people really do live in a different world. Meanwhile, I wonder if Tina can possibly be right about the hush-hush campaign. I don't like the idea of taking someone else's job, but I don't know Tina well enough yet to tell her. I'll have to do it later, when I'm not so new and she's more likely to listen to me.

When I explain it all to Ava, she gives me one of her megawatt movie-star smiles.

"Told you this would happen! I've heard of Rudolf Reissen. He could be the next Testino."

I nod knowledgably. I wish that when people said "Testino" now, I didn't automatically picture a black labradoodle in a basket, but at least I know who they're really talking about. And I know that I'm supposed to be impressed at this point, and I am.

A few days later, Frankie calls to book me for the casting with Rudolf's assistant.

"Eric's in town next week. He's got a shoot lined up for *i-D* and he's only seeing three girls. You're one of them. It wouldn't pay much, I'm afraid, but you know *i-D* . . ."

Nowadays, I do. It's a totally cool magazine and everyone wants to be in it. It's edgy and funky and it gets you noticed. I have several copies at home that various people have given me. *i-D*: seriously wow.

Wait a minute.

"Next week?"

"Uh-huh. Problem?"

"What about school?"

Frankie's voice is warm and reassuring. "Don't worry. School comes first. We'll work around it. But you're allowed a *few* days off, you know."

"Really? I've got my general certificate exams this year. I don't think I could —"

"Be calm, angel. I'll see what I can do. Eric gets here on Saturday, so I'll ask if he can see you on Sunday. You'll love him. He's adorable. I've got a few people interested in seeing you after that, but I'm just working out with Cassandra who's best for your profile. Leave it with me, OK?"

★

Frankie somehow gets Eric Bloch to agree to see me on Sunday morning. Even better, Ava's feeling well enough to be my chaperone today. We show up at a beautiful house in Bayswater. We are, of course, on time, and I'm "appropriately dressed," with spare shoes in my bag, my book (updated with some of the warrior princess photos that Tina took), and my unibrow freshly threaded by a professional, having recovered from Mum's emergency tweezer session.

Eric greets us in cutoff jeans, bare feet, and a rumpled linen shirt. He is short, French, with a slight American accent to his English, intense, addicted to strong espressos, unaware of the invention of the hairbrush, and, as promised, adorable. I don't sit in a damp, drafty waiting room this time: Today it's just him, me, and Ava. We lounge around a big scrubbed-pine kitchen table and he makes coffee for Ava and tea for me. We talk about movies — À Bout du Souffle is his favorite. Also music — he's a big fan of Blondie and is impressed I know all about New Wave (thanks to Daisy). After an hour of chatting, he sits me casually next to a tall window, with only natural daylight on my face, and takes a few pictures.

He doesn't give me much direction. "I just want to see what you can do."

I do some smiley faces, because he's supercute and it's easy to smile at him. However, I think I ought to show him the warrior princess, too, because that's what Tina wanted and it looked extraordinary in the photos afterward. It was like seeing pictures of another girl — maybe not what you'd call a traditionally beautiful one, but somebody fascinating, with a powerful story to tell. So I summon up Xena again and stare down the lens.

This is better. When I'm Xena I feel more in control. I know my eyes are doing the work and drawing attention away from my fat ankles. Not that I'm convinced they're so fat anymore.

"Yes!" Eric says. "More of that. Challenge me!"

I glare at him. I imagine he's Cally, rabbiting on to her posse about my "insane-asylum hair." He grins. He loves it.

"Tina was so right about you," he says.

Tina was right about a lot of things. She was the only person to explain that the camera is focusing on what's inside my head. I love the sense of control I get — telling the story using just my eyes, the angle of my shoulders, and the power of my imagination. Even though we're not talking much, it feels as though Eric and I are working as a team. He's certainly taking a lot of photographs.

Then, suddenly, he looks up and flashes me a smile.

"Great! I think that's it. Thank you, *chérie*."

And five minutes later, Ava and I are back on the street, heading for home.

"Well," she asks, "what do you think? It seemed like he liked you."

"I liked *him*," I admit, "but who knows? This is what it's like after go-sees. You're never sure till your booker tells you."

Ava grins. "You sound like *such* a model."

"Do I?"

"And you totally fancied him."

"I did *not*," I say hotly. "We just had a lot in common."

"Look at you! Your face is burning. You just go for guys with rumpled hair who talk about light levels. Don't fight it, Ted, it's sweet."

Oh, God. I am see-through and predictable and, worst of all, "sweet." And I did fancy Eric, just a little bit, although he's about ten years too old for me and based in New York, so it's not exactly relevant. And there are other people I've fancied more. Much more.

I continue to deny it strongly, and Ava continues to tease me about it, for most of the journey home.

THIRTY-ONE

What's happening may not be normal, but it's good. This time when I call Frankie, she says Eric liked my "killer look" and "instinctive approach." I've been optioned! We shoot *i-D* in two weeks. She's even organized castings for me with Miss Teen and Roxy in the meantime.

By the time I get to the Miss Teen casting, I'm starting to feel less like a freak, and more like a girl with a chance. They need someone to model their key looks for next season, to go in an in-store magazine and on enormous posters behind the registers. Only a few girls are invited to their headquarters to try for this job. They get me to pose in a couple of outfits to see if I can show them off properly, and the clothes are gorgeous. Soft leather boots, embroidered coats, wide belts, and high-necked shirts in earthy colors. There's a sort of warrior theme to the collection, which must be why they were interested in my new test shots. Now they've got me interested in embroidered coats and belts. They would need my hair to be a little bit longer, but it will have grown to the perfect length by then. The whole casting experience is wonderful. Then I get optioned. AGAIN.

I don't get the job at Roxy, but Frankie tells me they wanted me to know that they liked my look and they'll keep me on file. Ava was super-impressed when I told her about Roxy. They do the coolest surfing gear. I'd never have guessed that being "on file" could be so satisfying, but it is.

The *i-D* shoot with Eric takes place over fall break, in late October, so I don't have to miss any school to do it. Mum comes with me this time, and is treated like a queen by everyone who meets her, and assured how fabulous I am. It turns out they want me for the cover. The cover of *i-D*! Oh my God. Even Mum is impressed.

I even feel like a cover girl. My hair has been recropped, tinted, and gelled to look like a supersmooth swim cap. I'm wearing a variety of voluminous skirts and capes by, funnily enough, Laslo Wiggins, and having seen the catwalk show, I understand how he intended them to be worn. Eric wants the warrior princess look every time. Having seen it, he's obsessed with it. No problem. I spend the day imagining he's Cally Harvest with a French accent. He admits that he's already told his boss in New York how "extraordinary" I am, and that I might need to pack a suitcase soon. I pretend that Tina hasn't already told me her master plan about the hush-hush fragrance campaign, and that I have no idea what he means. But I'm starting to believe there is nothing in the fashion world that this woman cannot do.

A few days later, she calls from Moscow.

"SEE? I TOLD you. They ADORE you. Of course they do. Aren't I a megastar?"

I agree that she is.

"Eric's shown your pictures to Rudolf. They were as good as I'd said they'd be. Expect a call any minute. So what are you going to do with all the MONEY, baby girl?"

"What money?" I thought *i-D* didn't pay much.

"The Miss Teen money, my darling. Ten thousand British bucks. Not bad for a day's work, wouldn't you say? Hello? HELLO?"

Frankie hadn't mentioned the money. Not exactly. She'd said it would be "very good," and I thought after the TV thing that meant maybe three hundred pounds. Possibly four hundred. Ten THOUSAND pounds is Linda Evangelista money. I still can't talk. I'm gasping.

"If you think THAT'S good, just wait till you hear what they'll pay for this campaign." Tina cackles down the line. "You haven't even STARTED yet, sweetie. They suggested triple the Miss Teen figure, but Cassandra will get you more. I make my girls RICH."

"How much?" Ava asks.

We're on our way home from another visit to the pediatric oncology unit.

" 'Thirty thousand pounds. Maybe forty. On top of what I'll get from Miss Teen."

"Forty. Thousand. Pounds," she repeats. "It's enough to pay for your whole university tuition."

"I know," I say in a very small voice.

"So *that's* why you were so distracted just now."

Ava's been asked to help organize a head-shaving ceremony for some new patients in our group at the beginning of

December. The Director of Patient Services spent the past half hour going through various ideas with us and I was hoping she hadn't spotted that I wasn't completely concentrating, but Tina had just called.

"Did it really show?"

"You didn't answer about three questions. Don't worry, though. I answered for you. But hey — forty grand. What are you going to spend it on?"

"*If* I get the job," I remind her. "I don't know."

"You must have some ideas."

She's right. I have a few. For a start, there's a new phone. My old one is cracked and scuffed and doesn't always work. Then, of course, there's makeup, shoes, and handbags. Lots of them, to make up for all the years when I didn't take them seriously enough. And I wouldn't mind getting myself a decent camera and sponsoring a patch of woodland in the Cotswolds. Still, I think that would leave a lot left over.

"What do you think?" I ask her.

She pauses for a while and looks out of the bus window.

"A car. For Dad. It would be nice to travel by car sometimes."

That's true. How she drags her aching body on and off public transport on the bad days is a mystery to me. When she gets home, she's so exhausted she has to sleep immediately. Money doesn't make you happy, necessarily, but I bet it makes you a lot less tired.

"OK, a car," I agree. "What else? *I* know. Rose Cottage: We could move back to Richmond and get our old bedrooms back. And a vacation somewhere glamorous. Lots of vacations. What about Barbados?"

But Ava's still staring out the bus window. I can't see her face properly. It's not smiling, though — I can see that much.

"I miss the beach," she says eventually. Her voice sounds far away and sad.

Oh. *That* beach. With *that* surfer boy on it. The one she should have been on all summer. Jesse's back on it now, home from his Mediterranean yacht tour, but she won't let him see her. He's banished to Cornwall. It's still a stupid idea. We still don't talk about it.

"You can go there next year," I point out. "It'll still be there."

For the first and only time, she turns to me and gives me the look I've been dreading. The look that says "the beach will, but will I?"

So she does think about the other ten percent after all.

Of course she does.

Then she turns away again and all at once I realize how totally brave she is for dealing with this on her own and just focusing on the fun stuff with me. That's my job, I think: Fun-Stuff Girl. So I spend the rest of the journey picturing all the other things we could do with forty thousand pounds — or fifty, if you include my Miss Teen money, and once you get going, there are a lot of them. I'm still in the middle of completely reimagining Mum's thrift shop wardrobe, as designed by Frida at Gucci, when we get home.

If I get the job.

The thing is, with Tina on the case, things are different now. I'm in makeup for the Miss Teen shoot when she phones me again from LA. In fact, it's my sixteenth birthday today, but that's not why she's calling.

"I shouldn't be telling you this, princess. Frankie'll call you later. But I just wanted you to know, I'm a GENIUS. You've got the fragrance campaign. It's yours."

I leap so far out of my seat that Gemma, my makeup artist, sighs with frustration. She's going to have to completely redo my right eye. She gets on with it while Tina fills in the details. Then, as soon as the call's over, Gemma wants to know them all.

"They want me!" I explain. "Rudolf Reissen wants me! For this ad in New York."

"Oh my God. Really? The guy who just did that spread for Emmanuelle Alt?"

She high-fives me and we have a celebratory pastry. One of the good things about professional shoots is the amount of food everywhere. I have no idea how models stay so thin in the long run.

"So, when are you going?"

"Soon."

"And who's the campaign for?"

"Can't say."

I've been sworn to secrecy, but Tina told me it's Constantine & Reed — the first fashion store I ever paid any real attention to, and whose stuff I now want nearly as badly as I want to move back to Richmond Park again. This job is just too perfect. Tina says they're launching a new perfume called Viper, with a seriously impressive advertising budget. Massive. And some of that budget is going to be spent on me.

"My God, though," Gemma squeals, "if it's Reissen, that means it will be everywhere. Buses, billboards, magazines . . . you've made it, Ted! Go you!"

We both look at my reflection in the mirror. Today I'm a Mongolian huntress, with white hair and lips, and crystal-tipped eyelashes. I can't believe it. First the cover of *i-D*, now this. I've made it. I'm actually quivering with shock.

After that, the Miss Teen shoot goes really well. For the next six hours, I'm poured in and out of gorgeous clothes. They all fit perfectly and I feel I was made to jump and dance around in them, looking brave and heroic and being Xena for all I'm worth. Amanda Elat, the head of the brand, looks delighted.

"You captured the spirit of the collection perfectly. You just glowed."

I know. I could feel it.

Today, Dad was my chaperone again. On the way home, we talk about the money.

"We'll have to start a trust," he whispers wonderingly. "Make sure you're earning interest. Oh, and the taxes. We'll need someone to help with that." He trails off. I bet he never thought one day he'd be helping his teenage daughter manage her thousands. Then he shakes himself out of it. "Now listen, love. Are you sure you want to do this? Because you don't have to."

I put on my serious face and assure Dad that yes, I am perfectly comfortable about, oh, going to New York to model for a top photographer and earning enough money to last me till I'm thirty.

Seriously, I can handle it.

THIRTY-TWO

At school, I haven't mentioned what's been happening recently. Daisy and I talk about it at home — when we're not on the subject of Ava — but it all seems too weird to bring up in class. And I haven't forgotten Daisy's first reaction when I told her about modeling. It wasn't a good one. Anyway . . . since I found my inner Xena, I just don't feel the same need to impress everyone. Actually, I quite like having a secret double life. Nobody saw my TV disaster, luckily, and none of the pictures I've done have been published yet, so I thought I'd wait until they did before I said anything. That way, I also avoid Cally's "oh yeah?" look, which is good.

However, a few days after Tina gives me the news about the perfume campaign, a pair of long legs falls into step beside mine after school, as I'm walking to the bus stop. I look across. It's Dean Daniels. Who "just happens" — for the first time in history — to be going the same way as me.

"Hi, Ted. You off home, then?"

Two things: First, what happened to "Friday"? And second, of course I'm off home. Where else would I be going? And why does he seem so tongue-tied?

He coughs. "Er . . . someone said . . . that you were . . ." — *cough* — ". . . a model now. Is that true . . . or something?"

"What makes you think so?"

"Oh, nothing. It's just that Nathan King's cousin's temping at this model agency. And they're really excited about this new girl. And she sounds like you. And she's . . ." — *cough* — ". . . er, going to be, you know, like, famous."

"Oh, right. That's interesting."

We reach the bus stop. I check for the bus, which doesn't seem to be coming any time soon. Dean lingers.

"So?" he says.

"Sorry?"

"Is it you?"

"Why do you want to know?"

Dean looks down and scuffs the ground with his foot. "You know . . . *models* . . ."

No, actually, I don't. What does he mean, "*models*"? Which models? His face is scrunched up with embarrassment and he won't meet my eye.

"What?"

"Well, *you* know." His face scrunches up further. He looks almost as awkward as I did in choir last term. Then he catches my eye for a brief second and gives a dirty laugh. "You know . . . models. Sick."

"Sick?"

"In a good way. You know . . ."

He does the dirty laugh again, but apart from that, Dean is actually lost for words — for the first time since I've known him. Apart from "sick," obviously, which doesn't count. This is bizarre. And embarrassing, for both of us.

"Well, I'd better be going," I tell him, getting my bus pass ready.

Still no bus. Please don't let him notice I'm staring down an empty street.

"Yeah. Sure. Whatever. Cool. See you tomorrow." He trudges off, backpack bouncing on his shoulders.

I realize I never did answer his question, but it'll be around the whole school soon. If anyone thinks to check the Model City website, it'll be impossible to deny. Then I will officially be "Ted Richmond, model."

Just as I was getting used to being "Xena, Secret Warrior Princess." I was enjoying that. I wish I could hold that moment, but judging by the totally weird look on Dean's face just now, it's gone.

Sure enough, a couple of days later, thanks to Nathan King's cousin, the news about my trip to New York is all around our class. Cally looks so jealous it's like a physical pain, and lots of the girls aren't talking to me. This isn't the reaction I originally wanted at all. They seem to divide into the ones who are being bitchy about me behind my back, and the ones who are too stunned to say anything.

The boys are worse. "Models. Sick." I wish it would wear off. I imagined them being impressed for two seconds, then going back to normal. I didn't want them to ask for my autograph in math.

Miss Jenkins gives me a sad, crimson-lipped smile, as if I've just joined an opposing team. Mr. Anderson is more tongue-tied than ever and asks me to do more singing demonstrations than in the whole of last year put together. Even the headmaster calls me into his office for a long chat about academic success and fallback careers.

It takes Ava several nights of talking after lights-out to persuade me that all this is only temporary, and that anyway it's totally worth it for those moments when I'll get to meet the big designers and photographers. Not to mention earn some serious money. But I'm starting to realize why so many of the girls I met at castings weren't in school anymore.

The perfume shoot is set for the end of November. I'll have to miss a day of classes, but Mum agrees to this as a one-off, never-to-be-repeated exception to the rule, because I'm so excited and Dad has put it to her that it would be educational for me to see New York.

Mum will go with me, because Dad has some meetings lined up. I hope they're not with the attractive TV assistant, but it's not the sort of thing you can ask, and there's too much else going on at the moment to worry about it. Hopefully, when Ava's better and our lives are back on track, Mum will be less über-stressed and Dad can take *her* out for coffee instead.

Ava and I don't talk about that sort of worry. What we mostly talk about is me and Manhattan, and the money, and the glamour, and all the free Constantine & Reed stuff they'll probably give me, and whether any of it will fit Ava, and if so how much of it she can have, and how excited the patients in our head-shaving group at the hospital will be when we tell them. Which, when we do, is very.

★

Then, with a week to go, Cassandra Spoke calls me.

"Hi, my darling girl. Are you *thrilled* about your job? Listen, I need to talk you through some details. Can we do it at my place? It's much nicer than the office. I'm free this evening. Can you make it over?"

"Sure," I say nervously. Why is the head of the agency talking to me, not my normal booker? "Er, what happened to Frankie?"

"Oh, the usual. She's busy sorting out some lost passport in Stockholm. Besides, this is such a big deal for you, Ted. It could be the launchpad for your career. I always love to take a personal interest when it's something special."

Cassandra explains where she lives, which is a house not far from Buckingham Palace. I guess to many people that could sound like a perfectly normal address in London, but when you live here you learn that *nobody* has a HOUSE not far from Buckingham Palace. The area is full of abbeys, the Houses of Parliament, several other palaces housing various royals, and the Prime Minister. Maybe, if you're lucky, you get to live in a tiny flat squeezed in next to one of these places, but a *house*? This I have to see.

"Absolutely, fine," I say. "I'll be there."

"And call a cab," she adds. "I don't want you wandering around in the evening on your own. We'll pick up the tab."

I could really get to like this job.

Mum is out, Dad is writing, and Ava's asleep. Dad offers to come with me, but I don't want him to leave Ava on her own. He agrees I can visit Cassandra as long as I'm back by nine thirty.

And so, at seven o'clock, I draw up in my paid-for black cab outside a classic, tall Georgian house with five floors of glimmering windows. It is indeed so close to Buckingham Palace that I bet they get woken up by the sound of horses' hooves clopping by first thing every morning to guard the Queen.

I step out in my new skinny jeans and the long, shaggy vest they gave me at the Miss Teen shoot. I know I look a million times better than my hiking shorts days, but I'm still not sure I'm ready for Cassandra "at home." I mean, I'm not wearing anything made out of silk, or gold, or by a famous designer. This must be the house that houses the über-wardrobe. It looks as if it could house several. It also houses Nick Spoke, of course, but I tell myself to assume that he won't be there, because he's probably at art college by now, or out with his mates, or painting, or "dabbling in photography." And besides, he's not interested in me. So it wouldn't make any difference if he turned out to be the person who opened the door.

I stand there for ages after ringing the bell. Have I got the right house? Is anyone coming? Then I hear the sound of bolts being drawn. The door opens. He's standing there. In paint-spattered shorts made out of an old pair of jeans cut off at the knees, an old polo shirt, and bare feet. He makes me look positively overdressed. He sees it's me, with my mouth opening and closing like a goldfish, and smiles slowly. I guess at least I'm not semi-naked this time. It's a start.

"Come in." He turns back and shouts, "Eugenia! Guest for Mum!" Then he stands aside so I can enter the large hallway, which is lined with paintings. Away from his mother, he's more relaxed and positively polite. "Sorry. Big house," he says. "Nobody ever hears the door. Got a meeting?"

I nod. I am *so* articulate.

Nick looks at his watch and nods to himself. "She's working late again. Haven't seen her all evening." He hesitates and looks at me through his owlish glasses. "I like —" He stops.

"Yes?" I ask hopefully. I've never heard him say he likes anything before. Except Abstract Expressionism. And natural light.

He laughs. "I like your . . . shaggy thing."

I can't help smiling. He perhaps has an eye for fashion, despite himself, but certainly not his mother's vocabulary for it.

"Thanks. I like your . . ."

He stares at me. What was I going to say?

"Paint."

I indicate the artful spatter on his top and shorts. I am pointing at his shorts. I just said I liked his paint. Oh God oh God oh God oh God oh God.

His smile turns to a grin. Not Nightmare Boy at all, right at this moment. Although I am possibly Nightmare Girl. *I like your paint.* Honestly.

"Come on up," he says.

I follow him up a grand, curving staircase, so close we're almost touching. I can hear the sound of running steps on the landing above us. A woman in a comfy T-shirt and track pants meets us at the top of the stairs.

"So sorry!" she echoes. "I was doing the ironing —"

"No problem," he tells her. "Ted, this is Eugenia. She'll take care of you. Eugenia, this is Ted Trout. Actually, you're Ted Something Else now, aren't you?"

"Trout will do," I say. Knowing what I know about him, I'd rather he thought of me as Ava's sister than "aspiring model."

As if reading my mind, he looks concerned. "About your sister . . . Is she . . . ?"

"She's . . ." I shrug. I'm not going to tell him she's fine when she spent most of the afternoon trying to eat a tiny bowl of salad without throwing up.

He understands, and nods sympathetically.

From a nearby room, Cassandra's voice booms out. "Is she here yet? Show her to the study, would you?"

"Right," Nick says to me, with a small, awkward pause. "Anyway. See you."

"Yes. Great," I say — keeping up my reputation for witty conversation.

He heads on up the next set of stairs. I watch him go. Note to self: Do not point at the shorts of any boy you find interesting and admire their decoration. But definitely do wear the "shaggy thing" again. With a sigh, I turn to Eugenia, who leads me down the corridor to a wood-paneled room, furnished with leather armchairs and green velvet sofas.

Mario the labradoodle looks up at me from a Louis Vuitton dog bed beside the fireplace. By now, he's a friendly face, but I'm glad I know better than to try and stroke him. Besides, I'm too busy taking in my surroundings. I wasn't really concentrating before, but now I can't help noticing. Wow. Oil paintings in vivid colors. Furnishings that wouldn't look out of place in Claridge's. A massive brass coffee table in the middle, smothered in the latest magazines. Even the magazines probably cost more money than my family spends in a month. I'm grateful when Eugenia offers me a chair. All this luxury is making my knees go weak.

Cassandra comes in soon afterward, wearing glasses on her head and reading a document that she quickly finishes and folds with a sigh.

"Constant work! It never ends," she says by way of hello.

"It's worth it, though," I suggest, looking around. "I mean — this place is like a museum."

She sighs even more. "That's what Nick says."

"In a good way, I mean. Sorry. It's gorgeous."

I imagine Nick upstairs somewhere. In a house this size, he probably has a room he can just use as an art studio. Maybe he's doing another of those huge, splattery paintings . . .

"Thanks." Cassandra smiles. "But it's not all down to me. My husband's a banker and he works harder than I do." She looks around at it all with tired eyes for a moment, then puts her smile back on and pulls herself together. "But you have to make sacrifices if you want the best. And thank goodness for Eugenia. If it weren't for her, I couldn't function. Oh, here she is."

At this moment, Eugenia returns with a tumbler of clear liquid with ice in it for Cassandra and a choice of drinks for me. I pick an orange juice and Cassandra says, "Right. To work. The shoot. Rudolf's office has been on the phone and we have a lot to talk about. First things first: You're not snake-phobic, are you?"

I smile. "No. I don't like spiders, but snakes are fine. Why? Are they going to drape them round me?"

That would be quite exotic. I quite like the idea of posing with a python. I've always been a fan of snakes — ever since Ava threw one at me during a "meet the animals" visit to the zoo and I discovered they're not slimy, but smooth and dry, with delicate scales, and most of them can't kill you with a single bite, contrary to what horror movies tell you. *Snakes on a Plane* has a lot to answer for.

"No. You're going to be in a bath of them."

"I'm sorry?"

I take it all back. Who do they think I am — Indiana Jones? Are they *crazy*?

Cassandra laughs. "A bath of fake ones. Rubber ones, right up to your shoulders. Like bubbles, but much edgier. The perfume's called Viper, and the snake is the symbol of Constantine & Reed. They've got one winding round the perfume bottle. Here. Look."

She goes over to a side table and hands me a green glass bottle with a gold snake wrapped around it. It looks potentially poisonous. When I open the stopper, the smell is rich and pungent, like overblown flowers.

"They're going for a sensual, nighttime image," Cassandra says. "You know fragrance ads. They're not exactly selling milk and cookies. It's more . . . exposed . . . than you've done before."

"Er, exposed? How exposed? Because I —"

"I know you're still new to this," she interrupts me, flashing me a smile, "but you'll see when you get there: It will be gorgeous. Totally tasteful. And in a way, it will be easier, because you can focus on yourself, not the clothes. Besides, Rudolf is a photographic genius. He'll get shots of you that no one else could imagine. It'll be a master class."

I nod, not entirely convinced. But "gorgeous" and "tasteful" sound good. So does "master class." Actually, "master class" sounds great. How could I miss it?

Cassandra sips at her drink. "There's just one tiny detail," she adds. "He needs to reshoot a piece for Russian *Vogue*. They gave him the wrong kind of caviar to use and some caviar billionaire's gone crazy. The whole thing's been set back by a week, but that turns out to be a godsend, because between us, Tina and I have managed to organize some incredible go-sees for you straight afterward. Honestly — they'll set you up for New York Fashion Week next season. Then, as Tina says, your career will take off like a rocket."

"Er." My brain is frantically whirring. Cassandra seems to think this is all good, but I have a bad feeling about it. While I try to work out why, I ask who the go-sees are with. Cassandra lists them for me.

"Ralph Lauren. Zac Posen. Proenza Schouler. Rodarte. Vera Wang. If you walk for any of these houses in February, we can start naming your price."

Oh my goodness. After my summer fashion education, I recognize all these names. They are big. They are huge. So huge you need oxygen equipment to scale them. But I'm supposed to be busy with school next term, and anyway, I've just remembered why I can't see them.

"I'm sorry, but if you're talking about two weekends' time, I have to be in London then. I'm doing this thing with my sister."

Cassandra peers at me.

"But . . . Ralph Lauren. Zac Posen. Vera Wang."

I nod. I get that they're big names, but it doesn't change the problem.

"We've organized this head-shaving ceremony at the hospital. Four people are doing it. Vince from Locks, Stock, and Barrel has agreed to come and shave them for us. I promised I'd be there."

Cassandra takes another sip of her drink and frowns while she thinks. "And what would you be doing, exactly?"

"Well, nothing specific, but I've been telling them what it feels like, and how good it is to have people there to support you. And it was me who asked Vince if he'd come."

Cassandra smiles. "But that's wonderful! It sounds as though you've done your bit already. And look where your head shaving has got you! Now you can go to New York and celebrate!"

"I could, but not then. Couldn't we try and . . . ?"

"Darling, you're booked." Her voice is harder now. "Tina's had to call in huge favors to get you those go-sees. But they'll be worth it, you'll see. You've got to get known transatlantically or no one will take you seriously. Other girls would do anything for this chance. Believe me — anything."

I picture telling Daisy that I've got to get known transatlantically. She'd stick her fingers down her throat. Or Dad. He'd probably just look it up to see if it was really a word. Ava would grin with delight, though. New York . . . Milan . . . Paris . . . the clothes . . .

"Can I think about it? I need to talk to my family."

Cassandra looks tired again. "I don't think you get it, darling. Go and talk to your family if you need to. But just think who you'd be letting down. Some of the biggest names in fashion." She pauses. "Call me as soon as you've decided, OK?"

THIRTY-THREE

"You're not going. It's simple," Mum says briskly, clearing up the remains of the supper I've just missed. "You've got commitments. And besides, I've already booked two days off work next week and I can't change them. If I tried, they'd probably fire me and I really need that job, Ted."

"OK, but if I did go, I'd earn more money than you get in a year."

She whips around to face me.

"That's enough! How dare you? Don't you think it's bad enough for your father, with you going on about the money and getting Rose Cottage back? We don't want to live off our children, thank you very much."

I'm not sure what I want, but it's not this. I may be nearly six feet tall, but I feel about six inches. I hand her a tissue. She needs it.

Ava comes into the kitchen. She still doesn't look great. Thank goodness the chemo's nearly over and she doesn't have to go through this much longer. I don't think she'd have the strength for another cycle.

"It was ringing," she says, holding out my phone. "I answered it. I think it's Tina."

"Good," Mum says as I take the phone from Ava. "Tell her what we've decided, would you, Ted?"

I go into the living room, where it's quiet, and take the call.

"Princess?" Tina says. "Cassandra called me. Oh my God — drama! Where are we up to?"

She sounds bouncy and lively, but there's an edge to her voice, too. I can hear party noises in the background, and her shushing people who come too close.

"Um . . . I'm not sure," I tell her.

"Sorry, I didn't catch that. Are you EXCITED? Are you AMAZED? Have you any IDEA how incredible this trip is going to be?"

"It's just that . . . the dates have changed . . ."

"But we got you go-sees, princess. Go-sees with RALPH LAUREN! With DONNA KARAN! The other girls are going to be so jealous they'll want to scratch your FACE off. Hey, wait. They'll let you off school, right?"

"Yes, I think so, but —"

"Because that's what matters. School first. Then your career."

I have a sudden image of Nick Spoke saying, "I mean, it's life and death, right?" and the hard, cynical look he had when he said it.

"Yeah, maybe. But my mum can't come with me then, and things are complicated at home, and —"

"Complicated how?"

"My sister's got cancer and —"

"Oh, yes. Of course. Frankie told me. WAIT. Wait right there.

Just let me get out of this crazy place. If I just walk down this gangplank . . ."

Oh my God. She's on a yacht. She's at a party on an *actual yacht*, like the one Jesse crewed on, I can only imagine. And I'm sitting in a flat above a travel shop.

"You still there, princess? Get your parents. Put me on speakerphone. This is important. This is your LIFE we're talking about here. Get your mom and dad and we'll talk. I'll hold."

So I guess she hangs around on the dock of whichever beach cove she's in, and meanwhile I call Mum from the kitchen and Dad from his computer and sit down with them in the living room to listen.

"You there, Trouts?" Tina calls over the speaker. "OK. I need your attention. It's hard right now. I know that, and I don't want you to do anything for a MOMENT that isn't pure you. D'you think I don't get it? I totally get it. Mom and Dad, I know the story. You have someone precious who's sick, and you care about her, and you're focusing all your resources on her, and working to support her, and that's INSPIRATIONAL."

Mum looks at Dad as if to say, "Is she always like this?" and Dad shrugs, as if to say, "Usually worse."

"With my brother," Tina goes on, "it was a brain tumor. Inoperable. I can't tell you. Two years of sheer . . . But we won't talk about that. I want to talk about YOU. The thing is, you have someone *else* precious to take care of. She has to take a backseat sometimes, sure, but meantime, she's turning into an incredible young lady, and she needs to find herself as a person. But you don't need me to tell you that."

"Oh!" Mum flushes and puts a hand to her cheek. Dad goes pale. They both look guilty and stare at the phone. I suddenly wonder how Tina manages to get such great reception on a BEACH somewhere, but nothing about her will ever surprise me. And it's nice to think I'm an incredible young lady. Mum didn't seem so impressed with me in the kitchen earlier.

"We know Ted's precious," Mum says crossly.

Tina laughs, unperturbed. "Listen, you're a special family. Can I confide in you? You think I was always like this? I was a wreck, people. A sad, pathetic fat girl from Brooklyn with no friends, no life, just a passion for vintage *Vogue*s. When my brother saw me finally start to pull my look together and emerge from my chrysalis . . . well, the happiness it gave him. The pride. I bet your big girl's proud of her little sister."

"Oh, she is. In fact, Ava's been very supportive," Dad says.

"So, go, Ava! But Ted's more amazing than even you know. This is her one big chance and I'd hate for her to blow it. I know the dates aren't perfect, but these things are out of our control. Sometimes we have to make compromises to get the bigger prize. It'll be worth it, I promise you. And if she comes to New York, I'll look after her like she's my own."

Mum stares at me. Dad stares at me. Then they both stare at the phone.

"Thanks, Tina," Dad says. "We'll think about it."

"You got it," Tina says. "Gotta go now. They're starting the fireworks."

When Mum's sure the call's over, she stares at Dad again.

"Stephen, tell me that woman's not real."

"Apparently, she's totally self-made," Dad says. "I asked Cassandra Spoke about it when we were waiting for our taxis in the lobby of Claridge's, and she said the story goes that she was a teenager named Sue and suddenly decided she was going to be Tina one day — and here she is. She got the name Gaggia from a coffee machine, apparently. Explains a lot about her energy levels."

Mum nods.

"But what she can do in fashion is real," Dad goes on. "Cassandra said she's a legend. If she backs a designer, they make it to the top."

Mum turns to me with a worried, guilty expression in her eyes. She sounded cross on the phone, but I think what Tina said to her had more of an effect than she'd admit.

"I don't want to hold you back, darling. You've grown up so much over the last few months. And I haven't been able to look after you how I wanted."

She holds me to her and runs her hand over my tightly cropped hair. I can actually feel her teardrops running through it, but she doesn't need to cry. Yes, it's true, I've been feeling in the background at home, but Tina made it sound worse than it felt. I wouldn't have said Mum and Dad were holding me *back*, necessarily. However, Mum's tearful hug suggests that Tina has managed to persuade them to live without me for a few days.

I think this means I'm going to New York.

THIRTY-FOUR

"Are you sure?"

"Yes. Positive. Stop talking about it."

"Are you *sure* you're sure?"

Ava looks at me crossly. "For God's sake, Ted. Go. To. New. York. Do something interesting with your life. I don't need you at the hospital. It's all sorted out — it's just a bunch of haircuts after all. I'll be fine."

"Yes, but . . . are you *sure*?"

"Shut up!"

I'm feeling guilty — now that it's all arranged and Cassandra's thrilled and they've moved me onto a later flight.

Ava catches the look on my face and her expression softens.

"Vera Wang," she says, shaking her head at me. "I don't think you get what a big deal this is, T. You might get to meet the actual Vera Wang. She is totally *the* wedding dress designer. Then if you *do* run off with Eric Bloch, she could make your dress."

"I'm *not* going to run off with Rudolf's assistant!"

"So you say," she teases, pulling all of my stuff out of the closet and throwing it on her bed. "But think what's happened to you recently. You never know."

I open the suitcase that Dad has lent me. I have no idea what to pack, apart from the shaggy thing. Thank goodness Ava does.

"New York will be cold," she says. "Bitterly cold, so pick out all your best sweaters. Not that one — it's a crime against fashion. Oh God, they all are, aren't they? Look, I'll find some of mine."

Sharing. She is totally sharing. She really must want me to do this. As she rummages around for knitwear that meets her high standards for transatlantic travel, she runs through some of the designers I'll need to look out for on Fifth Avenue.

". . . and if you could bring me back one thing by Marc Jacobs — just any tiny thing, but preferably a bag — that would be good."

"Of course," I agree. Then it hits me, not for the first time, by any means, that the wrong girl is going to New York. "I wish you could come with me."

"So do I," she says lightly, folding a thin woolen sweater into a neat package. "But don't worry. I'll be busy. Oh, and Jesse's coming."

"*Jesse's* coming?"

"Yes. Didn't I tell you? He called this morning. He wants to see me."

"But you told him not to. Not till the treatment's over."

She cocks her head to one side. "I did. But he says he can't wait. He says the chemo's over and the radiation doesn't count. Ha! He should try booking himself in for some radiotherapy. It beyond counts." Her voice is suddenly brittle. "Anyway, he says we have lots to talk about, so that'll be nice."

Ava's last cycle of chemo finished a few days ago, but radio-therapy starts next week: the final stage in the treatment. According to the brochure they gave us, it involves high-energy X-rays, which they'll beam at the bits of Ava's body where they're worried that cancer cells might still be lurking. Dad's done his usual research on the internet and it says helpful things like "Don't worry, you will not become radioactive during this treatment." Which is perhaps less reassuring than they mean it to be. Ava found a NO RADIATION antinuclear T-shirt in the thrift shop and wears it with a certain flamboyant irony.

She shoves the sweater at me and starts folding another one, not noticing that it's inside out. The way she said "nice" just now makes me nervous.

"Er, what kind of 'lots to talk about'?" I ask.

She hands me the second sweater. "Who knows? There was that Barbie Girl from the yacht who put fifteen pictures of him on Facebook. Her, perhaps?"

"I don't believe it."

And I don't. Jesse just isn't the sort of person to say he's got a new girlfriend to someone about to be zapped with X-rays.

"I'm just being realistic," Ava says briskly. "Have you figured out which jewelry to take?"

But I refuse to be distracted. "Listen. I think it's great that he's coming. It won't be about another girl. I bet he just wants to see you. And soon your treatment will be over and you'll be able to go back to —"

"What?" she flashes at me, expertly folding up a pair of jeans. "You know, I've been thinking about the treatment for so long that I can't imagine when it's over. Anyway, I can't go back to anything. I've changed — I know I have. When Jesse sees me, I won't be some carefree surfer chick anymore."

"No," I agree. "You're different, but better, maybe."

"Rounder."

"Better."

"Balder."

"No. Better."

"You're just saying that because I'm lending you my parka."

"Partly," I agree.

But it's so much more than that. I'm quite certain that no boy like Jesse could possibly be mean enough to split up with a girl like my sister at a time like this. Surely he wants to be with her? That must be it. He can help her out with the head-shaving ceremony while I'm in New York, and it will be wonderful. Then she'll have him back in her life properly again. Though I'll miss us being warrior princesses together, because it's been very special for me. Not that I would ever have wished things to happen this way, but some of the side effects have been . . . strangely good.

"What?" she asks, chewing on her fingernail.

"I'll miss you, that's all."

"Oh, right," she says, breaking into her movie-star smile and shaking off her Jesse mood. "I'll miss you, too, T. But you'll have such a fabulous time while you're gone. Imagine — Ralph Lauren! Vera Wang! My si-ister is a supermod-el!"

She does her dance around the room, waving a pair of leggings over her head.

I wonder if life was ever this complicated for Lily Cole.

THIRTY-FIVE

Ava calls it NYC Day. The day I finally go to New York.

It starts with not much sleep, increasing panic, huge discomfort, and a lot of excitement — so basically, it's a typical day in fashion, as I'm learning. Frankie has arranged for me to travel with one of their more experienced girls, named Alexandra Black, so I'll have a guide and some company. But Alexandra arrives horribly late to pick me up. We get to the airport with minutes to spare, have to run past all the amazing airport shops with the snazzy makeup I was hoping to look at, and our seats end up being the worst on the plane, jammed up against the loos at the back. I guess non-super models travel coach. Alexandra then spends seven of the almost eight hours of the flight telling me exactly how evil her latest boyfriend is for possibly going out with a girl named Rain who opened for Prada in Milan last season, and by the time we land at JFK we are both hobbling after being crammed into tiny seats with no legroom.

At least there's a limo, sent by the agency, to pick us up. It whisks us through a knot of expressways until the road rises up and suddenly — over to the left — there it is: the Manhattan skyline. Suddenly, I can't quite believe that after all the stress and rush and drama, I'm really in New York. For the first time, I start to breathe normally and take it all in. I peer closer at the view, just to make sure it's not a mirage.

Alexandra yawns and stretches over to see what I'm looking at.

"Oh, that," she says.

"Do you ever get used to it?"

She yawns again. "Nope, not really. But now it always reminds me of jet lag. What are your plans, by the way? There's a club in the Meatpacking District I thought I'd check out. You can tag along if you want."

I drag my eyes away from the magnificent skyscrapers outside my window. "I don't think I'd be allowed," I point out.

She smiles. "I'm sure something could be arranged. You could pass for twenty-one with the right jacket. I've probably got one you could borrow."

"No, thanks; I'm meeting Tina di Gaggia," I explain, grateful that Mum and Dad weren't around to hear that little conversation. If they had been, I'd be on the next plane home.

Alexandra's eyebrows shoot up. "Tina? Oh my God. You've got *Tina* looking after you? That explains *everything.*"

The limo takes us straight to Model City's apartment in Manhattan. Alexandra says it's not far from Washington Square Park. This doesn't help me at all, as I've never heard of Washington Square Park, but she says it in such a way that I'm clearly supposed to look pleased, so I do.

I'm expecting something a bit like Cassandra's house, per-haps, except laid out horizontally in an apartment building. I picture rich velvets, fabulous paintings, and stunning views of famous places, like the Empire State Building. However, once we've squeezed ourselves into the tiny lift I discover that I'm wrong. So wrong.

The apartment consists of a small sitting area and three bed-rooms, with two bunk beds in each, and a view of another building's fire escape. No velvet or paintings, just basic furni-ture, which you can't really see because every spare surface is covered in clothes.

"Welcome!" Alexandra says. "Isn't it great? Awesome loca-tion. Who's here, honeys? Alexandra's home! And guess what? I've brought a girl who's in with Tina di Gaggia! Woo!"

I stay rooted to the spot for two solid minutes while I look around. It's like being on a school trip, but without the teachers. The place is chaotic and smells strongly of boiled hot dogs, deodorant, and hair spray. The bathroom door swings open and inside is a girl standing at the sink, brushing her teeth, while, oh, totally naked. She turns around and waves a friendly "hi" to me. Naked. Totally. Apart from a scrunchie holding back her hair. I miss my mum.

But I'll bet one thing: It probably *was* like this for Lily Cole — and Linda Evangelista — at least to start with. Wait till I tell Ava. This is *so* not what she described when she tried to picture the model life. It makes our bedroom at home look positively palatial.

"Message for you," Alexandra calls out. "It was on your pil-low. This is your bed, by the way." She indicates a bottom bunk with a relatively uncrumpled duvet, which somebody is using as a temporary closet at the moment. It's covered in miniskirts, jeans, ribbed tops, loose sweaters, and belted jackets. I'd happily wear almost any of it, but in the meantime I'm wondering how I'm supposed to sleep under it.

I read the message, which is written on thick white paper decorated with a shocking pink picture of a shoe:

WELCOME TO NEW YORK, PRINCESS!
MEET YOU AT THE HELPMAN AT 3.
TAKE A CAB.
LOVE YOU!
TINA

I check my watch. The time difference is confusing. It already feels like evening to me, but when I look at the time it's 2:30 PM in New York. That just gives me time to change into a fresh pair of jeans, touch up my lip gloss, and find a taxi that knows what and where The Helpman is. By the time we pull up outside a smart redbrick building, I have one minute to spare.

In a way, it's good to be in a rush, because it takes my mind off what's happening tomorrow and the day after. Constantine & Reed. Rudolf Reissen. Viper. A bath full of snakes. I know I told Mum and Dad I was fine, but it's pretty scary if I think about it, so I try not to.

Instead, I take a quick breath and admire the building. It is not, in any way, a New York skyscraper. It's only five stories high and, in fact, it looks like an old-fashioned warehouse, or a large school, maybe. It has arched windows, lots of ironwork, and a grand set of steps leading up to its double doors. I wish I had time to take a picture on my phone, but I don't. Any second now I'll be late, and that would be unprofessional.

As I go up the steps, a young man in a green uniform appears from nowhere to open the door for me. Oh, I see. Not a school or a warehouse. The Helpman is a hotel. Of course.

Inside, the lobby is dark and luxurious, smelling of sandalwood and spices. In the middle of it, Tina is waiting for me, dressed in a black wool cloak and what look like purple yakhair boots. There is a large, dark mauve shopping bag beside her, with MULBERRY printed discreetly in one corner. As soon as Tina sees me, she flings her cloak back over both shoulders and reaches up to air-kiss me.

"DARLING! You made it! Welcome to my city! Oh my God! What is that on your shoulder? You need this."

We perch on a couple of nearby armchairs while I open the dark mauve bag. Inside it is a matching cotton bag, and inside that is the latest, must-have Mulberry tote.

"It's just a little something," Tina says, waving a hand dismissively. "Don't thank me. I worked with them on it. It's a little present for being so INCREDIBLE. And now — YOU. Today we prepare. Tomorrow we shoot. Then we do some go-sees and have fun, OK? Or rather, you do. I've got to fly to LA first thing because Tyra needs to talk to me, but you're sixteen and you'll be fine, princess, won't you? You'll have the TIME of your LIFE."

As she talks, she leads me across to the elevators and up to the fourth floor of the hotel. We emerge into a corridor that appears to be completely lined with marble. Marble floors, marble walls, even marble wall lamps. It leads to a marble-lined room furnished with six chrome-and-leather chairs facing a bank of mirrors. A hair salon. The poshest salon I could ever begin to imagine.

"Meet Jake," Tina says. "Jake Emerson. He's doing you tomorrow so we're coloring you today. You are going to be MAGNIFICENT."

Jake Emerson is small, like Tina, with big hair, tight jeans, a skinny blazer, and a wide grin.

"Loving your bag," he says, admiring my new tote. "Off you go, Miss G. She'll be done in ninety minutes. Now, Ted, let me look at you. What a lovely face you have."

I like Jake. I like him a lot. He explains that his plan is to turn my hair into a particular shade of gold to match the Constantine & Reed logo. Then he gets a couple of assistants to apply chemicals and foil to my head under his guidance. At the moment, my hair is about an inch and a half at its longest. I wouldn't have said there was enough to dye, but he seems confident that it will look good. His own hair is about six different shades of blond, styled into a messy pompadour, and looks great, which is encouraging. Meanwhile, he chats away about all the models he's styled recently, and they include most of the girls I've heard of and several I haven't. It is totally like sitting through an episode of *America's Next Top Model*.

The results are incredible. My hair is shining gold, glossy, and gorgeous. Very short, sure, but styled close to my head like a snug-fitting, burnished helmet. The best it's ever looked in my life. I'm so grateful for my fabulous new head that I hardly know how to express it. Funnily enough, when Jake sees the happy, shocked look on my face, he's the one with tears in his eyes.

"I know, gorgeous, I know," he says, hugging me in front of the mirror.

The girl looking back at me is . . . quite arresting. Even better than I looked for the cover of *i-D*. I wonder what Tina has in mind for me next.

She reemerges at the perfect moment and guides me down into the basement, where there's a luxury spa. A woman in a pale green, Oriental-style jacket and cropped trousers leads me into a room playing soothing music, where I'm exfoliated, massaged, and generally pampered until I'm light-headed with the fabulousness of it all. That, and the hunger that comes from not having eaten since I was on the plane. In fact, I'm starting to get so hungry it's even helping to take my mind off the thought of posing for Rudolf Reissen, which I suppose is a good thing.

Even so, when Tina comes to collect me this time I point out that I could really do with something to eat.

She looks surprised, then checks her watch.

"OK. I guess it's later than I thought. Let's go find something."

That's a relief. The cab passed loads of yummy-looking little restaurants, cafés, and diners on the way here. I can't wait to explore.

"What do you feel like?" Tina asks.

I shrug. "Anything. Honestly. A burger, maybe?"

She shudders slightly. "How about a chicken club sandwich? I used to live on those in Brooklyn."

"Brilliant," I agree.

"I know the perfect place."

We head out of the hotel at top speed, back down the steps and past all the places I spotted on the way here, where yummy smells keep making my tummy rumble. Finally we get to a narrow, glass-fronted building with no sign on the door.

"Marcus's," Tina says with a triumphant smile. "Opened last month. EVERYBODY is trying to get in here. Follow me."

This doesn't look like my idea of a restaurant. Apple store, possibly, but not the sort of place you might find food. Inside, there's a tiny reception area and a sweeping staircase leading downward. I peer over the banister to see a vast room sprinkled with small tables, uniformed waiters, and customers in suits and expensive dresses. The air is full of the sound of tinkling glasses and loud conversation.

"Isn't it FABULOUS?" Tina shouts at me over the general noise.

It looks daunting. I would *so* much rather be in McDonald's, but that would be ungrateful. I stick with Tina as she wangles us a table, and wait while she orders.

"Two chicken club sandwiches," she says to the waiter who's in charge of our table. He's dressed in a dinner jacket and bow tie, and looks ready for a night at the opera. He doesn't look like the sort of man to serve sandwiches, and sure enough, his lip curls as he points out that the chef doesn't do them.

Tina flicks a hand dismissively.

"He does for me. Tell him it's Tina, and I want them the way he did them at Soho House. But extra arugula, only heirloom tomatoes, and hold the mayo. And this place is GORGEOUS. I'm telling all my friends about it. This is Ted Richmond, by the way. She's going to be the next hot thing in New York. Don't you just LOVE her?"

The waiter gives me a second glance, and this time his look lingers. I think he's admiring my hair. It is truly amazing tonight and I don't blame him. I give him a friendly smile and not long afterward he reappears bearing plates piled high with several layers of chicken, toast, and salad in a complicated arrangement. By now, my grin is dazzling. I really need this food.

"Isn't it heavenly?" Tina says, picking the chicken out of her sandwich with her fingers. "I always love it when a new place opens. It's almost impossible to get a table here, but you'll be able to, princess, because they'll remember you now. Don't eat that."

She takes my sandwich from my hand (where I've rather inelegantly been trying to squish the thing together — but how else are you supposed to eat it?) and removes the toast, piece by piece. She puts the pieces on her side plate, and puts the chicken and salad back on my plate with her fork.

"Why?" I ask. It's not as if I have a gluten intolerance or anything. I assumed she did. I mean, we're both super-skinny. It's not as if we need to lose weight.

"Carbs," she says simply.

"But I need them," I explain. "I'm starving."

"You won't be after all that chicken."

"I will."

I don't like arguing with Tina, but I hate arguing with my stomach even more, and a few bits of chicken and tomato aren't going to keep it happy right now — not at all.

Tina puts her fork down and sighs. "I don't want you to have a little pouch for Rudy tomorrow. God forbid. And you're going to have to learn to eat in moderation, princess. Look over there."

She indicates a woman at a nearby table with slightly wide hips in tight wool trousers, and shudders.

"But I have to eat," I explain. "I'm still growing."

"Sure," Tina says, waving the waiter over to take the plate of toast away — it's obviously bothering her. "But one day you'll stop. And then you'll have to manage every pound. Hours at the gym. Total carb awareness. It's best to start now, so you get into good habits. There's nothing wrong with being a little bit hungry. Cuts down on the gym time. We don't want you obese."

She makes it sound so reasonable, but my stomach strongly disagrees. In fact, I'm not really sure what else we talk about for the rest of the meal because mostly I'm trying to keep it from rumbling. I'm even distracted when she bids me good-bye, wishes me good luck for tomorrow, and reminds me to get an early night. And the second I get back to the apartment I race to the kitchen and eat half a pack of Oreos that I find at the back of a cupboard.

Then, suddenly, everything feels much better. I find my bed, dislodge the clothes on it and park them on someone else's duvet, and change into a comfy sweater. In the living room, a couple of girls are watching *America's Most Wanted* on TV. I wonder if it's going to be like *America's Next Top Model*, but it turns out to be about serial killers. Even so, there's something relaxing about being with the other girls, sitting quietly, not doing much. It reminds me of all the times I've sat next to Ava watching detective shows and old movies. She was seeing Jesse tonight. I wonder how they're getting on.

I hug my knees and shiver. It's hard to believe I'm doing this in New York.

★

Eventually one of the girls looks around crossly. Somebody's phone keeps ringing. It has a familiar, high-pitched tone and I'm surprised that nobody gets it, but it's only after about thirty seconds that I realize it's mine. Not the new, fancy iPhone that Model City lent me for my stay here, but my old, half-broken Sony, buried in the bottom of my old bag. Mum's already called me on the new phone to check I'm OK, so I wonder who'd be calling me on this one. With all the international codes tossed in, I don't recognize the number.

"Daisy?" I ask, amazed that she would risk spending so much money on a long-distance phone call.

"Hi, Ted? It's Nick. Nick Spoke."

"Nick? *Nick?* Er, hi."

Oh wow! He's phoning me in New York. I mean, why? But wow! I try to slow my heart rate and sound cool and sophisticated, not panicked and confused.

"I'm sorry it's so late," he says, after a pause.

I check my watch, confused as ever. "It's not that late."

"It's one in the morning!"

"No it isn't." I say. "It's eight at night."

"What? Where are you?"

"New York," I explain. "Why —?"

"*New York?* You're in New York?"

"Yes. I've got a shoot in the morning."

"Oh. Right." He sounded anxious before. Now he sounds totally cold. Absolutely Nightmare Boy again. "I see. I was calling to find out why your sister split up with Jesse just now. He's staying here and he just told me. But I guess if you're in *New York*, that doesn't concern you very much."

"What? No! You've got it wrong," I insist, quickly going into the bathroom of the apartment where I can get a bit of privacy. I lock the door and crouch in the shower stall — there isn't a bathtub — hunched down in the corner with my knees around my ears. "Jesse must have split up with *Ava*. How could he *do* that to her?"

There's another pause on the line. "No," Nick says in a clipped, hard voice. "I think Jesse got it pretty straight. The bit where she said to him, 'I've changed. We can't do this anymore.' Plus the bit where she told him not to call her. I'd say that was her splitting with him, wouldn't you? He's in pieces here. I had to find out what her problem was."

Oh, no. I see it clearly now. Poor Ava. She's been fending Jesse off all this time, worried that he'll be put off by her puffy face and tired bones. And now she's taken it too far.

"She didn't mean it," I start to explain. "When she says she's changed, she means she thinks he won't love her anymore. She's just frightened. But I'm sure she's wrong. Surely he's —"

"Hang on," Nick says. "So, you're in New York?"

"Yes. I said so."

"Which means you're not going to be around for this head-shaving ceremony thing Ava's doing? Jesse told me all about it. I thought that was partly your idea. D'you know what? I was pretty impressed by that. I thought you were different . . ."

"Well, I —"

". . . and you are, come to think of it. I've met some pretty evil models in my time, but you totally take the cake. I mean, not being there for a bunch of kids with cancer? That's a classic. Congratulations."

He laughs. He actually laughs.

I am so angry by now that I can't even speak. I have to breathe deeply for a second or two before I can get any words out.

"Listen, Nick. It was Ava who wanted me to come here. She loves that I got this job. The timing was rubbish, but that's not my fault. And what right do you think you have to tell me what to do —?"

But I'm pretty sure he hung up on me after "Listen, Nick." The line is empty. I'm pouring my fury into nothingness somewhere halfway across the Atlantic.

I sit for ages in the shower stall, shaking, until somebody knocks loudly on the door and makes it clear the bathroom is public property. Then I crawl into my pajamas and under my borrowed, scratchy duvet smelling of someone else's perfume, and lie there, still shaking, while Alexandra climbs into bed above me, and her breathing gradually modulates into sleep.

Or at least, it does to start. Soon she's snoring like an express train going through a tunnel. Normally I'd mind, but tonight it doesn't make any difference. Nick's rudeness and bitterness and pigheadedness are infinitely more annoying than any noise she could make.

Who does he think he is? He doesn't understand how small my role was at the hospital. He doesn't get how important this job is for me. It's my big chance to prove myself — to do something creative and be a real part of the world where people make jackets out of kite tails and dress up like Mongolian warriors. To find myself as a person, Tina said.

If I have a successful career, I can help everyone. Sure, I wish I didn't have to do it right here, right now, but I don't have any choice. I want to be amazing and make my sister proud of me. She wrote me a note and put it in my bag: *"Carpe Diem"* — Seize the Day. What else was I supposed to do? I didn't know she was going to do something stupid like break up with the love of her life the minute I stepped on an airplane.

I hate Nick Spoke. More than Cally Harvest and Dean Daniels squared. I truly loathe him.

Eventually, I hear two of the girls come in from a club, giggling and wondering how it can already be 2:30 in the morning. I can guarantee I'm not going to be looking my best first thing tomorrow, and it's entirely Nick's fault.

THIRTY-SIX

"My God, I have a pair of Prada stilettos this color, and it's not pretty under your eyes. Electric blue. What were you *doing* last night?"

Miranda, my makeup girl, is not impressed.

"Trying to sleep," I say. "I wasn't out clubbing, promise."

She purses her lips and checks her supplies for a thicker concealer. "Boyfriend trouble, huh?"

I shake my head violently.

"Oh, yeah?" She smiles. "I know that look. That's the look that says, 'He's not my *boyfriend*.' And that *definitely* means boyfriend trouble."

She laughs in a friendly way and doesn't seem to mind my grim expression, which means she's got it so wrong about me and Nick. Not that I'm going to tell her about Nick. How could anybody *be* that cruel? Anyway, Ava sent me a good-luck text this morning, saying how happy she is for me and how FABULOUS it's going to be today, which only goes to show how wrong Nick Spoke is about everything.

Ava's right. I'm in New York, in the studio of a top photographer, surrounded by makeup people, stylists, perfume-marketing people, assistants, technicians, and even a girl whose sole job seems to be to make sure I'm topped up with chocolate-covered strawberries to keep my energy levels going. I was whisked here first thing this morning by another chauffeur-driven limo, which arrived with fresh bagels, courtesy of Frankie's counterpart at Model City New York. (Pure carbs. Thank goodness Tina wasn't in the car with me.) There's jazz on the sound system, I can see the Statue of Liberty through the window if I crane my neck slightly from the makeup chair, and everybody LOVES my hair. Even the dark circles under my eyes are nothing that several layers of Touche Éclat can't cure. I am Xena again — I'm about to go on billboards and the back of every magazine you've ever heard of.

I am, it's true, slightly in awe of Rudolf Reissen. He met me at the door of the studio and radiated the gorgeous male beauty of Tom Ford combined with the boundless energy of Tom Cruise. He should really be in a magazine himself, or on a movie screen. In real life he's just too . . . big . . . somehow. He looked me deep in the eyes, kissed my hand lingeringly, and murmured, "Oh, yes. I can't wait to work with you, Viper Girl."

I had to resist the urge to giggle. But the urge soon disappeared when I saw the size of Rudolf's studio — bigger than our whole flat put together — the number of people moving around, the amount of expensive equipment and cables everywhere, and the massive oval bathtub at one end of the room. It's set up on a stage with ladders around it, so Rudolf can capture it from every angle. Perfect for Rudolf, but a bit intimidating for a schoolgirl from South London who would have quite liked her mum to hold her hand at that point and tell her it was all going to be OK.

Luckily, Eric Bloch came over, wandering across the cable-covered floors in a typical crumpled shirt and bare feet, and greeted me like an old friend. It was so good to see him. He introduced me to Miranda and she brought me to the dressing area at the back, where everything seems quieter and not so, as Tina would put it, INSANE.

Miranda has a mood board that she created for Rudolf showing how my viper makeup will look. It involves a lot of shimmery lipstick, green and gold eye shadow, and fake lashes. I watch in the mirror as my face is gradually transformed into something glittering and beguiling. A girl called Candy comes in to paint my nails to match. While they work, we chat.

"So, who else have you worked with?" Miranda asks.

"Hardly anyone," I admit. "My first proper shoot was for Eric and that was only a few weeks ago."

"*Really?*" Miranda muses. "My God, what happened? Who did you . . . I mean, you must know some pretty influential people to get this gig."

"I do. Tina di Gaggia."

She nods. "Gotcha. That is one seriously crazy lady."

"Did you know she used to be just a nerdy kid from Brooklyn?" Candy chimes in.

"Uh-huh, she told me," I say, remembering the conversation from the yacht with a smile.

"She went to high school with my cousin," Candy goes on. "One day: geeky girl in glasses; next day: hello, *Vogue*. She was like *Ugly Betty*, but in, like, one episode, not four seasons."

"She said her brother loved it when she transformed herself," I add.

Candy pauses and squints at my freshly green-painted thumbnail. "Brother? What brother?"

"The one who died."

She purses her lips. "Nuh-uh. No brother."

"Oh, yes, there was one," I assure her, surprised she doesn't know this bit of the story. "He had a brain tumor. It was awful."

"Not sure where you got that one from, sweetie." Candy frowns, starting the next nail. "My cousin knew her for years. Totally an only child. Can't you tell?"

"Now, close your eyes," Miranda interrupts, "'cause I'm going to dust some stuff onto you."

I sit there with my eyes closed, feeling confused. How could I possibly have misunderstood something as basic as whether Tina had a brother or not? She seemed to say it so clearly. I thought that conversation was important. It was all about me coming out of my chrysalis, wasn't it? Finding myself as a person. Now I'm not so sure what it was about at all. I wish Tina wasn't in LA right now, so I could check.

By the time Miranda and Candy have finished, my own mother would have to look twice to be sure it was me. I'm green and gold, glittery and dangerous. I look slightly reptilian, but in a hot way. It's otherworldly and absolutely NOT like my Uncle Bill the Royal Marine, or anyone who could possibly have the surname of Trout, or the nickname of Friday. I look like an artwork. Miranda is very, very good at what she does.

Jake Emerson arrives, accompanied by an assistant, and proceeds to burnish my pale gold hair to an extra shine, adjusting almost every strand. When he's working on it, a woman with scraped-back hair, in head-to-toe Armani, comes over to introduce herself. She's named Diane, and she's in charge of Viper's advertising campaign. She's very quiet and very intense, and everyone else in the room seems as scared of her as I am. She is the client today and the most important person in the place after Rudolf. However, even Diane seems to love my hair and makeup. Good.

Next, a much younger girl in an old sweatshirt and jeans comes over. She's Jo, the chief stylist, whose job is to look after my outfit. With a smile, she holds out a fairly small, flat box.

"You're gonna love this," she says. "It's from Myla, it's pure French lace, and it cost a couple hundred dollars. And you get to keep it!" She removes some tissue paper and lifts it carefully out of the box. It is flesh-colored, delicate, and, in its way, very beautiful. There is only one teeny problem with it.

IT is teeny. It's a thong. I could easily fit it in the palm of my hand.

There's a slight pause while the model (that would be me) does a double take. This season was all about volume. Everything I've worn on shoots so far has involved large amounts of voluminous fabric. This scrap of lace would fit through a buttonhole of a Miss Teen coat.

"I think there must be a mistake," I whisper.

"No mistake," Jo says. "Sexy, no? Shame no one's going to see it. It'll be covered in snakes. I've just seen 'em out there. Buckets of them."

This is a big relief.

"Are you sure? I mean, *sure*? I'll be covered up completely?"

"Oh, yeah. This is just to give you the right feeling."

O-kaaay. What sort of feeling is a lacy thong supposed to give you? Apart from discomfort. I keep staring at it in the box. It will categorically be the smallest thing I have ever worn.

Jake announces he's finished with my hair for the time being. It's time to get dressed. In the thong. There is nothing else.

"Want me to help you on with it?" Jo asks.

"NO!" I cough. "I mean, no, thank you. I'll manage."

"Be careful with it. That lace is delicate, you know?"

How does anyone help someone on with a THONG? I really don't want to know. There seem to be loads of people hanging about in the changing area, so I slip into the bathroom and put it on there, very carefully, all by myself. Then I wrap myself back up in the huge terry-cloth bathrobe they gave me and wonder how on earth people like Cally Harvest wear thongs to school every day for pleasure.

It would be so great if Ava were here now, to tease me about it and show me how to make it marginally less uncomfortable. I'll just have to remember the moment, so I can describe it in all its gory detail when I get home. Hopefully it will cheer her up a bit after the whole Jesse fiasco. I wonder how she's feeling about it now.

But I don't have time to think about it too much. By the time I'm ready, Rudolf has got the set prepared to his satisfaction. I go over to the bathtub, which is now half full of thin, rubbery snakes, with another couple of buckets of them on standby. Certainly enough to cover me up. I have never been so glad to see so many fake reptiles. Only trouble is — how do I get under them without everybody staring?

Jo senses my embarrassment, and somehow manages to get Eric, Rudolf, Diane, and the technicians to wait on the other side of the room. I like her slightly more now. She holds up the bathrobe for me as a screen while I step in and snuggle under the snakes, then she heaps more of them on top of me until I'm pretty much buried in them. Actually, now it's not so bad. They're warm under the lights and they cover me like a comfortable duvet. After my rubbish night, it would be fabulous to just lie here and go to sleep. But you don't get paid this much money for falling asleep in the bath.

"Ready?" Eric calls.

"Uh-huh," Jo calls back.

Gradually, everyone heads back to the set. I keep snuggled while Eric checks the light levels and Rudolf orders his assistants around, barking instructions.

I'm in a studio in Manhattan, lit by a dozen lights and hi-tech reflectors. Miranda is on hand to check that my face has the perfect level of shimmer. Jake is watching my hair like a hawk, in case a strand gets out of place. Jo is carefully arranging snakes around me. Now Rudolf is having a muttered conversation with Diane, occasionally glancing in my direction.

So this is what it's like to be a top model. Hot, nerve-wracking — and quite smelly; those rubber snakes are getting ripe under the lights. In fact, I'm just starting to wonder whether I can do it when Eric calls for the sound track to be changed. It switches from jazz to a familiar New Wave drumbeat. Oh my goodness: Blondie — just for me. The room is suddenly filled with Debbie Harry singing "Rapture." Eric catches my eye and winks at me. This is exactly what I needed: New York and Daisy combined. He's a seriously lovely guy.

We're ready. Diane sits by the monitor, poised to check the shots as Rudolf takes them.

"OK!" he says. "Ted, this is where you give me that viper stare. Show me why you're the hottest girl in New York. Sit up a bit. More shoulder. Let's have some fun here."

It's tricky, propping myself up among the snakes, making sure the right amounts of knee and shoulder are showing, and ensuring my eyes are reflecting the lights properly. When I'm ready, I empty my head of everything except Xena and flash him the warrior look.

Rudolf smiles back, but his expression is polite, rather than ecstatic. Oh.

After a few shots, he goes to join Diane at the monitor. She looks very prim in her smart jacket and French-braided hair. *She* should try sitting in a bath in a thong. She and Rudolf talk in low voices for a moment or two. They don't sound like happy low voices.

"OK, people, we need to get rid of some of the snakes," Rudolf announces. "Ted looks like she's drowning in oil here."

I breathe a sigh of relief. At least it wasn't my fault. Eric comes over, smiles at me apologetically, and gently scoops a few snakes out of the bath. Rudolf checks through his viewfinder.

"More. More. Still looking like oil."

Eric scoops. The pile of snakes on the floor beside him keeps growing, and another technician quickly moves in to get them out of the way. My rubber duvet becomes more of a blanket. My upper chest starts to show, as do my legs, up to the thigh, and some of my stomach. I take a quick peek at my body. It's the equivalent of being in a bikini. A strapless bikini. At least no one can see the thong. I think. But now Eric's gone and I'm looking at the camera again for Rudolf, trying to give him that magic shot of my eyes.

Concentrate. Concentrate, Viper Girl.

We get through several Blondie songs, but Rudolf still isn't really happy.

"OK, I'm bored now, baby. Don't glare at me, *smolder*. This Viper Girl isn't an ice queen, she's a volcano. Smolder at me, baby."

I pause, confused. I've never been a volcano before, and when I try and imagine it the first image that comes to mind is too-spicy Thai takeout. Surely that's not what Rudolf's after. "Volcano" feels a lot like "vamping," and that wasn't exactly my finest moment. This isn't what it felt like with Eric. This is bigger and more complicated and altogether more . . . exposed. I *wish* Tina were here to give me inspiration. And maybe she could explain about her brother. Surely she wouldn't lie to my parents about something that important? It's still bothering me.

"Focus!" Rudolf calls. "Where are you, Viper Girl? Look at me. Come on, honey — smolder! What's the problem?"

I'm glad he's asked. "Actually," I say, "I imagined this girl more like a warrior than a volcano. You know — brave, and hot, of course, but not too . . ."

Sleazy. I mean sleazy. Can I say sleazy?

"Not too what?" Rudolf asks in very clipped tones. He's not showing his teeth for once because he's not smiling at me now. Not at all.

"Too . . . smoldery."

Smoldery. What a stupid word. No wonder he's frowning.

"OK," he says, in a tone I haven't heard before. "We'll do it your way. How *you* imagined her. Because the editor of *Elle* hired you to do a shoot last month, didn't she? Because *you've* just got back from shooting ten pages for Russian *Vogue* in Siberia. Oh wait, no. That was me."

He laughs, and the crew laughs with him.

I feel exactly the way I felt back on Knicker Day. Or, actually, a thousand times worse. My eyes are stinging. I honestly didn't think I'd ever feel that way again. Where is Xena when I need her? Miranda comes over and pretends to fiddle with my glitter.

"Ignore him," she whispers. "He gets very sensitive. But you need to go with his vision. It'll be lovely, promise."

So I go back to trying to smolder, ignoring the fact that snakes are falling off me left, right, and center, and that the smell of hot rubber is making me feel slightly sick, and that if only I could do my warrior stare properly, I'm sure we'd get a much better picture. Rudolf runs off a few more frames, but he keeps going over to the monitor and looking disappointed.

"I'm sorry!" I call out. "I'm sorry. I've lost it. Can . . . can we stop for a minute?"

He sighs, checks his watch, and puts the camera down. It's obvious that I'm wasting everyone's very valuable time.

Jo, the stylist, comes over. "What do you need, babe? Can I get you anything?"

I shake my head. "Just my robe." She holds it for me while I climb out of the tub and head for the changing room. Diane joins us there, smoothing down her Armani skirt and looking worried.

"What's the problem? Aren't you feeling well?" she asks.

"This isn't what I expected," I explain. "He wants some-thing . . . different. I know how to be a warrior, but not a volcano. I'm not sure I can do this."

"Of course you can!" Diane says firmly. "You can do more than one expression, surely? You really shone in those test shots. You're perfect for the brand. You've just got to be professional, that's all."

There's an edge to her voice now, too. But she sees the look in my eyes, and the wobble on my lip, and somehow she squeezes out an encouraging smile.

"Come on! You'll enjoy it." She stretches out a hand to flick a tear from the corner of my eye. "Thousands of girls would crawl over their grandmothers to work with Rudolf. I know it feels like he's pushing you, but that's because he wants a great pic-ture. It's not just an ad campaign — it's art. You just have to be brave and take a risk, Ted. That's how you get noticed."

Five minutes and three chocolate-dipped strawberries later, I'm back under the lights, having my hair and makeup tweaked, and being professional. The snakes are rearranged over me. Not so many snakes now. Maybe a string bikini's worth. A crotcheted string bikini. I look down to check that nothing's showing and it isn't — just. But even Dad hasn't seen me in this little covering since I was small. If Dean Daniels could . . . Ew. Sick, definitely. The thought makes me nauseous. And they want to put the picture on the back of a million magazines . . .

Eric gives Rudolf a thumbs-up. Blondie goes back up to full volume.

"Better," Rudolf says. "Go again. OK now, gorgeous, I'm getting the scary glare. Enough of that. I need more smolder. Think of your boyfriend. Think of that good-bye kiss he gave you . . ."

Out of nowhere, I think of Nick. I instantly remember every word of his call last night, and how wrong he was about Ava, and how furious he made me. Rudolf looks up from his camera, horrified. "OK, not him. We need something . . . someone . . . Who's hot around here?"

"Hey!" Diane giggles, still staring straight into the monitor. I had no idea she could giggle. She's so not the giggling type. "No need to ask, Rude."

Everyone laughs. I wonder why. Then I catch sight of Eric out of the corner of my eye. He's shrugging and looking slightly embarrassed, but only slightly. He's clearly used to being told how cute he is, and I'm not surprised, because he really is the most adorable —

"THERE! That's IT!" Rudolf whips the camera back into position and starts snapping. "How does that look, Diane? Hold it there, baby."

He goes over to check the monitor again, while I try to maintain my expression. I do my best. I really do. I think of the money. I try to pretend I'm not staring at the fiancé of some supermodel I've never met, and that a room full of fashion professionals now know that I secretly fancy him. And that I'm not doing semi-naked in a bath of smelly fake reptiles. While wearing a lacy thong. And pretending to be a volcano. And that I'm not TOTALLY MORTIFIED.

I want to be professional. I tell my brain to tell my eyes to smolder. Instead, my brain goes off on its own and thinks about Ava. She said exactly the same thing to Jesse that she said to me: *Go do what you want to do — it's better this way.* But she didn't mean it about Jesse — she missed him desperately while he was away. So of course she didn't mean it about me, either. She's frightened and alone right now, and she needs me more than ever. And instead here I am, practically nude, in a bath full of hot snakes, "smoldering," because I somehow got talked into "finding myself." I mean, honestly. Where was I?

And then suddenly it hits me.

From the moment I put that thong on, I've been disappearing.

I'm in a room full of people and they're all staring at my face and body as if their lives depended on it (and maybe their jobs really do), and none of them understands how I feel. This isn't like working with Eric, or the kite-tail designer. I might as well be a piece of expensive fruit.

Meanwhile, my sister is coping with chemo, radiotherapy, that terrible "ten percent," and a broken heart, with only my parents for company. Mum will no doubt be crying. I can hardly bear to think what Dad will have broken by now. Without Jesse, I'm all Ava has. The warrior princesses. We were starting to make a real team.

"Oh, COME ON!" Rudolf says, coming back from the monitor and looking through his viewfinder again. "Concentrate! It's one simple expression, baby. Surely even your tiny brain cells can process it for ten shots!"

My "tiny brain" is getting angry now, but I can't help more tears of frustration from forming. The lens picks them up instantly. Rudolf hands the camera to an assistant and storms off, exasperated. "Deal with her and tell me when she's ready."

I think I just found myself.

I ask Jo for my robe again. Turns out Daisy was right about "standing around in your undies" after all. I loved being Xena, but Xena doesn't do this. Any day that starts with a self-conscious girl and a lacy thong is liable to end badly. Diane was right, too: I just have to be brave and take a risk.

THIRTY-SEVEN

An hour later, I'm on a ferry that goes around Liberty Island, with sea spray in my hair and tourists staring first at my green-and-gold face, then at the Statue of Liberty, then back at me. It's New York. Anything goes.

I get out my fancy new iPhone to dial Ava's number. But she's not answering, so I call home.

"Hello?" Dad's voice. I could cry with relief.

"Hi," I say, sounding as cheerful as I can.

"Ted? Is that you? How's it going?"

"Fabulous," I lie firmly. I don't want to have this conversation right now. "Where's Ava?"

"She went out," Dad says. "Ages ago. She seemed very . . . Don't worry about it. Have a great time, love."

Oh, God — Ava's so bad that he's trying to spare me by not talking about it.

"Will do. Tell her . . . Give her lots of love from me and tell her I'll see her as soon as I can. And Dad? She's got this new thing for butterscotch ice cream. Can you make sure we've got some in the fridge?"

"Of course. Butterscotch. Bye, love," Dad says, sounding puzzled. He doesn't like long-distance phone calls. I think a part of him still lives in Civil War times. Complicated technology makes him nervous. Plus, why did I call him from New York to talk about ice cream? Poor Dad. I can't explain it to him right now. Ava needs a whole lot more than the right flavor of ice cream, but from this far away, it's the best I can do.

I put the phone back in the new Mulberry tote that I *so* haven't earned, and slump back into my seat on the ferry. I'm not Xena anymore. I've used up all her energy and she's gone. Instead, I start replaying the last hour's worth of conversations in my head.

Me finding Rudolf and explaining, very politely, that I can be a warrior princess, but I can't be a sexy volcano, because I don't know how and I didn't realize what I was getting myself into, and I really have to get home because my family needs me.

Rudolf storming off again and shouting at Eric, someone, *anyone* to deal with me.

Diane, desperate, reminding me about my contract and trying to get Model City on the phone. Then Diane, disgusted, explaining exactly how much money the shoot is costing and how much *I'm* costing them with my "silly, selfish, juvenile, unprofessional" attitude.

Eric telling me earnestly that thousands of girls would run through fire for the chance of this shoot, and assuring me that it's "artistically valid," or he wouldn't have put me up for it. Me agreeing to every point. It's just a shame that Rudolf's idea of "artistic" is my idea of "sick." In a bad way.

Rudolf, storming back in, seeing me still in my robe, threatening to sue Model City *and* me, and shouting at me that he'll personally see to it that I never work again. I'm just a *model*. I do what I'm *told*. Without the photographer, the model is *nothing*. He can't have his whole schedule turned upside down because the stupid girl wasn't *listening* when the shoot was explained to her.

Diane, on the phone, already trying to book another model at short notice.

Miranda saying, "This way."

She guided me back into the changing room and found my clothes for me. She offered to help take the makeup off, but I was too desperate to get out of the building to wait. As I dragged my jeans and sweater on, she was full of reassuring noises about how I'd get over it, and so would Rudolf, and it was just his temperamental genius that made him do all that shouting. Then she hugged me to her, just like Mum, and kissed the top of my head.

If I ever worked in New York again — which I never will — she's the makeup girl I'd ask for. She's the one who told me about the ferry, slipped me some dollars, and suggested I sneak out the back door to get some air. She was right. I really don't need the others flapping around me right now, reminding me how much trouble I'm in.

The ferry trip is just what I need to start breathing again after what happened in the studio. The sea spray cools my face. The chugging noise of the boat is reassuring. And Lady Liberty herself reminds me that a woman can look bold and brave and inspirational without having to smolder, or do it in a thong. I'd look ridiculous in a bikini anyway: three triangles on a plank of wood. What *was* Simon thinking when he spotted me?

When we return to the ferry terminal, I still feel the need for fresh air. I decide to walk up through Manhattan, following my nose toward the model flat. I buy a hot chocolate to keep the cold out, and after about fifteen minutes' walking I stumble across a little patch of grass and trees, where I can sit down and finish drinking it.

There's a woman already sitting on the only bench, with an enormous plastic bag beside her. She's enormous, too. Her hair is matted, her face isn't tanned, as I thought at first, but ingrained with dirt. There's an "interesting" smell coming from her direction and I'm guessing it's not Viper. She's guarding the plastic bag with dogged determination, probably because it contains everything she owns.

I ask if I can sit beside her, and she nods. We recognize each other: two strange people in a strange city, making our own choices — sometimes wrong ones — and not taking grief from anyone. She even smiles.

"Nice hair," she says, passing the time.

I offer her what's left of my hot chocolate.

"Nice socks," I tell her.

They're long, with multicolored stripes. Over them, she's wearing red shorts that come down to her knees and electric-blue clogs. She should be wearing a coat in this cold weather, but instead she's making do with several hoodies, worn in layers, and matching scarves. I don't know where she found them, but they match the colors of the stripes on her socks and even — when I look further — in the right order. Nestling in her hair is a small felt hat with a flower. She looks like a very well-put-together clown.

"Nice outfit altogether," I admit.

She stares at me.

"You German?"

"No."

"French?"

"No."

"Italian?"

"No. English."

"Uh-huh." She stares at me. I can't believe my accent sounded French or Italian, but I guess you never know. Whatever it is, I'm not what she expected.

"Easy on the eyes," she adds.

"I'm sorry?"

But she doesn't answer. She said it as if it was a warning. Does she mean I'm easy to look at and that's a problem? Or that I should do something about my eyes? I suddenly remember that they're still covered in glittery snake makeup. I probably look like I should be clubbing, not going for a walk in the park.

She finishes the hot chocolate, shifts closer to her bag, and stares resolutely ahead. There's something grand about her. Undefeated.

"Erm, I hate to be rude," I say, "but would you mind . . . Could I possibly take your picture?"

I pull out the iPhone that Model City gave me. It has all the latest features and a great camera.

"Be my guest," she says with a low, rumbling laugh. "They do it all the time."

I crouch down a short distance away and take a few shots of her with the bag and the bench, but mostly trying to bring out the incredible way she plays with color.

"Nice meeting you," I add. Simon and Tina have very narrow vision. If I were picking someone to take photographs of today, it would definitely be this lady, not me. "And if you don't mind me saying, I think you look . . . amazing."

"Right on, sister," she says, smiling.

I put the phone back in my bag and, to my surprise, find I'm grinning. It's just occurred to me that I spent most of today at the wrong end of the camera. But at least I managed to rescue it in the end.

THIRTY-EIGHT

When I get back to the model apartment in the late afternoon, Frankie calls from London, asking what's gone wrong. Whatever I've done, it's too late to change it now. I tell her I want to go home as soon as possible so I can get back to my sister. Frankie agrees. After the way I behaved today, I don't think she trusts me to go to any go-sees and we both seem to agree that I'm better off in London than here.

Somehow, she gets me on the last flight out of JFK. By the time I find out the details it's after midnight in the UK and too late to call home, so I send Mum a text with my flight times. When she gets it, I'll probably be halfway there.

I'm busy squishing everything back into my suitcase when my phone goes again. I grab it, wondering if Ava has somehow got hold of my new number, but no: It's Tina, at LAX Airport, waiting for her flight back to New York from LA.

"Princess, tell me that didn't just happen."

I tell her it did.

"But nobody walks out on RUDOLF REISSEN. The guy's a genius!"

"I couldn't do what he wanted," I tell her. "I'm sorry."

"That's not what I heard. I heard you had your own ideas. You were trying to tell him what to do. NOBODY tells Rudolf what to do. Especially not some girl I picked out of the gutter."

"I was not in the gutter!" I protest. "I was at Somerset House. It's a historic building."

"It was the gutter compared to where you are now, baby. Or where you were this afternoon. I put you on top of the world. What were you — suicidal?"

"Tina," I break in, suddenly remembering, "about your brother —"

"What brother? Oh, him."

"Was he really —?"

"Ted, I don't have time for him right now. I only have time for . . . HOW UNGRATEFUL YOU WERE. And how spoiled. And how much you've wasted everything I've done for you. I can't believe it. I'm shaking. I'm literally standing here in the middle of LAX, shaking. I'm not sure I'll get over this."

She is quite frightening when she's annoyed. Her voice has gone up several notches and her Brooklyn accent is very strong. There's no hint of Rio or Rome now. But there's more than a hint of anger. Even so, I really need to understand about her brother. You don't invent someone with a brain tumor just to make someone go to a modeling appointment, surely? I mean, I'm living with someone with a serious disease; it's not something you mess around with.

"Can you just tell me his name?" I ask.

"Oh, for God's sake. I'm ending this call!" she shouts. "But you haven't heard the last of this, Ted Richmond. Believe me. I haven't even STARTED to finish with you yet."

She did. She invented someone with a brain tumor.

Wow. *That's* how she performs her miracles: by doing whatever it takes. I admire her tremendously — I really do. I just never want to see her again.

The plane takes off into the dark skies over the city. Soon afterward, I'm flying high above the ocean. I spend the flight not sleeping — undoing all those dreams I had in the days before I came over. The shops I was going to visit on Fifth Avenue. The people I was going to meet at Zac Posen and Vera Wang. The things I was going to buy. Why couldn't I just smolder? The money was going to change my life, and now I can't even afford a new phone. Oh, wait. I still have my Miss Teen money. But what if Rudolf sues me? *Can* he sue me? There were all those people rushing about, costing all that money. It could wipe my new savings out in a moment. What if I'm broke?

And I abandoned Ava to get myself into this mess. My sister with cancer. Nick Spoke said I was evil — actually, I think he implied I was beyond evil. Why do I cry every time I think of Nick? He was so thoughtless and mean. He has no idea about me, and he never tried to find out. I hate him so much.

I wish Mum could be sitting here beside me. She'd be telling me off for something, probably, but it would still be better than how I'm feeling now. Better still, I wish Ava were here. I'm not used to trying to get to sleep without her anymore. We thought it was so terrible when we had to share a bedroom — Ava especially — but we've done so much talking at night. It's how I've gotten to know her. It's how she's talked me into most of my stupid adventures. If I'd been at home, I could have told her how silly she was being about Jesse. I could have comforted her. I could have made it OK somehow. And, somehow, she'd have made it OK for me, too.

The flight attendant keeps coming over to check on me. She can obviously tell that something's not right, but I huddle under my blanket and pretend to be asleep. At least there's one good thing about not "getting known transatlantically": I'll never have to cram myself into one of these airline seats again.

Mum calls me as the plane is pulling into its gate at Heathrow Airport.

"Ted! Where are you? What happened?"

"I'm fine," I tell her, wondering whether "fine" is an accurate description of how I feel right now, which is aching, scared, and angry with myself. "How's Ava?"

"Oh," Mum sighs. "It's pretty bad. I think Jesse broke up with her. After he left she just . . . shut down. But what about you?"

I try to find the words to describe the last couple of days, but "They didn't get the photo" doesn't seem to cover it, and anything else just seems too complicated.

"Can I tell you when I see you?" I ask.

"All right," Mum says. "I've got to work, but your dad's here. And Ava will be back from the hospital later. Maybe you can talk to her."

Suddenly my heart is in my mouth.

"Hospital?" She didn't have a radiation treatment booked today.

"It's the ceremony," Mum says. "Remember? It's starting around now. Anyway, are they sending someone to pick you up?"

With everything that's happened, I'd forgotten that the head-shaving ceremony was this morning. Oh, yeah: "not being there for a bunch of kids with cancer." Go me. Except maybe I've still got a chance. I think of the glamorous New York limos. If I'm lucky, the car might be able to get me there before the styling session finishes. I could at least take a picture or two to help out.

I tell Mum the plan and she likes it. But it takes ages to get through passport control, and this time no one is waiting for me. No man with a sign. No limo. Of course no limo. Why would they send a limo for the "stupid girl who wasn't listening"? The one with the "silly, selfish, juvenile, unprofessional attitude"?

I dig out my old handbag from the bottom of my suitcase, extract my trusty metro card, and head for the Underground.

I have never known a Tube train to travel so slowly. It seems to take pleasure in stopping between stations, just to spite me. As the minutes tick by, I imagine Vince and his team performing their head-shaving transformations on the four patients we've been talking to, then the styling session with Ava, then the families wrapping themselves around their children, admiring their new looks and taking them home.

As soon as I get to the hospital, I drag my suitcase up the steps and race toward the day ward where the ceremony was due to take place. But I was right: The room is silent and empty. Only the heady smell of scented candles still lingers in the air. Along with the cheerful Christmas decorations, there might as well be a banner up saying TOO LATE.

One of Ava's scarves lies abandoned on a chair. I pick it up and it smells of her perfume. I was going to buy her more perfume in New York — something else I didn't do. As I stand there, holding the scarf and hating myself, Vince appears in the doorway. He immediately walks over and envelops me in a bear hug.

"Darling creature! You look incredible! Check out your *hair*! But you missed the most gorgeous event. It was beautiful. Quite beautiful."

"I bet it was," I sigh. "How was Ava?"

"Marvelous. What a star. But, my God, so exhausted. That must be why she —" He stops and lowers his voice. "It hasn't *spread*, has it?"

I shake my head. "We don't know yet. The thing is, she's just dumped her boyfriend."

"The fool!"

"I know."

"Someone needs to sort her out."

"I know."

He puts a hand on my shoulder. "Do you want me to take you to her?"

"To her? Is she still here?"

At this point, a nurse pops her head through the door. I recognize her from my earlier visits. She nods at me.

"You got here very quickly," she says.

"Well, actually, I'm late. I —"

"I'm glad she called you. Don't be alarmed: She's not as bad as she looks."

Don't be alarmed? And as bad as what? The panic I felt back at the airport when Mum mentioned the hospital instantly returns. It's like it's always lying in wait, ready to strike, making up for all the times we should have noticed something serious and didn't. What's she still doing here?

The nurse motions to me to go with her. I abandon Vince and my suitcase in the day room, and follow her rapidly down a couple of corridors.

"She was brilliant just now," the nurse says chattily, "but as soon as everyone left she just collapsed. It's probably her red-cell count again. She's having a rest while we check it out. Here we are."

She opens the door to a side room, where there's nothing but a bed and a chair. Ava's lying on the bed with her clothes on. Her skin is quite colorless, and her eyes are closed. She doesn't move when I come in. Her beautiful face looks infinitely sad. I perch on the chair beside her and wonder how the medical profession can't tell the difference between a low red-cell count and lovesickness. It seems obvious to me. Mind you, it could be both. Who knows what's going on inside my sister?

The nurse smiles and leaves us in privacy. I take Ava's hand and stroke it gently. Instantly, her eyelids flicker. She opens them slowly.

"You're here," she whispers, and she gives me the ghost of her movie-star smile. Then she frowns. "Why, though? Are you OK?"

"Don't be silly." I don't know whether to laugh or cry. "Of course I'm OK. Are you OK?"

She squeezes my hand weakly. "Better now. Sorry about this. Don't tell Mum."

"What? That you fainted?"

She nods. "I was going to call Dad to come and get me, but now you're here. No need to worry them."

I laugh. She's her usual stubborn, determined, generous self — wonderful and annoying in equal measure.

"You've got cancer, Ava. They're worried, trust me."

She sighs. "Good point. I don't want to worry them *more*. Anyway . . . like I was saying . . . you're here. Shouldn't you be in New York?"

"Buying your Marc Jacobs bag? Yes, I should. Sorry."

She gives me the movie-star smile again and lays her head back on the pillow. Her face relaxes and loses some of its pale fragility. And finally, I know for certain: She doesn't want me to be in New York, shopping at Marc Jacobs, and she doesn't care why I changed my mind. She just needs me to be with her, and she's too tired to pretend otherwise anymore.

"It was good, you know," she says softly, thinking back to this morning's ceremony. "Vince made everyone look amazing, and feel it, too, just like we did. I'd like to do more of that kind of thing, maybe . . ."

She trails off. Serious Ava. She's still not quite sure about this new aspect to her personality. I know some young cancer patients who are extremely grateful for it, though. And someone else who probably doesn't mind it as much as she thinks.

"You look wiped out," I say.

"Thanks. You don't look so great yourself."

I giggle. "It was a long flight. Tell me when you're ready and I'll take you home."

"Now, please."

With perfect timing, the nurse comes back to say that Ava's red-cell count isn't the problem.

"You can go, but I hope you're not coming down with something," she says sternly. "We need you in good form for radiotherapy next week."

I look at Ava again. All the brightness has gone out of her. I wonder what the cure is for idiotically breaking up with the one person who gave you hope for the future. She still looks frail — not ready for London public transportation. This is when a waiting limo would really come in handy. I can't help thinking that what Nick Spoke would do at this moment is call up the cab company and get one on his mother's account. But I'm not Nick Spoke, thank goodness. We'll just have to make do with a taxi, paid for out of what's left of my travel money.

As we gather up our things, I sense that something's bothering me. It's to do with Nick. But so much about Nick bothers me that I can't pin it down. Passing one of the nurses' stations, I catch sight of our reflections in a pane of glass: two distracted warrior princesses with stuff on their minds. I'm thinking about Nick; Ava's thinking about Jesse. Then it clicks. That cure. I know what it is — or, at least, I know what it could be.

I wait until we're safely in a cab. The tricky bit is going to be persuading Ava to go along with my unlikely plan. I decide to take a page out of her book and try lying. I know I'm not good at it, but I think she's still too depressed to notice, and I might as well take advantage while I can.

"There were a couple of things I needed to straighten out with Model City," I say as casually as I can. "Do you mind coming with me? It's sort of on the way home."

Ava agrees without really thinking. I explain that, since it's the weekend, Cassandra has asked to see me at her house instead of the office, and I give the driver the address near Buckingham Palace. Ava shrugs. I'm actually praying that

Cassandra *isn't* there. I really, really don't want to see her right now, but it's a risk I've just got to take.

We don't talk much in the taxi. Ava's too wrapped up in her blanket of post-Jesse misery, and I have too much else on my mind. When we draw up outside the big Georgian house, I leap out and promise I won't be long.

Please, please let him be in. Please, let him know the answer to my question. Please let his mother be out.

Eugenia, Cassandra's housekeeper, opens the door.

"Yes? Can I help you?"

"Is Nick in?" I ask.

"No. Sorry."

All the air sighs out of me. Not that I particularly want to see Nick Spoke again, ever, but I need to, if this is going to work.

"You don't know where he is, do you? I've tried his phone," which I have, in the taxi — "but I think it must be off or something."

Eugenia purses her lips and shakes her head. "I've no idea. He left the house fifteen minutes ago. But they didn't say where they were going. The other one had his bag with him, though, if that helps."

It takes a moment for the thought to process, but then I grin at her.

"Thanks. Yes. It does."

I rush back to the taxi and ask the driver in a low voice which station trains go to Cornwall from.

"Paddington," he says. "Want me to take you there?"

"Yes, please."

Back in the cab, Ava is still silent and morose. She watches the London sights pass by without showing much interest. It reminds me that I didn't get to see much of New York, apart from the Statue of Liberty, and that's quite a long way to go to see one statue. I'm going to have to find a way of going back again one day to fill in the gaps.

"Hey, wait a minute!" Ava says after a while. "This isn't the way home. This is Marble Arch! Where are you taking us, T?"

She's getting some of her energy back. Enough to stare at me accusingly, anyway. I definitely preferred tender, smiling Ava. Then she sees the road the taxi takes off the roundabout and her eyes narrow even farther.

"*I* know where this road goes. Wait! I came this way to see Jesse off last time. We're not going to Paddington, are we?"

"Yes," I say, as defiantly as I can manage.

"Why?"

"Because he's there. At least I think he is. He might be. You have to see him, Ava."

"I certainly don't. How *dare* you, T? You swan around New York and you think it gives you the right to mess around with my life? And how do you know about me and Jesse anyway?"

"Long story," I sigh. "But, listen, I did a lot of thinking and you need to hear him out. I bet you didn't give him the chance to say how he felt about you."

"Well maybe I don't want to," she hisses angrily. "Maybe there are some things it's better not to hear. Turn this taxi round. I need to go home. Now. Do it."

A few months ago, I would have done it. A few weeks ago, even. But this time·I've had enough. This time I think my big sister needs to listen to someone other than the frightened voice inside her head.

"Talk to him," I plead. "Don't ask me how I know it's worth it, but trust me. Please? Just trust me?"

She looks at me sadly for a long time, before reaching out a hand to stroke my smooth, shiny hair.

"It's too late," she says. "But thanks for trying, I suppose. There are just a lot of things you don't understand."

The driver pulls up outside Paddington Station and, after paying out most of my travel money to him and dragging my suitcase out of the cab, I manage to persuade Ava to come as far as the station concourse with me. She doesn't have much choice, because I don't think either of us has enough cash left to pay for a taxi home from here. In fact, when we get inside she heads slowly for the entrance to the Underground, reaching into her bag for her metro card. Meanwhile I wildly check the departures board. There's a train leaving for Penzance in seven minutes from Platform 3. That must be the one.

"Wait!" I call to her.

Ava turns to look at me. I'm guessing I have about one minute to spot Jesse in the crowd of people heading for the train before she heads down the escalator to the Underground and out of sight.

I look around frantically for Jesse's sun-bleached hair and tanned face. Thank goodness he's the kind of guy to stand out in a crowd. Except . . . he isn't in this one. Wherever I look, there are just pale-skinned, dark-haired people. Loads of them. He would shine out like a beacon if he were here, but —

"Ted?"

I whip around.

Nick Spoke, one of the pale-skinned, dark-haired people, has materialized from the crowd and is gaping at me like I've just landed from space or something. I'd sort of forgotten he'd be here, too — or at least tried to keep it out of my mind. But here he is, in a thick navy coat and scuffed boots, looking sad and tired behind his glasses.

"What are you doing here?" he asks.

"Looking for Jesse," I say desperately. "Ava's here, but not for long. Where is he?"

Nick glances over my shoulder and catches sight of my ghostly sister, hovering in the middle of the concourse, about to turn and go.

"Hang on!" he shouts.

Ava sees him and looks surprised. She looks even more surprised when he darts off and leaps over one of the ticket barriers, swiftly pursued by a station official in uniform, before running full tilt down the side of the train. We both watch as he slows about halfway down the train and starts peering into the windows of the car. He beats his fists on one of them and shouts loudly. Moments later, Jesse appears with a big duffel bag, jumping down from the train doorway and tearing back up the platform with Nick in his wake.

At this point, the station official catches up with Nick and puts a heavy hand on his shoulder. Nick urges Jesse on, and he quickly heads back through the barriers, spotting first me and then Ava. He rushes toward her as if he's about to rescue her from an oncoming train. Meanwhile, the one he was supposed to be on pulls slowly out of the station in the opposite direction.

Ava doesn't move. She stares at Jesse, utterly confused. He throws his bag down and squeezes all the breath out of her.

He bends his head to ask her something, but before she can answer he shuts her up with the longest, sloppiest kiss I've ever seen my sister publicly indulge in. She tries to resist at first, but soon she gives in to the inevitable, and after a while she's kissing him back, fiercely, making up for all that time when she was . . . well, when she was incredibly stupid and didn't realize how much he loved her. But that's the thing: Sometimes you just don't know how much other people need you. Sometimes it takes someone else to make you understand.

It hurts, I know, until you realize where you're wanted. If Nick hadn't called me in New York, I wouldn't have found out what Ava was going through in time. He was still mean and pigheaded and didn't know what he was doing. But it's thanks to him that we're here, I suppose.

He extracts himself from the clutches of two very burly officials, and heads in my direction.

"Right," he says with an embarrassed cough, still panting slightly. "So, you're back."

"Yes," I say tightly. I am "evil," after all.

"Good time in New York?"

"No."

"You're home sooner than I expected."

"Really?"

He pauses. I glance across at him. Even his *coat* has flecks of paint on it. What does he do? Work in the garden? Use his studio as a closet? What?

"Look, Ted, I'm sorry if I said things . . . Anyway, it worked out. He'd waited all this time . . . Thank you for bringing her."

Yes, it worked out. The way Jesse is kissing my sister, there is no way he ever looked twice at any of the Red-Bikini Babes. Even now Ava looks gorgeous, in a big, furry vintage coat of Mum's and a massive red wool hat. It helps that she's melting into the arms of a stunning blond surfer god, of course. They make a gorgeous couple.

Nick and I stand there, waiting, while they finish their reunion. Then they smile at each other, Ava giggles, and they come over to join us.

"Well, I've totally missed that train," Jesse says, "so I might as well enjoy London. Where shall we go?"

"Come back to my place," Nick suggests. "Mum's working, as usual. But Eugenia'll cook for us. We can hang out there all day if you like."

Ava grins. Right now, she's happy to be anywhere that Jesse is. "What do you think, Ted?"

"Enjoy it," I tell her, picking up my suitcase. "I'll see you at home later."

Nick looks as if he's about to say something, but he just stares. First at my eyes. Then at my gleaming gold hair. It's time to go.

I wish them all good-bye and head for the Underground by myself, dragging my suitcase behind me. Ava calls after me, but I pretend not to hear her. Now that she's OK, I finally realize how bone-tired I am. I need sleep and I need to be by myself. I certainly don't need to spend any more time hanging out with rumple-headed, paint-flecked boys in glasses who think I "take the cake."

It's only lunchtime, but it's already been a very long day.

THIRTY-NINE

When I get home, I curl up in Ava's bed. I always thought I'd hate sharing, but the room now seems so empty without her. I spend most of the afternoon sleeping. In the evening, I briefly give Mum and Dad a few more details about the shoot. I was sure they'd be furious with me for being unprofessional and walking out on a job, but instead they seem . . . impressed.

"Darling, you're amazing!" Mum grins at me over supper (where my plate is loaded with extra potatoes, just because I can). "After we stupidly let you go all that way on your own. I can't believe that woman talked us into it. But look at what you did, all by yourself. I had no idea you were so strong."

She wouldn't be saying that if she'd actually been there. I didn't feel particularly strong as I sat shaking on the Staten Island Ferry afterward.

"I wouldn't recommend it as a regular career strategy," Dad adds with a twinkle in his eye, "but I'm proud of you, love. I really don't like the sound of that photo from the way you describe it. That's not you at all."

No, it isn't. The girl Rudolf wanted would never sit at home with her parents, loading up on carbohydrates and worrying about being sued by a top photographer. She would be lying around, smoldering somewhere, or off on another plane to a new location, ready to do it all over again. She would be getting rich and famous, and one day maybe she'd have a house as big as Cassandra's, and an über-wardrobe, and possibly even a yacht.

She was never me. I have so many other things to do with my life.

Ava gets home late from Nick's house, just as I'm getting ready to go back to bed. I'm not sure what she and Jesse did all that time, but her lips look sore and chapped, and her eyes have got some of their sparkle back.

"I didn't really thank you properly," she says, popping her head through the bathroom door where I'm brushing my teeth. (With my pajamas on, I might add. I am not a naked teeth-brusher. I didn't know anybody was until I went to New York.)

"Oh, don't worry about it."

"Jesse said to thank you, too."

"Cool."

Nick probably pointed out that I'm an evil, selfish diva, just like Sheherezade. Actually, worse. He must be the person who put Jesse off models in the first place. But she doesn't mention that bit.

"By the way," she adds, "Dad says you've got an e-mail from Model City. It's probably important. D'you want me to read it to you?"

"No, thanks."

I'm really not in the mood to hear how much Rudolf's suing me for right now. But Ava ignores me. She comes back five minutes later.

"Here it is. I've got a printout. It says —"

"Stop! I don't want to know."

"Don't be silly. It's not that bad. It's from Frankie. She says she tried to get you on your phone but she couldn't."

"I turned it off."

I sensed that my old phone was filling up with messages I didn't want to see. So, apart from trying to call Nick in the taxi, I buried it in the bottom of my Mulberry handbag, and I've been avoiding it.

"Well, anyway," Ava continues, "Frankie says Cassandra's pretty annoyed with you, but not to worry, it will blow over. She says she had a girl last week who missed a whole shoot because she booked her own ticket and she flew to San Diego in California, instead of Santiago in Chile. That's quite funny, actually." She pauses to snicker.

"And?" If she insists on reading this thing out, I might as well hear the "getting sued" part.

"She says she'll contact you later in the week. Apparently, Rudolf Reissen has a certain reputation and she thought you might not be ready for him yet. Cassandra could have said so at the time, but there we go. Anyway, she'll take care of things. Oh, and she remembers me and she wants me for *Vogue Italia* when I'm better."

"REALLY?"

"No! Of course not, you idiot! God, Ted . . . sometimes . . ." Ava shakes her head in despair and her scarf wobbles dangerously. "Anyway," she adds, "I'd call her back tomorrow, if I were you. She's worried about you."

I call first thing in the morning, and Frankie tells me to delete all texts from Tina without reading them — she is famous for her texts to people who have displeased her — and wait for further news. I'm still pretty tired, so the "do nothing" option works for me. Besides, I have Ava's final week of treatment to worry about, and dealing with all the weirdness at school, so my brain feels pretty overloaded as it is.

When I get to Richmond Academy, the day seems to pass by in a jet-lagged dream. If anything, the weirdness is worse. For some reason, Cally Harvest looks dazed and upset, and spends most of the morning passing notes to her posse. Half the girls in the class stare daggers at me during gym. It can't just be because I went to New York. Boys give me strange, shy looks in the corridors, and high-five each other when they think I'm out of view. Cally's in floods of tears at lunchtime. Weirdest of all, Dean Daniels keeps grinning at me for no apparent reason.

I fall asleep during math and Daisy has to prod me awake with her pencil. By the end of the day, I'm just desperate to get home and rest.

But on the way to the bus stop, a now-familiar pair of legs falls into step beside mine. Dean gurgles and coughs. The prelude to a conversation.

"So, like, they're saying you turned down this mega-job and, like, you lost a hundred grand," he begins.

"A hundred grand?"

"So, did you?"

"No! Of course not!"

It wasn't *that* much.

"So you kept it? Cool. That's, like . . ." He pauses, searching for the right word.

"Sick?" I offer.

"Yeah, sick. And Ted," he rushes on, before I can correct him about the money, "I've been thinking. About you and me."

Oh, dear. This sounds very bad. He turns to look at me with the same lovesick-puppy expression Dad has when he thinks about Claudia Schiffer.

"What about 'us,' Dean?"

"Well, like, things between me and Cally haven't been . . . you know. And she's, like, a bit . . . So I dumped her yesterday. And, you know, you and me . . . We're, like, similar, you know? Like with art and jokes and stuff. And you're hot, so . . . What I mean is . . ."

We reach the bus stop. I put my bag down. He looks at me hopefully.

"Dean?"

"Yes?"

"You called me Ted just now, which was nice. I think that's the second time, ever, that you've used my name. Do you remember when you first met me, five years ago?"

"Er, just about." He looks shifty and fiddles with a buckle on his backpack.

"You called me E.T."

"Did I?"

"Yes. And then I grew two inches and you changed it to Freaky Friday. And everyone else called me that, too. In fact, I think there are still some people in our class who don't know my real name."

"Er, right."

"And I didn't like those names, Dean. I really didn't. Whereas Cally . . . Well, Cally has your initials tattooed on her neck."

"So?"

He can see this is leading somewhere — he's just not sure where.

"So, what I'm trying to say is that Cally is probably still the girl for you. And no, I didn't keep a hundred grand. I didn't get any money. I'm not a model, OK? I never really was. And to be perfectly honest, I fancy someone else. Not that it matters."

"Oh, right. Cool." He won't catch my eye, but he looks, if anything, slightly relieved. I think I came across as a bit scary. I am, after all, the girl who reminds her own mother of a Royal Marine.

"But no hard feelings?" he says, perking up a bit. "You can't blame a man for trying. 'Cause you're, like, quite a cool chick now, if you don't mind me saying."

"No hard feelings, Dean. And no, I don't mind you saying."

He holds out his hand. This feels totally bizarre, but I shake it. Then he wanders off and leaves me standing at the bus stop, staring after him, wondering if I really just said all that stuff. And how come, if I'm such a cool chick now, I still feel so depressed?

★

When I get home, Dad's sitting at the dining table, trying to fix the toaster.

"Dad! What happened this time?"

He grins at me. A huge grin. Much too big for someone who's just broken one of the most vital pieces of family equipment.

"I was making a celebratory grilled cheese sandwich. I forgot that cheese melts. Don't worry, it won't take me long to fix it."

"Celebratory?"

"Yes." He grins smugly some more. "I've just booked our vacation."

"What?"

"Our New Year's vacation. In Polzeath down in Cornwall, so Ava can remain glued to that boy she's obsessed with. At a lovely hotel overlooking the sea, with plenty of room for all of us."

He grins even more, waiting for me to ask for more details, but my blood's running cold. Meanwhile, Ava comes in and asks for an update, so he tells her, too, including the name of the hotel.

"Ooh, swanky!" She grins back. Then she sees me. "Ted? What's the matter? Don't you want to go?"

Normally Ava picks up on things before I do, but she seems to have missed a massive problem this time. I sit down at the table.

"Dad," I say quietly, "you do realize they won't be paying me?"

"For what?"

"The shoot. I know I mentioned trips and things, but that was before I messed up. I still don't know if they're going to sue me."

He's staring at me, doing his trademark hand-in-hair stance, still not getting it.

"What's your shoot got to do with it, love?"

So I explain how I was planning to pay for a big vacation, but I can't now, and the blood drains out of Dad's face. Ava looks pretty shocked, too. I hadn't realized they were counting on the money so much. I thought I'd be saving most of it for university, or to get Rose Cottage back. Maybe I *was* being selfish by walking out on Rudolf. I should have gone through with it after all.

"Ted!" Dad says. "I can't believe I'm hearing this."

"I know. I'm sorry, Dad. I just couldn't —"

"Don't be ridiculous! I'm paying for this trip. For God's sake, Ted. I thought you realized by now. We'd never ask you for money."

"So where . . . ?"

I'm so confused.

Which is when Dad explains about the attractive assistant producer he met during my "very nothing" TV job. And how she told him she was working on a new history series.

"She's chief researcher for a show about the Restoration. You know, when Charles II came back from France?"

We do. You don't live with my father for sixteen years without knowing what the Restoration is.

"So. We got started talking history," he explains. "She asked if I wanted to be a consultant on the program. Of course I did. We weren't sure it was going to happen, but it got the green light while you were in New York, Ted. It doesn't pay mega-bucks, but it'll pay for the hotel, OK? And your mum can scale back her hours. She's had too much on recently. In fact, we all need a break."

"Oh, Dad!"

Ava hardly ever cries. Nor does Dad. It's funny: Ava's diagnosis just made the three of us go quiet, but hearing we're going on holiday . . . *that* sets us all off.

Of course, if I'd done the New York job, I could have paid for lots of holidays, but I don't think Dad would have let me. Besides, I kind of helped as it was: If I hadn't done the TV job, Dad would never have met the researcher. Not so "very nothing" after all.

FORTY

By the middle of the week, I'm feeling better. I'm still pretty stressed about what the consequences will be of walking out on Tina di Gaggia's FAVORITE photographer, but Dad's news has helped a lot, two good nights' sleep have lifted the fog of tiredness, and on top of that, with some help from Ava, I've finally managed to get my art project the way I want it. I hope Miss Jenkins is going to be impressed with what I've done. It's certainly better than those shaded bananas.

I'm starting to think about art in a new way, now that Miss Jenkins has challenged me to take it more seriously. I'm interested in the idea of documentary photography. Finding fascinating people, wherever they happen to be, and taking portraits of them in a way that brings out what's unusual about them. People like the bus driver on my route to school who always gives me the saddest smile when I get on, as if we're in the middle of some tragic story. Or Mr. Anderson, even, the way he stares after Miss Jenkins in her pencil skirt when he thinks people aren't looking. Or Daisy, spiky-haired, chatting animatedly to Cally about something music-related — until her face falls when she sees me watching and her expression becomes guarded.

Now that I'm starting to think of myself as the girl behind the camera, not in front of it, I see things differently. I notice the nervous look Cally flashes at Dean the moment I enter our homeroom, for example, and the sad sigh Daisy gives when she moves away from Cally to say hello to me. I notice that they don't look hostile, but wary, and something about me is making them feel that way.

After what happened the other day with Dean, I finally understand about Cally. Her boyfriend seems to like me more than I could have imagined. Maybe Ava was right about people being jealous of the way I look. In spite of everything, I still think of myself as freaky, but even Daisy seemed to think I might be model-ish, and now Dean seems to agree. It's clearly hurting Cally. And Daisy's torn between us. Perhaps I need to be gracious after all.

It's like a picture coming into focus. While it's still sharp, and while I've still got the courage to go through with it, I walk over to Dean and give him a friendly but totally nonflirtatious smile.

"Hi," I say. "You know that . . . er . . . advice you were asking me for the other day. Did you take it?"

He looks at me nervously. "Er, no."

"Well, I'd do it soon, if I were you. Before it's too late. She's right there."

He gives me another nervous glance. I give him the warrior stare. He knows what he needs to do. And he does it. He goes over to Cally and has a quiet word in her ear. Somehow she hears it through her clouds of poufy hair and she looks across at me, surprised. I was supposed to be stealing the boyfriend, not giving him back. I smile at her. The first friendly smile I think I've ever given her. She gives me a long double take, to check if I'm being sincere. Then she smiles back. Cally's got a lovely smile: bright and open. But Dean cuts off my view of it, moving in to talk to her more closely and putting his arm casually around her, as if it's always been there.

Daisy doesn't say anything until art, when Cally moves off to a different class.

"What got *into* you?"

"With Cally? I just thought I'd try being nice for a change. See if it helped. Did it seem too strange?"

"Yes!" She frowns. "And no! It was lovely. You've always been so standoffish with Cally. She hated it. She just wants to be friends with you, really. She thinks you're so . . . beautiful. She always worried that Dean fancied you more than her."

Seriously? Wow. She hid it well.

"Well, I can assure you he doesn't," I tell Daisy.

He doesn't now, anyway. That's the second time I've brought those two together. And this time, I didn't even need to reveal my underpants to do it.

"You're looking cheerful, Ted," Miss Jenkins says, coming over. "Are you ready to talk us through your project now?"

I am. I stand at the front of the class and explain my approach to "Still Life": how I started with the idea of fruit, as depicted by the Old Masters, and moved on to my sister, who embodies the idea of life to me at the moment. I talk about all the raw fruit and vegetables she's eating to help combat the side effects of her treatment, and how her beautiful shaved head matches their smooth contours.

My project covers a large piece of poster board, on which I've stuck my inspirations, from Dutch paintings to the photograph of the princess and the flowers by Richard Avedon. In the center is a black-and-white portrait of Ava, her head resting sideways, perfectly still, among a selection of exotic fruits and berries. It's a very peaceful picture, until you think about why her head is shaved, and notice the faraway look in her eyes.

Miss Jenkins studies it for a long time.

"You've captured her beautifully, Ted," she says. "Her head tells a difficult story, but overall, it's uplifting. It reminds me of a photograph by Sam Taylor-Wood, actually."

She goes to the computer and searches the internet until she finds the image she's looking for. It's called *Self Portrait in a Single-Breasted Suit, with Hare*. She brings it up on the whiteboard and we all check it out. It is, indeed, a woman in a suit, holding what looks like a longhaired rabbit, taking a picture of herself.

"I'm sure you see the play on words," Miss Jenkins says. "She was suffering from breast cancer at the time, and about to lose a breast and her hair. This is her response. Yours is similar, Ted."

"Copying, more like," Nathan King grumbles at the back. Dean pokes him with a pencil. He may be slightly scared of me now, but at least he's loyal.

"No, not copying," Miss Jenkins corrects Nathan. "Taking a similar approach. And Sam Taylor-Wood is a highly respected contemporary artist. I think Ted should be proud to be in her company. Well done."

I chose the most artistic-looking picture of Ava for my project, but we took loads. I love the one of her pretending to be a pineapple, with her chin resting in a shallow dish and a couple of bunches of grapes draped over her ears. She also made a very convincing mango (left cheek on the table, eyeing up a nearby bowl of raspberries). And an impressive oversized avocado (right cheek on the table, lots of green eye shadow, nestled under a bunch of bananas). Unfortunately, we were laughing so hard by then that the avocado has a rather scary — under the circumstances — full set of teeth.

The pictures are quite Surreal, and very Man Ray, but we decided the exam board wasn't ready for "chemo patient impressions of larger fruits." Instead, Ava's let me put them on my new blog, where I'm experimenting with different photographic styles. It's early days, but I'm loving it. I still want to be a part of that crazy, artistic world I encountered, but I want to be the one who decides what's beautiful. One day, I will have an exhibition in New York. And I want Ava to be beside me when it opens.

Because what she's going through now is a blip, and it's nearly over. That's what we tell ourselves. It's what we have to believe.

FORTY-ONE

Friday is the last day of her radiation treatment. She's going in with Jesse, who has stayed behind specifically to help her through this final week. I've hardly spoken to her, because she spends most of her time hanging out at Nick's house with Jesse, or going on smoochy walks, or taking him off to see old films at the movie theater and introduce him to some of her favorite stars.

I suppose it's going to be like this from now on. Of course, Jesse will go back to Cornwall, but they'll be in touch again properly, like they used to be. Assuming the results from the hospital are what we want to hear when the treatment is over. Assuming Ava's in the ninety percent. It really is a big number, isn't it? Ninety percent. I guess if you're in the ten percent you have to go through all of this again, and I don't know how we'd do that. But ten percent is tiny. That's what I keep telling myself.

We don't talk about the ten percent at home, of course. But something has shifted. We don't talk about the ten percent *together*. We know we're all thinking about it and worrying about it, and we somehow support each other by talking about different things. But we're not spinning off in our own directions anymore. Mum and Dad are hyperaware of me since I got back from New York, and making sure I'm OK. So now we talk a lot. About our vacation. About my new blog. About how things are going at school. About Dad's history program ideas and whether he might even get a TV host job one day. And how good he would have looked in his fedora . . .

Luckily, they laugh when they get to this bit. I hope I don't get *too* sued, because I really owe him another hat.

I'm about to find out, because toward the end of the week Frankie calls and asks if I want to come into the office on Saturday morning. I might as well. If she has bad news and it's complicated, it might be better if she can explain it to me face-to-face.

So on Saturday I make my way to Charlotte Street in Soho, where Model City is based. Frankie takes me to the café in a chic hotel nearby, so we can be away from the office atmosphere. I sit back while she speaks to the waitress in fluent Italian and manages to send five texts on her iPhone as she explains the latest situation to me. If you combined the pent-up energy of Frankie and Dad, you could probably create a small nuclear explosion.

"Has Rudolf calmed down yet?" I ask.

"No," she says, smiling. "But then, he's famous for holding a grudge."

"And legal action?"

She stares at me. "What?"

"He said he'd sue me."

"Oh, don't be silly! I mean, they won't *pay* you, but they're not going to sue you. He wouldn't sue a sixteen-year-old. Cassandra would come down on him like a ton of bricks. He might have threatened to, perhaps, but that's just his artistic temperament. He was being a bit naughty."

A bit naughty? If a teacher stormed around like that, making threats, they'd be sacked. Then I remember: At school I'm a student. In that studio I was supposed to be a professional. You don't get paid fifty thousand dollars a day without being expected to put up with . . . artists.

"What about Tina?" I ask. I did as advised and deleted all her voice mails and texts.

"She's furious," Frankie says. "Incandescent. She put her reputation on the line for you, Ted, and you let her down. Nobody does that."

"No," I say. "I imagine they don't." For a moment I'm scared, but then I remember: Tina does whatever she needs to do to make things happen. She's tough and she'll cope. And so am I now. I don't really care what she thinks.

"But she'll get over it," Frankie says, echoing my thoughts. "I had two girls come into the office today with the Ted."

"*The* Ted? What's that?"

"The supershort blonde crop. It's the new look. Not many girls can carry it off. One of these girls couldn't, actually. You've got to have the right face, but if you've got it — wow. It's what everyone wants, ever since the film from the *i-D* shoot came in. So there's more work if you want it. Lots more, actually — as long as you do what you're told next time. But I promise you won't have to do it in a thong."

"They told you about the thong?"

"Oh, yes. The thong is famous."

Oh God.

There's a long pause.

"Do you want the work?" she asks, going back to her phone — no doubt e-mailing some VIP about something urgent that's gone wrong somewhere. "Because if you don't, there's plenty who do."

I shake my head. I've considered it, but I only really do warrior princesses. If they need temptresses, for example, they need another girl. Besides, I have other things to think about right now. Even so, perhaps this won't be the last I see of Frankie.

"You don't know any photographic agents, do you?" I ask.

She looks at me, surprised.

"Yes, loads. Why?"

"Oh, nothing. It's just . . . in case I might need one, one day."

She laughs. "For you?"

"Yes."

She thinks about it for a moment while she types. "Cool. Sure. Why not? If you do, call me. Stay in touch, Ted."

I promise I will.

After the meeting's over, I make my way to another café around the corner. Ava asked me to meet up with her and Jesse here. They're celebrating her first day of total freedom after her second round of treatment. I agreed to have a hot chocolate with them. But they must have got stuck somewhere, because I'm ten minutes late and when I get there there's still no sign of them.

"Ted?"

I know that voice. Right under my nose is a head of rumpled hair, a pair of glasses, and a paint-speckled jacket. Every single item of clothing . . . I'm beginning to think he does it deliberately.

"Nick?"

"Are you here for your sister?" he asks.

"Yes."

He nods. "Take a seat. You might as well. I'm here for Jesse. There must have been a mix-up or something."

He's managed to grab a round table by the window. It's the best one in the place and it seems silly to go anywhere else, so I sit down awkwardly beside him. We both stare out the window, not talking, apart from my order of a hot chocolate when a waitress comes over. Five minutes go by. Then ten. Presumably Ava's lips are becoming more chapped from Jesse's attentions somewhere. They must have lost track of time. I wish they hadn't. I'm sure Nick doesn't want to be sitting next to the most evil model he's ever encountered, and I'd certainly rather be anywhere than next to his brooding face.

He looks at his watch. It's a Disney one, with Mickey Mouse's arms for hands. Not the jeweled, designer affair I might have imagined from a boy who practically lives next door to the Queen. He glances across at me and I pretend I wasn't looking at his wrist. Then I look back. Mickey's hand ticks along as five more minutes pass agonizingly by.

Eventually he coughs.

"Look, Ted, I know what you must be thinking of me."

I stare at him. I was actually thinking that I really like his watch. But that isn't the point. "No — isn't it about what you think of me?" I correct him. "Don't worry. You made it pretty clear."

He coughs again. "Er, Ava told me about the shoot. I assumed you'd come back on schedule, not . . . what happened. And she told me it was her fault you were there in the first place, really."

"Did she?"

"Yeah. She said she kept on encouraging you to do these crazy things, and you did, and she's kind of sorry, but you were just so . . . *amazing*."

"She said that?"

"Yeah. She talks a lot about you. I suppose because . . . I suppose because I was asking."

There's a very, very long pause while my hot chocolate goes cold, four people go in and out of the café — none of them Ava and Jesse — and I try to tell myself Nick was asking about me because he was curious about just how evil I was. Not for any other reason. And that the expression in his eyes right now is disgust, not . . . not something I can't even dare to imagine, because my heart ties itself in knots at the thought of it. I may feel like I loathe Nick Spoke, but my heart doesn't. My heart fancies every tiny detail of his face, his hair, his clothes, his voice, even his use of the word *dabble*, despite everything I do to tell it not to bother.

"And I suppose I kept asking about you because . . . you're fascinating, Ted. I mean, beautiful girls are normally so boring, but you don't even seem to know how gorgeous you are. And then I thought you'd got the whole thing worked out, and you were off in New York, being as boring as the rest of them. But you walked out. Why?"

I'm pretty sure that when I open my mouth my voice isn't going to work. My brain is processing too much information here, including "beautiful" and "gorgeous." Coming from a boy whose mother deals with supermodels on a daily basis. However, speech comes out somehow. Not much of it, but as much as I can manage.

"I couldn't do it. And . . . because of you. You told me Ava needed me."

He winces at the memory. "About all that . . ."

He's leaning in toward me. He's looking at my lips. They've probably got hot-chocolate foam on them or something, but I can't seem to move any of my muscles to wipe it off.

"I was an idiot," he mumbles. "And you are the most . . ."

Then his lips are on my lips, and my whole body catches fire. It doesn't last long, because he pulls away anxiously, to see how I took it. But my eyes are good at explaining things for me now. So he moves in again, puts his hands gently on either side of my face, and does it for longer. So long, in fact, that by the time he's finished, Ava and Jesse are standing beside our table, looking down on us, criticizing our technique.

"I never understand how people with glasses do it," Jesse says curiously. "Don't they steam up?"

"Shut up, Surfer Boy," Nick grumbles, sliding back into his seat.

"I didn't even know Ted *could* do it," Ava observes. "Not properly, anyway."

Nor did I, actually. Not like that. But it's never felt like that before.

They sit down and join us.

"We thought you'd never get round to it," Jesse sighs. "We've been standing out there for ages. I'm frozen."

"I hope he apologized first," Ava says to me. "He was totally vile to you when you were in New York. He's told us all about it. And I've explained to him that it was probably his phone call that cost our family forty grand. Fine if your dad's a banker. But we needed that money."

She's grinning. She doesn't entirely mean it. And now that I think about it, I still have that money from Miss Teen, and Rudolf isn't going to sue me for it, so hopefully our busking days are over. Besides, if I'd stayed in New York I wouldn't be here now, with all of them, having this silly conversation. And if I had to put a price on this moment it would obviously be more than forty thousand pounds, because I don't regret what it took to get here for a minute. Meanwhile, Nick's fingertips have just found mine, and I have a sneaking sensation that, under my bulky winter outfit, I might finally be smoldering.

FORTY-TWO

It's the picture on the back of every magazine, the side of every bus.

A girl with a pure, oval face and tightly cropped hair sits in a bath of (fake) snakes and stares sexily into the camera. Her skin is dusted with gold and green shadow. Her expression is sheer lust. One of the snakes rests on her bare shoulders and points suggestively down toward her left boob.

You can't actually see anything, but you can . . . you know . . . imagine.

She looks interesting. Her name is Jovana, apparently, and she's an exciting seventeen-year-old from Serbia. She used to be known for her long, dark hair, but she's had it cropped super-short and dyed blonde for this shoot. She's the talk of New York. Everyone loves the look, although true fashion insiders wonder whether it was inspired by Ted Richmond, that teenager from London, who was tipped to be a top model herself one day.

No one knows what happened to Ted Richmond and no one really cares. Fashion is a fast-moving business. You come. You go. Ted was requested for *Teen Vogue*, but apparently she turned the job down because she was on some family vacation. That's hardly dedication. No problem, though. There are lots of girls to take her place.

Meanwhile, I have my own pictures:

I'm standing with my arm around Daisy, while Dean predictably does rabbit ears above Cally's head. It's the school Christmas dance and we've all dressed up in hot pants or flares, star-shaped sunglasses and crazy seventies Afros. Under my costume, I'm also wearing my new signature stripy socks and electric-blue Mary Janes. Actually, my legs don't look as bad in the socks as I thought they might. Nick thinks that they're my best feature. After my eyes and my hair and my smile, apparently. And my use of natural light.

Me and my boyfriend snogging, eyes closed, with his hands on either side of my face. Ava took that picture on her phone when we weren't looking. We appear to have Snoopy lying across both our heads. My sister is a totally rubbish photographer. I don't know why I keep it, really.

The cover of *i-D* magazine. Photographer: Eric Bloch. Model: Ted Richmond. Agency: Model City. My first and only cover. My hair is micro-short and color-washed rose pink for the shoot. I love it. I'm doing my warrior stare, and I look somehow tough and ethereal at the same time. Still nothing like Lily, or Linda, or Kate, or Claudia. But then, I guess every model needs her own look, and this was mine. Despite the fact that Nick hates the modeling business, he likes this picture of me because I look so strong and challenging. Although he generally prefers the pictures he takes of me, or the ones I take myself.

New Year's Eve, at night. I'm on the beach at Polzeath with Mum and Dad, Ava and Jesse. The sky is black and it's freezing cold. We're all dressed up in coats and wellies and wool hats, posing for Ava's camera — now mine (I swapped it for the Mulberry tote) — which I've screwed onto the new tripod I got for Christmas. We're huddled together for warmth, trying to ignore the icy drizzle and pretend it's surfing weather. Dad has one arm around me and the other around Mum, who's cuddling Ava, who's snuggling up to Jesse on her other side, while he shouts, "Work it, baby! Work it!" He's making her laugh so much she can hardly breathe.

Everything about us is lit up from inside. After six months of chemotherapy and radiation, Ava's test results were clear and now we can celebrate, together. She made it into the ninety percent. We've never felt so alive as in the cold, wet Cornish air.

I had to rush back from setting the self-timer and the flash went off too close to my moon-shaped face. I look like a blob. A carefree, happy blob.

This is my favorite picture. I'll keep it with me forever.

AUTHOR'S NOTE

When I started to research Ted's story online, I was instantly targeted by advertisements from model "agencies" that turned out not to be agencies at all. That is why I found myself writing about scams. They exist. No joke. To help promote safe and fair practices in the American fashion industry, model Sara Ziff has even formed the Model Alliance, an organization dedicated to protecting models' rights.

In researching Ava's story, it was good to hear about the work of the American Cancer Society (www.cancer.org). They know how to help, and are looking for fund-raisers and volunteers. Could that be you?

Sophia

ACKNOWLEDGMENTS

This book is also dedicated to Elizabeth W., a fan of *Threads* who once asked me about modeling. Elizabeth — here's my answer. It might be slightly longer than you expected, but I hope it helps.

Thank you to Caroline at Christopher Little; Barry and Rachel H. at Chicken House, who supported me all the way through; and Rachel L. and Imogen, my editors, who worked on it with me. I'll always think of this as our book.

Then there is the yoga sisterhood: Kasia, Jen, Rebecca, and Clare. I couldn't have done it without you and I'm sorry I was thinking about modeling disasters when I should have been concentrating on downward-facing dog.

The Reeds: Thank you for Cornwall.

The writing sisterhood: Cat, Fiona, Gillian, Kay, Keren, Keris, Luisa, Susie, and Tamsyn. You're always there when I need you. Thank God for you.

Lara Williamson, Amanda Howard, and Kika-Rose Ridley: my fashion advisers. Thank you, all of you, for giving me your time, and telling me some seriously amazing stuff.

Celia and Felicity Pett: You know the scenes you gave me. Felicity — I seem to be thanking you in every book. You really are a *top* goddaughter.

Dr. Stephen Daw and Stephen Cox at University College Hospital. Thank you for your brilliant, succinct medical advice, just when I needed it.

And lastly, but totally not leastly, Alex, Emily, Sophie, Freddie, and Tom. Thank you for putting up with the times when I wasn't really there, because I was busy being Ted and Ava. This is your book, too.